Her F...

Miss Valeria Harwood ... shameful, at least shocking. Valeria engaged in an activity no proper young lady would dream of: she wrote lurid adventure novels under a male *nom de plume*.

Now Valeria was immersed in her latest creation, bringing to life her most irresistibly infamous villain: the elegantly attractive, infinitely evil Marquis de Moreau. Her only problem was how to defeat this fascinating figure in the final pages.

It was then that Valeria met the Earl of Traverhurst—and to her horror realized that this legendary lord of licentiousness was the perfect twin of her imaginary marquis.

Valeria knew from the way her eyes met the earl's at their first encounter that her powers as a woman would have to be greater than her powers as an author if this man in truth were not to prove far, far more dangerous than fiction. . . .

(For a list of other Signet Regency Romances by Margaret Summerville, please turn page. . . .)

Knave's Gambit

Margaret Summerville

A SIGNET BOOK

NEW AMERICAN LIBRARY

NAL BOOKS ARE AVAILABLE AT QUANTITY DISCOUNTS
WHEN USED TO PROMOTE PRODUCTS OR SERVICES.
FOR INFORMATION PLEASE WRITE TO PREMIUM MARKETING DIVISION.
NEW AMERICAN LIBRARY. 1633 BROADWAY.
NEW YORK. NEW YORK 10019.

Copyright © 1986 by Margaret Summerville

SIGNET TRADEMARK REG. U.S. PAT. OFF. AND FOREIGN COUNTRIES
REGISTERED TRADEMARK—MARCA REGISTRADA
HECHO EN CHICAGO. U.S.A.

SIGNET, SIGNET CLASSIC, MENTOR, ONYX, PLUME, MERIDIAN AND
NAL BOOKS are published by New American Library,
1633 Broadway, New York, New York 10019

First Printing, September, 1986

1 2 3 4 5 6 7 8 9

PRINTED IN THE UNITED STATES OF AMERICA

1

VALERIA HARWOOD stared thoughtfully into space as she sat at the carved oak writing desk in the library. A dreary March rain pelted against the windows and the gray sky darkened the room, giving it a melancholy aspect. At the best of times the library at Melbury was not the cheeriest of places. The wainscotted room contained heavy antique furniture and the walls that were not lined with books were adorned with implements of medieval warfare.

Miss Harwood, however, was unaware of the shortcomings of the room's decoration. Having lived all her life at Melbury, Valeria loved the manor house's library. As a girl she had spent many happy hours there, devouring the books in her father's collection.

Indeed, certain relations feared that Valeria was far too bookish, an opinion they had never dared venture to her late father. The fourth viscount had been a man of decidedly strong character and his daughter was not unlike him. Lord Harwood had encouraged Valeria's interest in a number of unconventional pursuits, and when at the age of ten the young lady had announced her intention to be a writer, the viscount had been delighted.

Now at the age of six and twenty, Valeria was an accomplished authoress. She had three published works, all of them tremendously popular, and among her readers was the Prince Regent himself. Since Valeria's novels were exciting tales of derring-do and not what one would have expected from a lady's gentle hand, Miss Harwood had taken on the masculine pseudonym Verrell Hawkesworth. The identity of Verrell Hawkesworth was a mystery and the subject of much speculation in literary circles. Indeed, only a handful of people knew that the respected author was, in truth, a pretty country miss.

Valeria continued to stare into space for a few moments longer, and then she seemed to suddenly receive an inspiration. Taking up her goose quill pen, she scratched rapidly at the paper, pausing only to dip the writing instrument in ink.

Anyone observing the young lady at her work, her brow knitted in concentration, would have been favorably impressed by her appearance. It was Valeria's custom to scoff at those who declared her a beauty, for she considered her curly dark hair unmanageable and her features a trifle off the mark. Yet, less severe critics praised her fine hazel eyes and charming smile and proclaimed her figure quite admirable.

Although never overly concerned with fashion, Valeria always appeared well dressed. That morning she was attired in a simple frock of dove-gray muslin with a prim white cap atop her dark curls.

Valeria's pen stopped suddenly and she frowned. Perhaps her villain would not have made such a remark, she reflected. After considering it for a moment, she crossed out her last sentence and replaced it with another. Rereading it, Valeria seemed satisfied and continued on.

The novel seemed to be going very well. A sequel to her very popular *The Queen's Champion*, the new book was entitled *The Villain of Versailles*. It continued the adventures of the dashing English soldier of fortune, Captain Hannibal Wolfe, in seventeenth-century France. The intrepid captain was pitted against his nemesis, the treacherous Marquis de Morveau. Of late, the marquis was giving Valeria some trouble. He threatened to dominate the book with his Gallic charm and unspeakable villainy, overshadowing her virtuous English hero.

Well aware of this problem, Valeria continued writing. She was so lost in her work that she did not notice the entrance of a stout maid. "Oh, miss! Her ladyship is here! I saw her carriage pull up."

Valeria turned and regarded the servant in confusion. "Her ladyship? Whom do you mean, Sally?"

"It is Lady Harwood! Oh, no, I mean to say your stepmother, the Princess Lubetska!"

"Here now? I did not expect her for another week." Before the servant could reply, a short, plump, middle-aged lady appeared at the doorway.

"Valeria, my darling girl!"

Valeria hurried to her feet and rushed to enfold the newcomer in an exuberant embrace. "Maria!"

After disengaging from this joyous greeting, the older woman regarded her stepdaughter affectionately. "How I have longed to see you, Valeria. How lovely you look."

"Such stuff, Maria!" said Valeria, smiling. "But look at you! You look wonderful! You have not changed in the slightest all these seven years."

"That is, as you would say, 'bosh,' my dear."

"Do not contradict me, Maria. You look very well indeed and very much the princess in such finery."

The Princess Lubetska did, in fact, appear quite grand. She was dressed in a loose-fitting coat of fine black cloth, lined and trimmed with ermine. On her head was a bonnet of black silk ornamented with black feathers. A woman of fifty-four years, the princess bore her age well. She had a pretty round face dominated by sparkling blue eyes. Peeking from beneath her bonnet were bright, henna-reddened curls.

The Princess Lubetska's merry countenance belied her mourning dress and few would have guessed that she had been widowed just three months ago. Those who disapproved of her, and there were many, would have suggested that the princess's ability to bear up under her bereavement was due to her having had so much practice at widowhood. The late Prince Lubetsky had been Maria's fourth husband. Her other husbands had been an Austrian count, a Prussian baron, and Valeria's father, the late Viscount Harwood.

There had been many who had been shocked when the

sixty-one-year-old fourth viscount had married Maria. Few
of the Harwood family relations had approved of the match,
for not only was the lady a foreigner, Viennese by birth,
but she had a rather scandalous reputation. Her affair with
a Hapsburg prince had been the talk of several courts of
Europe.

One might have expected Valeria to have been unhappy
with her father's second wife, but the young lady had
taken an instant liking to her Austrian stepmother, much to
the displeasure of her older brother, Julian. Julian, now the
fifth Viscount Harwood, had never reconciled himself to
his father's remarriage. He had been very happy when his
stepmother had returned to Europe after his father's death.
Julian had been even more pleased when he had heard that
Maria had married a Polish prince and had relinquished the
Harwood name.

"Maria, let us sit down. Do take off your things. Sally
will take them."

The princess turned to the servant and smiled at her.
"Ah, Sally Miller. I do hope you still make that delicious
cocoa."

The maid, very pleased that Maria had remembered her,
grinned and made an awkward curtsy. "I do, m'lady. I
mean, your highness."

"Would you like some now, Maria?" said Valeria.

"That would be wonderful," said the princess, taking
off her coat and bonnet and handing them to the maid,
who hurried out of the room.

The two ladies sat down on the sofa near Valeria's
writing desk. "What a happy surprise, Maria. I did not
expect you for another week."

The princess nodded. "My dear girl, I did not think I
could bear it another day. How I miss my poor Stanislaw!
But you cannot know how difficult it was to remain at the
castle without him. I have told you his son did not like
me." Maria sighed. "I fear I have little luck with my
husbands' sons. Indeed, I do fear your brother Julian will
be most displeased knowing I am here at Melbury."

"Oh, bosh, Maria. But in any case, it does not signify
what Julian thinks. I may have whom I please at Melbury.

After all, Julian and Fanny are scarcely ever here. It seems he has left Melbury to me, at least for the moment.''

"And are you happy here, my dear?"

"What a question, Maria. Of course I am happy here. Between managing the household and my work I am kept very busy.''

"Oh, your work. You know how much I love all your books. Stanislaw loved them, too. Of course, he could not read English so I had to translate them into French. I fear I was not very good at it. You know my French has many flaws." The princess smiled mischievously. "Such agony it has been for me to keep your secret. What a triumph it would be to reveal that you are Verrell Hawkesworth!'' She laughed at Valeria's expression. "Oh, do not fear. I shall do no such thing." She glanced over at the desk that was piled with papers. "You are working on another book, no? How bad of me to disturb you."

"You are a most welcome interruption, Maria." Valeria reached over and took her stepmother's hand and pressed it fondly. "I have missed you so much."

"And I you."

"You must be very tired after such a journey. I hope it was not too arduous.''

"Oh, it was not so very terrible," said the princess, "and my dear little Putti enjoyed the trip immensely."

Valeria smiled, remembering the little white dog her father had given Maria. "And where is she?"

"Oh, I had the footman take her to the kitchen. She was so hungry.''

"I beg your pardon, miss." Valeria looked over to find her butler had entered the room.

"Simms?"

"A letter has arrived for you, miss. It is from Lady Harwood." The butler, a somber, dignified looking man, approached the ladies and extended a silver salver toward Valeria, who took up the letter from it.

"Thank you, Simms." The butler nodded and departed. "I shall read it later," said Valeria, putting the letter aside.

"Oh, no, you must read it now. It might be important.''

"Oh, Fanny's letters are never important. Her only subjects are my nephews' progress at their lessons and my niece's new gowns."

"I always liked Fanny," said Maria, "and I believe she liked me in spite of your brother. Do read her letter. I do not mind."

"As you wish." Valeria took up the letter again and broke the seal. She then quickly scanned the contents. "Oh, dear, it appears that Fanny is in high fidgets."

"Whatever is the matter?" said Maria.

Valeria shook her head. "My niece Kitty has a *tendre* for a most unsuitable gentleman."

Maria's interest was piqued. "Little Kitty? When I last saw her she was not out of the schoolroom. She was such a pretty child. I fancy she is a great beauty now."

"Yes, she is a very lovely girl, but, according to her mother, not a very sensible one."

"But all young girls form attachments to unsuitable men," said the princess.

Valeria looked amused. "They do, Maria?"

"Do not say that you never did."

"Indeed, I've never formed an attachment unsuitable or otherwise."

"My poor Valeria."

"Do not waste your pity, Maria. I assure you I am very glad that I have never acted the moonling." Valeria looked back at the letter. "I do not know why Fanny flies up into the boughs over such trifling matters. Listen to what she says. 'It is a great disaster. Kitty thinks herself in love with the man and indeed, he shows marked interest in her. He is the most notorious gentleman in town and many blush simply at the mention of his name.' "

Valeria smiled at Maria. "Shall I tell you the gentleman's name or would it put you to the blush?"

Maria laughed. "My darling girl, you may put aside your fears. What is this gentleman's name?"

Valeria looked down at the paper once again. "He is Rohan Warrender, the Earl of Traverhurst."

"Traverhurst? Interested in Kitty? *Gott in Himmel!* He

has never before been interested in—how do you say?
—green girls. Yes, that is right.''

"Are you well acquainted with him, Maria?''

"I know him but slightly. I am, however, well acquainted with his reputation. I can see why dear Fanny
would be upset. He bears watching, that one. He is a
charming rogue. Do you not remember him, Valeria?''

"I remember hearing about him, but, I daresay, I have
never met him. Of course, as you know, for some years
now I have had little to do with society. I much prefer
Melbury.''

Maria shook her head. "I wish you had not abandoned
society, my dear. It is not good to hide yourself away here
in the country. How will you ever meet a man and get
married?''

"My dear Maria, I am not seeking a husband. I am
perfectly content as I am, which is fortunate as I am very
firmly on the shelf.''

"Do not say that!'' cried Maria.

Valeria laughed. "It is not so tragic.'' The Princess
Lubetska, who thought Valeria's attitude incomprehensi-
ble, prudently made no reply and the younger woman
continued, "But tell me more about the infamous Lord
Traverhurst.''

"His mother was French, the daughter of the Duc de
Châteauroux. She was very beautiful and they say that
every man at the French court was enraged when she
married an English lord. But then the late Lord Traverhurst
was so handsome and so very rich!

"It is said that Rohan, the present earl, has inherited his
mother's French temperament as well as her charm. He is
also handsome as his father and a devil with the ladies.
You remember my dear friend Lady Howison? She has
written to me since I left England and has kept me informed of the latest *on-dits*. She often mentions Traverhurst.
His name has been linked with all the great beauties in
town. I recall he fought a duel once over an actress.''

An ironical smile crossed Valeria's face. "He sounds
like an admirable fellow. I fear Kitty is enough of a
pea-goose to fancy such a man.''

"He is the sort of man most young girls would fancy, my dear. But it is odd he would play up to Kitty. Of course, he must be nearly five and thirty, and perhaps he thinks it is time he married. What else does Fanny say?"

"She wants me to come to town." Valeria once again began to read from her sister-in-law's letter. " 'I beseech you, my dear Valeria, to come to my aid. You know how Kitty admires you. You are the only one to whom she will listen. You cannot refuse me. I am desperate.' " Valeria looked over at Maria. "There is a postscript. 'The linen draper has the most delightful blue sarcenet from Paris. I bought you some as it would make an admirable evening dress for you.' "

The princess laughed. "Dear Fanny. I do hope you are going to her assistance."

"Certainly not," said Valeria firmly. "I should be of no use whatsoever. I do not know how Fanny got the hubble-bubble notion that Kitty would listen to me. My niece is too much like my brother Julian, stubborn and strong-willed."

Maria laughed again. "That, my dear, is a Harwood characteristic."

"I fear you are right, Maria," said Valeria with a smile.

"But you should go to London, Valeria. It would be most diverting."

"For one thing, I wish to stay at Melbury with you. And for another, I hardly think it diverting to stay with Julian and Fanny in town. Julian and I invariably quarrel."

"But we could go to town together, my dear. I have taken a house there."

Valeria looked surprised. "You have?"

"I have always loved London—it is so exciting. Indeed, aside from Vienna, it is my favorite city. My dear Stanislaw made generous provision for me, and I can do as I please. What fun it would be if you could stay with me. Do say you will. Dear Fanny needs you."

Valeria hesitated. She had been working hard on her book and needed a rest. A short sojourn in town would be enjoyable and probably do her good, she reflected. Also,

Valeria's curiosity and novelist's instincts had been aroused by Traverhurst. "Very well, I shall go, Maria."

"Oh, that is splendid!" cried the princess.

"But I insist we stay here at Melbury long enough for you to rest properly. Oh, here is Sally with the cocoa." The maid brought in the tray and the two ladies continued their animated conversation.

❧ 2 ❧

LESS THAN two weeks after the Princess Lubetska had
arrived at Melbury, she and Valeria Harwood were settled
into Maria's stylishly appointed London townhouse. Lo-
cated in an exclusive neighborhood favored by the *haut
ton*, the fashionable residence had been designed by the
well-known architect John Nash.

Valeria was very impressed by the house, although she
thought its Egyptian decor a trifle outlandish. It was certainly very different from Melbury, just as the hectic pace
of the great city was so different from the country. Although Valeria loved country life, she had to admit that
being once again in London was quite exciting.

The day after their arrival, Valeria prepared to visit her
brother and sister-in-law. Knowing that Julian set great
store by appearances, she dressed with care, putting on her
best walking dress of jaconet muslin with a rose-colored
spencer. The ensemble was set off by a French bonnet
trimmed with rose-colored satin and an ostrich plume.
Thus attired, Valeria proceeded to the drawing room where
she found Maria ensconced on the sofa with her tiny white
dog.

"So you are going now, my dear?" said the princess.

"Yes, Maria. I do wish you would come. I know Fanny
and Kitty would want to see you."

"But your brother would not. No, Valeria, it is best you
go alone. Perhaps if you find that Julian is not so opposed

to the idea of my being in London, I might visit another time. But do tell Fanny and dear Kitty they must call upon me."

Valeria nodded. "Very well. I shall not be long." She turned and left the room. Outside a footman assisted her up into Maria's stylish phaeton and it was not long before she arrived at her brother's house.

Met at the door by Julian's butler, Eliot, Valeria was quickly admitted into the viscount's drawing room. Her brother and sister-in-law rose to greet her. "Valeria! I am so glad you could come," said Fanny.

Valeria smiled and kissed her sister-in-law on the cheek. She then turned to her brother. "Julian, you look well. Indeed, you both look wonderful."

The viscount and his wife did, in truth, make a handsome couple. Julian was tall and slim, with Valeria's dark hair and hazel eyes. His wife Fanny was blond and exceedingly fair. A prominent lady of fashion, Lady Harwood looked very attractive in her high-waisted silk gown with its tiny puff sleeves.

"It is nice to see you, Valeria." Julian took his sister's hands and kissed her affectionately. "Do sit down. You will stay to tea?"

"Oh, I think not, Julian," said Valeria, taking a seat. "I told Maria I would be back soon."

At the mention of his stepmother, the viscount's face clouded.

"And how is dear Maria?" said Fanny, oblivious to her husband's change of mood. "It has been so long since I have seen her. Fancy that she is a princess."

"Princess," sniffed Julian. "These foreign princesses are to be found everywhere. It is not at all the same as an English princess, to be sure."

"Oh, I know you are right, my dear," said Fanny quickly. "But still, to be even a foreign princess is quite above the ordinary. Poor Maria. How tragic for her to be widowed again!"

"Do not fear, Fanny," said Julian. "I do not doubt that my stepmother will soon set her claws in some other unsuspecting fellow. She has never had any difficulty securing husbands.''

"I would appreciate it, Julian," said Valeria severely, "if you would refrain from such ungentlemanly talk. You know how fond I am of Maria.''

"And you know the nature of my feelings for her," replied the viscount. "I find it particularly galling that you are staying with her in town and not with your own family.''

"I consider Maria my family," said Valeria coolly.

"I hope you do not intend to foist her upon us. I have never considered her fit company for Fanny or Kitty. Indeed, I do not think her fit company for you, and I must insist you leave her house and stay with us.''

Valeria's hazel eyes flashed dangerously. "You insist? Brother, you forget yourself. I am far too old for you to order about.''

"Then you should be old enough to realize how unacceptable it is for you to reside with her. Her name is a scandal throughout Europe.''

"What fustian!" Valeria rose quickly to her feet. "I will hear no more of this, Julian.''

"Valeria, please! Do not rush off!" cried Fanny. "Julian did not mean to vex you.'' Lady Harwood cast an imploring look at her husband. "Do tell Valeria you wish her to stay.''

Julian looked at his sister. "It was not my intention to set up your back. Please sit down. I shall say no more about Maria.''

Valeria hesitated, but noting her brother's conciliatory expression, she nodded and sat down once again. "And how are my nephews?" said Valeria, turning the conversation away from her stepmother.

Fanny was very happy to enlighten her sister-in-law about the progress of the two young Harwoods, who were away at Eton. She talked for some time, her face filled with maternal pride. However, when Valeria inquired about Kitty, Fanny's expression grew worried. "How glad I was to receive your letter saying you would come to town. I am hopeful that your advice to Kitty will be most helpful.''

"My dear Fanny, as I said in my letter, I do not think that I shall be of much use in this matter. Surely Kitty will listen even less to her maiden aunt than she would to her parents."

"But she ignores me completely," said Fanny. She glanced over at her husband. "And I fear she only quarrels with her father."

A slight smile appeared on Valeria's face. "That does not surprise me. But are you certain that the matter is so serious? A young girl like Kitty may be expected to have such infatuations. I daresay she will soon transfer her affections to another. Surely there is no cause for so much concern."

"I assure you, there is," said Julian. "Your niece is not a level-headed girl. She has been flirting outrageously with Traverhurst and her behavior has occasioned comment. And Traverhurst! The man is so unprincipled that he would have no scruples about compromising an innocent girl."

"Is he in love with Kitty?"

Julian regarded her as if she were the greatest ninny-hammer. "I doubt he knows the meaning of the word."

"But he is no fortune hunter," said Valeria. "I am told he has great wealth. If he does not love Kitty, why is he pursuing her?"

"I don't know. I sometimes think it is to spite me. Traverhurst knows that I despise men of his cut. When I told him that he must cast aside any ideas of connecting himself with our family, he had the audacity to laugh in my face. The man is a devil's cub."

"So you see it is serious, Valeria," said Fanny. "Kitty is totally unmanageable."

"And where is my unmanageable niece?"

"Upstairs in her sitting room."

"Then perhaps I should go see her," suggested Valeria.

"Yes, I think that would be a very good idea," said Fanny.

Valeria nodded and proceeded to her niece's rooms. Finding Kitty's door shut, she knocked. "Who is it?" came the reply.

"It is Valeria."

The door was quickly flung open. "Aunt Valeria!" Kitty threw her arms around her aunt's neck. "What a splendid surprise!"

After the exuberant young lady released her, Valeria regarded her niece fondly. As always, she was struck by Kitty's beauty. Her niece was perhaps the most lovely girl in society. She had inherited Fanny's fair good looks but had far eclipsed her mother. Kitty had a face of classical perfection and eyes of the clearest blue. Hers was the ethereal beauty of an angel and, indeed, many ardent suitors had compared her to those heavenly creatures.

"Do come in," said Kitty, taking her aunt's hand and leading her into the room. "Oh, how well you look. Do say you are staying for the Season. You must not go back to Melbury."

"I shall be in town for a time."

Kitty clapped her hands in delight. "Oh, good, it shall be such fun! You will stay in the room next door!"

"Oh, I am afraid I will not be staying here."

Kitty's face fell. "Not staying here?"

"I am staying with Maria."

"Maria! Mama said she had returned to England. Did she not come with you?"

"No, but she wants you and your mother to call upon her as soon as possible."

"Oh, that would be famous!" Kitty hesitated. "But then, Papa does not like Maria. Perhaps he will not allow me to visit her." Kitty sighed. "He can be so unreasonable. I suppose he and Mama have told you how I have distressed them."

Valeria nodded. "They have told me about Traverhurst. I should very much like to hear what you have to say about the matter."

"Oh, Aunt Valeria!" Kitty's face took on a dreamy look. "Have you ever seen him?"

"I have not had that pleasure."

"When I first saw him he took my breath away."

"Is he so very handsome?"

"Oh, yes! As handsome as a Greek god!" Valeria tried to refrain from smiling at this effusive remark as Kitty continued, "And he is more than handsome. He is the most charming man and so very dashing. Why, he once fought a duel! He is a crack shot and the most famous whip! His clothes are perfection itself. His boots are the envy of everyone!"

"Indeed? I should certainly like to see them," said Valeria, her hazel eyes expressing her amusement.

"And they say he is the best judge of wine in all of England," added Kitty.

"He sounds like a veritable paragon," said Valeria with mock solemnity.

"Oh, he is!" Kitty shook her head. "I cannot understand why Papa is so opposed to him. I think he would make the most wonderful husband."

"I am sure it is only that your parents would like you to consider other gentlemen as well. After all, Lord Traverhurst is a good deal older than you."

"That does not signify in the least. My dear aunt, I could never look at any other gentlemen. Traverhurst has taken my heart completely!"

Valeria paused and wondered how she should proceed. "But, Kitty," she said finally, "there is the matter of Traverhurst's reputation. You cannot blame your parents for being unhappy about that."

"Oh, fiddle faddle! Few gentlemen have spotless reputations, and those who do are so very dull. Mama and Papa do not understand. They are trying to ruin my happiness."

"It is your happiness they are concerned about. I do wish you would try to view the matter through their eyes."

Kitty regarded her aunt with a trace of petulance. "Aunt Valeria, I thought you would be on my side."

"It is not a matter of taking sides, Kitty."

"But I think it is. It is clear you are against Traverhurst." Kitty adopted a tragic pose. "It should not surprise me. Everyone is against him."

"Kitty, do not fly up into the boughs. I don't even know this Traverhurst. I just do not want you to make a cake of yourself over the man."

Valeria's niece looked indignant. "You are just like Mama and Papa. You do not know what is like to be in love!"

Thinking she had made a muddle of things, Valeria decided it was best to retreat. "I did not mean to upset you, Kitty. I shall say no more. Do promise you will call on me."

Kitty seemed to consider this and finally nodded. Valeria then smiled at the girl and took her leave.

Returning to Maria's townhouse, Valeria took off her bonnet and spencer and handed them to a maid. "Princess Lubetska is in the drawing room, miss. She has visitors."

"Visitors?"

"Two gentlemen, miss. Her highness wished you to join them as soon as you returned."

"Thank you," said Valeria, dismissing the servant. Wondering who Maria's callers might be, she made her way to the drawing room. The sight that greeted her eyes through the doorway made Valeria stop in some surprise. There was her stepmother and two rather unusual looking gentleman. The elder of the gentlemen was standing in the center of the room. He held a daffodil in his upraised hand. His other hand was placed upon his brow in a melodramatic pose and he was reciting what appeared to be a poem.

"Ode to the First Daffodil Lately Bloomed in Chelmsford Square," he said in stentorian tones. Then, clearing his throat, he continued, "Oh, yellow goddess, harbinger of spring. So lovely and so modest, Thy praises I do sing. There is none fairer, than this sweet flower, that shows to its bearer, nature's rapturous power."

At the conclusion of this recitation, the speaker bowed his head as if in anticipation of the accolades he would receive. They were soon forthcoming as Maria clasped her hands to her bosom and exclaimed, "Mr. Kingsley-Dunnett, how beautiful!"

The other gentleman, a pale young man, sighed. "A work of true genius, sir," he said.

Mr. Kingsley-Dunnett acknowledged the praise with a

nod. He then gallantly handed Maria the daffodil. "For you, Princess. A fair flower for a fair lady."

Maria smiled sweetly and took the flower. Then, noticing Valeria in the doorway, she called out, "My darling Valeria! What good fortune you are back! You must meet these gentlemen."

After hearing the older gentleman's lamentable verse, Valeria was intrigued. She entered the room and looked expectantly at her stepmother to make the introductions. "My stepdaughter, Miss Valeria Harwood. May I present Mr. Kingsley-Dunnett and the Marquess of Merrymount?"

During the introduction, Valeria had the opportunity to scrutinize the two visitors. Mr. Kingsley-Dunnett was a slight man of middle years who wore deplorable clothes. Valeria noted his baggy trousers and ill-cut coat and concluded that it was obvious Mr. Kingsley-Dunnett was oblivious to fashion. His black hair was long and wild looking and the only remarkable feature of his sallow face was a pair of piercing blue eyes. Valeria met his gaze and felt vaguely uncomfortable.

Lord Merrymount was a serious looking young man. His stylish clothes were a sharp contrast to those of his companion. Blond and fine featured, the marquess was quite good looking. Valeria judged him to be about twenty years of age. "How do you do, Miss Harwood?" said Merrymount in well bred accents.

Valeria extended her hand to the marquess, who bowed politely over it. Then she rather reluctantly gave her hand to Mr. Kingsley-Dunnett. To her horror, that gentleman raised it to his lips. Then still holding her hand, he gazed at her with his piercing blue eyes. "You are a vision of loveliness, Miss Harwood. I am so very pleased to meet you."

"Mr. Kingsley-Dunnett is a poet, Valeria," explained Maria. "He has just recited the most lovely poem. I am certain you could persuade him to do so again."

"Oh, I heard the poem," said Valeria hastily. Since Mr. Kingsley-Dunnett was regarding her expectantly, she felt some comment was necessary. "It was most . . . springlike."

"Precisely!" cried Kingsley-Dunnett. "That was the essence of it! What a perceptive young lady you are."

"Indeed," said Maria. "That is because Valeria is herself a literary person." Valeria directed a warning look at the princess, who realized her indiscretion and appeared apologetic.

"You are a fellow poet, Miss Harwood?" said Kingsley-Dunnett.

"I have not the talent for it, I assure you," replied Valeria. "My stepmother exaggerates, sir. I did once write a short essay that appeared in a ladies' magazine."

Kingsley-Dunnett cast a look of benevolent condescension at Valeria. "How wonderful, Miss Harwood. I think it charming that ladies amuse themselves by dabbling in literary endeavors. I should be very happy to assist you with any future efforts."

"You are too kind, Mr. Kingsley-Dunnett," said Valeria sweetly. "But, in truth, I should never wish a man of your obvious capabilities to see my poor efforts."

Mr. Kingsley-Dunnett smiled and revealed his uneven yellow teeth. "How I wish we might stay with you delightful ladies. Alas, I have another engagement and so we must reluctantly take our leave."

Maria expressed distress at this announcement, but Valeria was very happy to see them go. After the gentlemen had departed, Valeria sat down beside her stepmother. "Wherever did you find them?" she asked.

"Are they not fascinating? Mr. Kingsley-Dunnett had a letter of introduction from my dear friend Lady Balderston. I so love being in the presence of literary persons. How I missed such stimulating company at the castle. We were so very remote and had only the prince's dreary relations for society. But in London it is so very different. It is possible to be surrounded by artists of renown." She smiled at Valeria. "Why, I have a most distinguished authoress in residence."

"Just take care you make no mention of Verrell Hawkesworth, my dear Maria."

"Oh, you have my word. Now, tell me, how was your

visit to dear Fanny? Was your brother well? And what of Kitty?''

"Fanny and Julian are well. I fear Kitty is most adamant about her affection for Traverhurst. Nothing I could say could dissuade her from that. She has truly lost her head over the man. Julian is very opposed to the idea of a match between them and Kitty thinks him a terrible villain.''

"How sad,'' said Maria. "Love always has its difficulties. But I do not think it is so serious. With the Season just starting, a pretty girl like Kitty will have scores of suitors. I do not doubt that another handsome fellow will soon turn her head.''

"I cannot be so hopeful, Maria,'' said Valeria. "Kitty appears to be most constant in her affections. After all, Traverhurst is the best judge of wine in England.''

Maria directed a quizzical look at her stepdaughter and Valeria burst into laughter.

❧ 3 ❧

VALERIA found the early morning hours the most productive time to work on her book. Maria was a late riser and the household was relatively quiet then. A fine Queen Anne desk graced one corner of the princess's fashionable drawing room and Valeria soon commandeered it for her writing.

The next few mornings Valeria went down to the drawing room to work on *The Villain of Versailles*. She wrote diligently, quitting only when Maria appeared at noon. One day, however, Valeria had a difficult time accomplishing anything. She kept thinking about Kitty and wondering why she and Fanny had not called. It had been three days since Valeria had seen her brother and his family. A frown appeared on her face. She did not doubt that Julian was preventing them from coming to Maria's, and Valeria was very annoyed with him. Obviously, he expected her to do the visiting. Although tempted to stay away from her brother's townhouse, Valeria very much wanted to see Fanny and Kitty and she decided to call upon them that afternoon.

Having made that decision, Valeria turned her attention back to her writing. She reread the pages she had written the previous day and found the villainous Marquis de Morveau prominent in the story. Valeria looked thoughtful. Perhaps it was time that the marquis met his well deserved fate.

Valeria envisioned her hero Hannibal Wolfe locked in mortal combat with the treacherous Morveau. She heard the clash of their swords and saw the marquis's mocking smile as he goaded the virtuous captain to do his worst. She imagined Wolfe's triumphant look as his final sword thrust dispatched her villain to the netherworlds.

Valeria frowned. For some reason, she had no desire to kill Morveau. The book would seem so very flat without him. Indeed, perhaps it might be better if the ruthless Frenchman escaped to return in another sequel. Valeria pondered this, thinking it an admirable idea, and then she began to write once again.

Some time later Maria came down to the drawing room, her little white dog cradled in her arms. The princess greeted Valeria warmly. "My darling Valeria, you are so industrious. However can you rise so early?"

"I have kept country hours since I was a girl," replied Valeria. "I enjoy the morning most of all. Really, Maria, you must come down early some time. We could take a walk. I know Putti would like it very much."

Maria, who abhorred exercise nearly as much as she did rising early, expressed little enthusiasm for the idea. "My Putti is as much a slugabed as her mistress, aren't you, darling?" The princess planted a fond kiss on the top of the dog's head. "And besides, you need the mornings for your work. I trust it is going well?"

"Well enough. I shall be finished soon."

"How splendid! We will have a party when you are all done." Maria sat down on the sofa and placed Putti down beside her. The little white dog promptly curled up and closed her eyes, making it very clear that she did not want any part of morning outings. "Now, what shall we do after luncheon, my dear?" said Maria. "We should see the dressmaker, do you not think? You must arrange for your ball gown."

"Oh, Maria, I don't need a ball gown. If I do attend a ball, and, I daresay, I doubt I shall do so, I can wear the dress I wore at the Melbury ball three years ago."

The princess looked horrified. "You must be, what you

would say, 'gammoning' me. Wear a dress three years old in town? It would be a scandal!''

Valeria laughed. ''I suppose it would at that.''

''Do not argue with me, my darling. You must have a new ball gown.''

''Very well. I do not wish to shock society.''

Maria appeared relieved. ''Then we will go and consult Madame Gauthier this afternoon.''

''But I had planned to call at Julian's house today, Maria. It seems that Fanny and Kitty are not going to call here.''

''I would not be surprised if your brother would not permit them to do so. But do come with me to see Madame Gauthier. There will still be ample time for you to call at Harwood House. I shall not even consider accompanying you, for I know I am not welcome there.''

Valeria wished she could contradict her stepmother, but unfortunately, Maria's words were true. However, the princess seemed unperturbed and discoursed animatedly on the new spring fashions until it was time for lunch.

After the visit to the dressmaker's establishment that afternoon, Valeria set out to call at her brother's house. She appeared at Julian's door looking very stylish in a pelisse of green silk and matching bonnet. The butler admitted her. ''I am sorry, Miss Harwood, Lord and Lady Harwood and Miss Harwood are out.''

''Oh dear,'' said Valeria. ''Are they expected back soon?''

''I expect her ladyship and Miss Harwood shortly. I am uncertain as to his lordship's plans.''

''I shall wait for them in the drawing room, Eliot.''

''Very good, miss. Might I get you anything?''

''Oh, no. I shall be fine.'' Valeria went into the drawing room and, after casting off her bonnet, sat down on the sofa. She looked about the room, noting for the first time how much Fanny had changed it. It had been repainted a fashionable mauve hue and all the furniture was new. Valeria smiled, knowing how much Fanny liked to be in vogue.

The house was certainly very different from Melbury. Indeed, the Harwood ancestral manor was dreadfully old-fashioned, and Valeria wondered why her sister-in-law had never redecorated the country house. The reason quickly occurred to her. Fanny thought of Melbury as Valeria's home and she would never try to change it without leave. "Dear Fanny." Valeria spoke aloud and then smiled. She must suggest that Fanny make some changes at Melbury.

Valeria waited for some time, and then, having grown tired of sitting, rose from her chair and paced about the room. After scrutinizing all the paintings and artifacts, Valeria returned to her seat and waited a while longer. Finally, glancing up at the mantel clock, Valeria realized she had been there almost an hour.

Having no desire to remain any longer, Valeria took up her bonnet and rose to leave. Entering the hall, she heard the butler speaking to someone in the entry hall.

"I am sorry, my lord, but no one is here but Miss Harwood."

"Miss Harwood?" returned the apparent caller. "That is whom I have come to see. Tell her I am here."

"But, my lord . . ."

"Where is she?" demanded the imperious voice.

"In the drawing room, my lord, but . . ."

"Stand aside, then. I'll announce myself."

Valeria hurried back into the drawing room and sat down to await the brash visitor. A few seconds later a gentleman entered the room. "Kitty." Seeing Valeria, he stopped and regarded her in confusion.

The stranger's appearance startled Valeria and her eyes widened in surprise. There standing before her was the incarnation of her fictional character, the Marquis de Morveau. Indeed, in all of her imaginings of her villain, Valeria had pictured him looking exactly like the man who had just entered the room.

He was tall and exceedingly handsome with curly dark hair arranged in the Brutus cut. His countenance had a decidedly roguish appearance due to the dark eyebrows that framed his gray eyes and the slight smile that played upon his lips. On his cheek was a faint scar. Valeria stared at it, noting that it ran in a straight line from his left cheekbone to the corner of his mouth. It was precisely like the scar the villainous marquis had received in an earlier encounter with the redoubtable Hannibal Wolfe.

The stranger's clothes marked him as a proper Corinthian. He wore an impeccabley cut coat of olive green superfine which, due to the broadness of his shoulders, required no padding. His muscular legs were encased in fawn-colored pantaloons and on his feet were a pair of sparkling black Hessian boots.

"Is it that you don't like my neckcloth, or do I have gravy on my chin?"

"What?" asked Valeria in some bewilderment. Then, realizing that she had been staring at him, she colored with embarrassment. "Forgive me. It is just that for a moment you looked familiar to me."

"Well, I regret, madam, that you do not look familiar to me. I was expecting Miss Harwood."

"I am Miss Valeria Harwood."

The gentleman's dark eyebrows arched in surprise. "You cannot mean you are Kitty's spinster aunt?"

"I am Kitty's aunt, and my niece is not at home," she replied coolly.

He laughed. "The way Kitty talked of you, I thought you were ancient. She respects you so. It is always Aunt Valeria said this and Aunt Valeria said that. You sounded like the oracle of Delphi. I never expected you to be a girl hardly older than she is."

Valeria bristled. "I assure you, sir, I am far beyond my girlhood."

"I apologize, but most of the ladies of my acquaintance are very glad to appear younger than their years. Oh, I must introduce myself. I am Traverhurst."

"I scarcely needed the introduction, my lord," said Valeria, frowning disapprovingly at him. "Your reputation precedes you."

He laughed. "Then I hope I do not disappoint you."

"On the contrary, I see you are all that people say."

"I am gratified to hear it, Madame Oracle." He grinned and then, without as much as a by your leave, sat down opposite her. "And why have I never had the pleasure of meeting you before, Miss Harwood?"

"I am rarely in town. I prefer the country."

"That is society's loss, ma'am. And you are paying one of your rare visits?" A flash of insight came to him. "Of course, Harwood has brought you here to talk sense into Kitty."

"It appears she is in need of it."

Traverhurst laughed. "You are too hard on me, Madame Oracle. I am not such a bad fellow. My old nanny would give you a dashed fine character reference." Valeria smiled in spite of herself and the earl grinned. "Ah, your smile is very becoming," he said. "You should smile more often."

"I shall smile when I please," said Valeria testily, "and at present I do not think there is much cause for smiling. I shall be blunt, Lord Traverhurst. I share my brother's concern for Kitty. I wish to know your intentions regarding her."

"My intentions?" Traverhurst raised an eyebrow and regarded her quizzically.

Valeria nodded. "I wish to know if your intentions are honorable."

He grinned. "My dear lady, my intentions are never honorable."

"I do not think this is occasion for levity, sir," said Valeria severely.

"Do forgive me," he said, but the amused glint in his eyes belied his contrition.

Valeria frowned and continued. "You cannot blame my brother for worrying about a man whose only virtues appear to be the shine of his boots and his taste in wine."

Traverhurst smiled. "You forget that I also tie a devilish good cravat."

"You are incorrigible!"

"And you are a meddlesome maiden aunt. Cannot Harwood handle his own affairs? Why must he summon the provincial oracle?"

"I am not in the least amused by your remarks."

"Then you are as humorless as your brother."

Valeria rose from her chair. "I think you had better go, Lord Traverhurst."

"As you wish, madam." The earl made an extravagent bow and then, casting one last smile at her, left the room.

"What a dreadful man," said Valeria aloud. "And how uncannily he resembles Morveau." She went to the window and watched the earl leave the house, jump nimbly into an awaiting phaeton and, taking up the reins, drive recklessly away.

The carriage had scarcely gone when another vehicle pulled up to the curb. Valeria observed her brother and another gentleman descend from the equipage and enter the house. A few moments later they appeared in the drawing room.

"Valeria," said Julian. "Eliot said you have been waiting. I hope you have not been dreadfully bored."

Valeria smiled. "I have scarcely been bored. Indeed, I have been richly entertained." Julian looked perplexed and his sister laughed. "Lord Traverhurst was just here."

"Traverhurst here? How could you have admitted the fellow?"

"I did not admit him. He simply barged in."

"That is so like him," said the other man.

Julian, seeming then to remember the presence of this gentleman, hastened to make an introduction. "Valeria, may I present Sir Rupert Netherton. Rupert, this is my sister Valeria."

"How do you do?" said Valeria, extending her hand to Sir Rupert. As that gentleman bowed politely over it, she took the opportunity to study him. As tall as her brother, Sir Rupert was of heavier build, inclining toward stoutness. He was very well dressed and his bearing was dignified. His countenance was pleasant, although not particularly handsome, and his graying hair was neatly cropped.

"It is a pleasure to meet you, Miss Harwood," said Sir Rupert.

"I am very glad to meet you, sir," said Valeria. "Julian has mentioned you so often that I believe I know you. You are lately back from India?"

"Yes, I returned some months ago."

"How exciting that must have been. Julian has told me you were on the Viceroy's staff."

"Rupert always has the exciting life," said Julian, breaking into the conversation. "He has lived in all the exotic places."

"Exotic?" said Sir Rupert with a smile. "In truth, Miss Harwood, exotic means hot and deuced uncomfortable."

They all laughed and then Julian suggested they sit down. Once settled, they continued the conversation. Valeria turned to Sir Rupert. "Then will you be in England long, sir?"

"For a time. But, then one never knows in government service."

"I imagine this bobbery with Bonaparte escaping from Elba makes matters so uncertain," said Julian.

"Indeed, yes," agreed Netherton. "One does not know what will happen next."

"What do you think will happen, Sir Rupert?" asked Valeria. "I expect working in the government you have a better understanding of the situation."

"I fear, Miss Harwood, I am not at liberty to discuss the matter."

"Oh yes," said Julian, "Rupert is privy to all manner of government secrets. He advises the prime minister, you know."

Valeria appeared impressed. "How thrilling to be in the thick of things," she said.

Julian steered the conversation away from his friend. "But what is this of Traverhurst being here?"

"He came to see Kitty."

"The audacity of the man!" Julian looked over at Rupert. "I have told you of Traverhurst's attentions to my daughter." Netherton nodded gravely.

"He is all you have said," said Valeria. "His impudence knew no bounds."

Julian looked startled. "Did he dare offend you? By my faith, he will have cause to regret it!"

Valeria was amused by her brother's reaction. "I assure you, there is no cause for you to have to defend my honor,

Julian. He thought me a meddlesome old spinster and had the boldness to tell me so."

"The fellow should be flogged," said Sir Rupert indignantly.

Julian nodded. "An admirable suggestion."

Valeria laughed. "You gentlemen are a trifle harsh."

"I think not, Miss Harwood," said Netherton. "It is infamous that such a fellow can behave so shockingly and still be accepted in society."

"Indeed," said Julian, "he is quite popular. That is what galls me."

"Well, he is not popular with me, I assure you," said Valeria.

"You show admirable judgment, Miss Harwood," said Netherton, smiling at her. He then turned to Julian. "I fear I must be going. I have an appointment."

"Affairs of state?" asked Julian.

"One might say that," replied Sir Rupert, rising from his chair. The viscount rose, too.

"I'll see you at the club tonight," said Julian.

Rupert nodded and then looked over at Valeria. "Such a pleasure to have met you, Miss Harwood. I am hopeful that I shall see you again when I next call at Harwood House."

"Oh, I am not staying here. I am staying with my stepmother, Princess Lubetska, on Chelmsford Square."

Sir Rupert's face registered surprise. "I do not think I have ever met the lady."

"She has only recently returned to England. Perhaps you might call upon us one day."

"I shall endeavor to do so." Sir Rupert then took his leave. When he had gone, Julian looked at his sister.

"You see what response there is to your Maria's name. My old friend Rupert was undoubtedly quite appalled to know that you would be staying with her. I don't know if any respectable persons will wish to visit you there."

"Julian, pray do not start on this again. I have no desire to quarrel with you."

"Nor I with you. Let us speak of something else. How is your novel progressing?"

"Very well. It is nearly completed."

Julian smiled. "Good. I am eager to read the further adventures of Captain Wolfe. Fanny was in raptures over *The Queen's Champion*. I so wanted to tell her the identity of Verrell Hawkesworth. When are you going to reveal your secret to Fanny?"

"It is not that I consider Fanny a gabblemonger, Julian. But I think it best that few people know about it. Perhaps sometime later."

"As you wish. But I know your niece would be especially thrilled to find out her aunt was a famous authoress."

Valeria smiled. "I had hoped to see Kitty this afternoon."

"I am not certain when she and Fanny will return."

Valeria rose from her chair and took up her bonnet. "Then I think I shall be off, Julian. Do give Fanny and Kitty my love. And do allow them to call on me."

"I don't know," said Julian.

"Oh, do not refuse now. Take some time to think on it."

"Very well." Valeria smiled and kissed him on the cheek. "Why don't you dine with us tomorrow night?" asked Julian.

"You know I could not do so without Maria."

Julian frowned. "I shall think on that, too."

"Oh, Julian," said Valeria happily. "I knew you would come around!"

"I have scarcely done that. I have simply said I would think about the matter."

However, sensing that her brother was thawing, Valeria smiled again and, kissing him once more, departed.

4

THE NEXT morning Valeria sat at her desk in the drawing room, writing the concluding chapters of her book. Deep in concentration, Valeria was oblivious to her surroundings. Her pen raced across the paper, rapidly filling page after page.

After finishing a particularly exciting scene, Valeria felt exhausted. She glanced at the clock and realized with some surprise that it was almost noon. Maria would soon appear. Glancing back at her work, Valeria started to reread it. "Oh dear," she said, as her eye fell upon a word. She had written "Traverhurst" instead of "Morveau."

Valeria quickly scratched out the name Traverhurst and corrected it. It was not surprising that she had made such an error, she reflected. Since meeting the earl the previous afternoon, she had thought of him often. It was such an odd coincidence that the earl so closely resembled her fictional character. Indeed, it made Valeria a trifle uneasy.

In her thoughts, the two of them were now so interwoven that she had difficulty separating them. Like Morveau, the earl possessed a roguish charm, and she did not doubt that Traverhurst was every bit as unscrupulous as her villain. Certainly he was as dangerous.

"Valeria." Maria's voice brought Valeria from her thoughts of Traverhurst. The princess entered the room with Putti tucked under her arm.

"Maria, I did not hear you come in."

"Of course not. You are too much involved with *mon capitaine* Wolfe."

Valeria smiled. "Actually, I was more involved with my villain."

"Ah, the wicked marquis. Sometimes a scoundrel has great appeal to a woman."

Valeria reddened and she was glad that she had not told Maria how Traverhurst resembled the fictional Morveau. "Perhaps to some women such a man is attractive."

"And not to you?" said Maria. "Do not tell me that you did not find Traverhurst rather attractive."

"Certainly not!"

The vehemence of Valeria's response caused Maria to laugh. "Pardon me for suggesting it, my dear. But I must confess I would like to see the earl again. I remember thinking him an extremely handsome young man."

Valeria switched the subject away from the earl. "Shall we go to the linen drapers today?"

"No, there are much more exciting plans."

Valeria regarded her stepmother with interest. "Indeed?"

"Yes, I am having some fascinating visitors for tea. You met two of them, Mr. Kingsley-Dunnett and young Lord Merrymount."

Remembering these gentlemen, Valeria tried to appear pleased. "They are calling again?"

"Certainly, I think they shall be frequent callers. Indeed, I hope to gather all manner of artists about us here. It will be so stimulating. In time, we shall rival the salon of Madame de Stael."

Valeria tried to refrain from laughing. "It sounds very diverting."

"Oh, yes, I shall be a great patroness of the arts. Indeed, Mr. Kingsley-Dunnett has begged to dedicate his epic poem to me."

A mischievous smile crossed Valeria's fair countenance. "How very generous of him."

"He is generosity itself."

"Oh, I am certain of it," replied Valeria.

"My dear, would you be so kind as to come with me

upstairs? I need your assistance to decide what to wear this afternoon. It is important that I look my best."

Valeria nodded and the two ladies left the drawing room.

The Princess Lubetska looked very handsome in her black crepe gown as she greeted her guests. Standing beside her, Valeria was surprised at the number of persons arriving. She had not expected such a sizeable party.

The drawing room was filled with all manner of personages, some of them decidedly eccentric. Among them were a formidable looking Prussian sculptress, a nearly unintelligible Scottish poet, a dissolute Italian count, and a sultry Venetian opera singer. The company was so diverse and amusing that Valeria was enjoying herself immensely.

Her enjoyment was cut short when Mr. Kingsley-Dunnett attached himself to her and showed no inclination of wanting to leave. She found the poet a very unappealing gentleman whose conceit was nearly as great as his lack of talent. His conversation consisted of reciting a catalog of his works, each of which he declared a masterpiece.

"Doubtlessly you are wondering about my epic poem, Miss Harwood," said Kingsley-Dunnett. "Everyone is."

"Indeed, how curious. No one has mentioned it," replied Valeria.

He ignored the setdown and continued. "I have entitled it, 'Gloriana, or the Divine Elizabeth.' "

"It sounds so very . . . historical."

"Your astuteness amazes me, Miss Harwood. It is indeed historical. It is the very essence of the Elizabethan age. The virgin queen is its focus, of course."

"I did suspect as much," said Valeria.

"Perhaps you would like to hear a portion of it. There is a brilliant section in which Robert Dudley meets the Queen's barge."

Valeria shook her head. "I shall prefer to wait until your work is finished. I fear hearing but a morsel would be unbearable."

The poet, unaware of the sarcasm in the lady's remarks,

nodded. "I can well understand that. You may be glad to know I am quite near completion."

They were suddenly joined by the Prussian sculptress, an enormous blond woman with the look of a Valkyrie. She fixed her pale blue eyes on Kingsley-Dunnett. "Your face, *mein herr*, it belongs in bronze."

"Thank you," said Kingsley-Dunnett, perceiving the remark to be a great compliment.

Valeria valiantly managed to keep from laughing and the giantess continued, "I am the Baroness von Mecklenberg." She extended a brawny hand to Kingsley-Dunnett and, taking his, shook it vigorously. "I have long wished such a great poet to meet. Your work is . . . *sehr* beautiful."

Kingsley-Dunnett appeared well accustomed to such praise. "You are kind, madam."

"*Nein*, not kind, *mein herr*. I am only truthful." Then, pointedly ignoring Valeria, the baroness forcefully led Kingsley-Dunnett away. Rather than being offended at the Amazonian sculptress's appropriation of her companion, Valeria was delighted. She smiled and joined Maria.

The princess appeared to be thoroughly enjoying herself. She was standing with Lord Merrymount and a frail old gentleman in a powdered wig. "Ah, my dear Valeria. You have not met Herr Schnitzler. He is an old friend of mine from Vienna. This is my stepdaughter, Miss Harwood."

"How do you do?" said the elderly man, bowing low over Valeria's hand. Then, protesting that his English was very bad, he switched to French and the conversation proceeded in that language. When, after a time, the Austrian gentleman appeared weary, Maria solicitously led him to a chair, leaving Valeria with young Lord Merrymount.

"It is such an interesting gathering, is it not?" said Valeria. "I had not expected the princess to have so many guests this afternoon."

"The Princess Lubetska is a very gracious lady."

Valeria nodded. Glancing across the room, she espied Kingsley-Dunnett in animated discussion with the Prussian sculptress. "It appears that the Baroness von Mecklenberg is very much taken with your friend Mr. Kingsley-Dunnett."

"Mr. Kingsley-Dunnett has many admirers, Miss Harwood."

"But, I daresay, there are not many who wish to cast him in bronze."

The marquess smiled.

"Are you also a poet, Lord Merrymount?"

"Oh, I dare not call myself that, Miss Harwood. One day I hope to be one."

"That is admirable."

"My father certainly does not think it admirable. He thinks being a poet a cork-brained notion."

Valeria smiled. "That is a pity, but perhaps in time he will change his opinion."

The marquess shook his head. "I fear the Duke of Westbridge never changes his opinions."

"Your father is the Duke of Westbridge?"

Merrymount smiled. "I thought everyone knew that."

"I am much in the country and do not know many people."

At that moment, the butler entered the drawing room and announced Sir Rupert Netherton. Valeria turned toward the doorway in surprise. She had not expected to see her brother's friend again so soon. "Oh, Sir Rupert is my brother's good friend. Do excuse me. I must go and greet him."

Valeria approached Netherton, who smiled warmly at seeing her. "Miss Harwood."

"Sir Rupert. How good of you to call."

"I did not expect such a crush of people."

Valeria smiled. "Nor did I. My stepmother has been in England such a short time. Of course, she has many acquaintances throughout Europe."

Netherton surveyed the company. "It appears a good many of them are here. I do not believe I know anyone. Oh, but there is Merrymount."

"You are acquainted with Lord Merrymount?"

Sir Rupert nodded. "I know his father well. The cub had given the duke no end of bother. Who would have expected Westbridge to have such a son?"

Valeria, although not well acquainted with Merrymount,

had found him a pleasant young gentleman, and she rather resented Netherton's comment. "I just met him, but I thought him very nice."

"He is nothing but a silly mooncalf," said Sir Rupert scornfully. "His younger brother, Lord Andrew, is more the man. Pity he was not born first."

Before Valeria could reply to this unkind remark, they were joined by the princess and two of her guests. Maria eyed Netherton with some interest and Valeria hastened to introduce him. "Oh, Maria, may I present Sir Rupert Netherton? Sir Rupert, this is my stepmother, Princess Lubetska." Netherton made a polite bow. "Sir Rupert is a good friend of Julian's."

Maria raised an eyebrow. "Any friend of Julian's is most welcome here. But I must introduce Count Renzetti and Signora Borguesa. The signora is the most talented singer. I saw her in *Don Giovanni* in Prague and she was magnificent."

The signora, a voluptuous dark-haired lady in a low-cut gown, beamed at the praise. "You are too good, *principessa*."

"No one can do you justice, *carissima*," said the count, a thin man with a sallow complexion and bulging eyes. "She sings like an angel. And such beauty as well. How the gods have favored you!" He took the signora's hand and kissed it, and then he looked adoringly into her face.

"I should very much like to hear you, Signora Borguesa," said Valeria.

"And you shall, my darling," said Maria. "The signora is singing in *Così Fan Tutte*. We will go at first opportunity."

"Indeed, you must," cried the count. "She is divine."

The signora cast a fond look at Count Renzetti, and then she turned to Maria. "We must take our leave, dear *principessa*. And do not forget my little party on Thursday."

"No, indeed not," returned Maria, and then the count and Signora Borguesa left. "Such charming people," said Maria. "And they are as much in love as they were twelve years ago when first she became his mistress."

Sir Rupert, who did not think such talk fit for Miss Harwood's ears, frowned. Looking over at Valeria, he was

a trifle surprised that the young lady did not blush or
appear in any way offended. "It would be fun to go to the
opera, Maria," she said. She turned to Sir Rupert. "Do you
enjoy the opera, sir?"

Netherton shrugged. "I fear I do not find it to my
taste."

Maria shook her head. "You Englishmen do not have
musical souls. The only music you enjoy is the baying of
hounds."

Valeria laughed, but Sir Rupert looked unamused. "You
cannot blame a man for enjoying hunting," he said
defensively.

"Yes, yes, I know so well the English fondness for
sport. But I must leave you. There are so many guests and
I must see them all." Maria hurried off and Valeria did not
fail to note that Sir Rupert watched the princess's retreating form with obvious disapproval.

Netherton returned his attention to Valeria. "Will you
be in town for the Season, Miss Harwood?"

"I really do not know how long I shall stay. I suspect
that after a time I shall miss the country. But at present, I
am enjoying myself very much."

Sir Rupert seemed to be happy to hear that Valeria had
no immediate plans for leaving London. He began to talk
about various upcoming social events. Valeria soon found
her attention waning and was happy to see the arrival of
her sister-in-law Fanny and Kitty. "Oh look, Sir Rupert, it
is Fanny and Kitty."

Netherton turned and they watched the two ladies enter
the drawing room. Fanny looked very well in a stylish
walking dress of blue kerseymere, but she was far out-
shone by her daughter. Kitty was an enchanting vision in
lavender. All heads turned and watched her as she and
Fanny approached Valeria.

"Fanny, Kitty, I am so glad you have come."

Fanny smiled at her sister-in-law. "I did not expect a
party."

Kitty surveyed the crowd with wide eyes. "How famous
to find so many interesting people."

"And Rupert," said Fanny. "How nice to see you here."

Netherton seemed to find it necessary to provide an explanation for his presence. "I met Miss Harwood yesterday, Fanny. She invited me to call."

"I see," said Fanny, eyeing Sir Rupert with some interest. "But where is dearest Maria?"

Her question was immediately answered by the princess herself. "Fanny, my darling!" Maria hurried to embrace her and then looked at Kitty. "*Himmel*! How you have grown, *liebchen*. And what a beauty you are! So many broken hearts you will leave."

Kitty blushed prettily. "Oh, Maria."

The princess opened her arms and embraced Kitty. "How wonderful for you to come."

"We have been eager to see you," said Fanny. "And you look perfectly lovely. And so many guests! What a squeeze!"

"Oh, you must meet everyone," said Maria, taking Fanny's arm. "Valeria, see to Kitty. Introduce her about."

Since Maria and Fanny had hurried off, Kitty looked expectantly at her aunt. "I fear I do not know that many people here," said Valeria.

"They are all so different than the people I usually see at parties," said Kitty, looking across the room. "Why, look at that gentleman with the wild black hair and that large lady. Do you know them?"

"They are among the few I do know," replied Valeria, smiling at Kingsley-Dunnett and the Baroness von Mecklenberg. "The man is Mr. Kingsley-Dunnett. He purports to be an eminent poet."

"Poet," said Netherton distastefully. "He looks the part."

"And the lady?"

"She is Baroness von Mecklenberg, a sculptress. She rather frightens me."

Kitty laughed. "She is a veritable gorgon. I should swoon if she talked to me."

"I daresay there is little danger of that," said Valeria.

"It appears she wishes only to talk to Mr. Kingsley-Dunnett."

"He looks rather frightful himself," said Kitty. "But I have never met a poet. Indeed, I would very much like to meet one."

"I doubt that your father would approve of him, or of most of the other people here, Kitty," said Netherton.

"Then I should like to meet them all the more," laughed Kitty. "Come, Aunt Valeria, you must introduce me to some of them."

"Well, I do know Merrymount," said Valeria, espying that young gentleman standing by himself. "I shall introduce you to him." The three of them made their way to the marquess. "Lord Merrymount," said Valeria. "I should like you to meet my niece. I believe you know Sir Rupert Netherton. Kitty, this is the Marquess of Merrymount. Lord Merrymount, my niece, Miss Kitty Harwood."

The young man stood staring at Kitty as if transfixed.

"How do you do, Lord Merrymount?" said Kitty politely. "I believe I know your cousin, Lady Helena Gilroy." The marquess did not seem to hear her. "Lady Helena is your cousin, is she not, my lord?" asked Kitty, regarding him curiously.

The young man appeared flustered. "She is," he said finally, and then seemed incapable of any further utterances.

Kitty appeared amused. "Do you know Princess Lubetska, Lord Merrymount?"

"No, that is, yes. I mean to say, I know her slightly."

"And are you acquainted with the others here, Merrymount?" asked Netherton. "Perhaps you know the odd-looking fellow over there. I am told he is a poet. I would have taken him for one. Egad, can you imagine the fustian such a fellow would write?"

Merrymount directed an icy look at Netherton. Drawing himself up to his considerable height, he seemed to lose all trace of his former awkwardness. "Mr. Kingsley-Dunnett is a very good friend of mine. sir," he said in a manner worthy of the son of a duke. "He is a well-respected poet."

Netherton was rather startled by Merrymount's imperi-

ous manner. Although thinking the marquess a ridiculous
cub, he decided it was unwise to alienate someone of his
rank. "I meant no offense, Merrymount." Looking unconvinced by Netherton's words, the marquess eyed him coolly.
Sir Rupert looked at his watch and then turned to Valeria.
"I fear I cannot stay any longer. I hope to see you again
soon, Miss Harwood. Kitty." He bowed to the ladies and,
after nodding to Merrymount, departed.

Kitty watched him go. "I do not think Sir Rupert likes
poetry. He is just like my father."

"And do you like poetry, Miss Harwood?" asked
Merrymount with a trace of his former bashfulness.

"Oh yes, very much! I adore poetry. Shakespeare's son-
nets are my favorites. Aunt Valeria gave me a volume of
them for my last birthday." The marquess seemed very
much encouraged by this reply and ventured his opinions
of the bard's immortal works. They continued to chat
pleasantly for a time and Valeria was most happy to see
that the sensitive young marquess was beginning to enjoy
himself.

❦ 5 ❦

VALERIA straightened the pages of her manuscript into two neat stacks and then looked at the mountains of paper with satisfaction. Her book was finally finished. Captain Hannibal Wolfe had triumphed and his enemy Morveau had fled.

She carefully wrapped each thick stack in brown paper and then tied them with string. Now she had only to deliver the book to her publisher, and she hoped to accomplish this that very morning.

Leaving the manuscript on the drawing room desk, Valeria went up to her room to get ready to go out. After changing into a walking outfit and putting on her bonnet, she headed for the stairway. As she passed Maria's rooms, the princess called out to her. "Valeria!"

Not expecting her stepmother to be awake at such an early hour, Valeria was surprised. She entered Maria's bedchamber and found the princess sitting up in bed. Little Putti, lying at her feet, uttered a shrill bark.

"Hush, darling," said Maria. "It is only Valeria."

"Yes, it is only I." Valeria reached down and stroked the tiny creature's head.

Noting her stepdaughter's attire, Maria regarded her questioningly. "But you are dressed to go out."

Valeria nodded. "I am taking my book to my publisher's office."

"So early?"

Valeria smiled. "I am anxious to be rid of it. I shall feel better when it is in Mr. Burden's hands."

"Would you like me to accompany you?"

"Oh, no. There is no need for that."

Maria did not seem too unhappy, for in truth she did not relish the idea of rising at this hour. Valeria, well aware of her stepmother's fondness for sleeping late, smiled. "I am surprised that you are awake. Could you not sleep?"

"I could not. I am so very excited. Everyone is coming this afternoon. All the wonderful guests who were here last week are returning! Mr. Kingsley-Dunnett has agreed to read a portion of his 'Gloriana,' and the signora will sing. I know you will enjoy it."

"Oh, dear," said Valeria, "I fear I cannot attend. I promised Kitty that I would go shopping with her."

Maria appeared disappointed. "Oh, what a shame!"

"But I know there will be many other opportunities to hear the signora. After all, it appears you have established a salon here. It is very exciting."

Maria brightened. "Yes, you are right. We shall miss you."

Valeria patted Putti again. "I must be going. It is all right if I take the carriage?"

"But of course, my darling."

Valeria smiled. "Thank you, Maria. I shall be back well before luncheon." Valeria went to the drawing room and scooped up the bulky packages. Soon she was on her way through the streets of London.

Sometime later she arrived at the office of Hollingshead and Burden, Publishers. Valeria was quickly ushered into the office of Mr. Jeremiah Burden, an owlish little man, who appeared delighted to see her. "My dear Miss Harwood," he cried, hurrying over to her. Noting the bundles in her arms, he beamed. "Might I hope that this is *The Villain of Versailles*?"

"Exactly so, Mr. Burden." She handed him the manuscript.

"You cannot know how happy this makes me," said Burden. "Our readers have been clamoring for a new work by Verrell Hawkesworth. How delightful that you came in person. It has been so long since you have visited our office. Are you staying in town?''

Valeria nodded. ''I am staying with Princess Lubetska on Chelmsford Square.''

''Princess Lubetska?'' The publisher looked quite interested.

''She is my stepmother.''

''Indeed? I have heard so much about her and I would dearly love to meet her. By all accounts, she is a fascinating woman.'' He paused and appeared to be considering something for a moment. ''Do you think, Miss Harwood, that the princess might be persuaded to write her memoirs? We would be most interested in publishing them.''

Valeria smiled, thinking of how her brother Julian would react to seeing his stepmother's reminiscences in print. ''I do not know. But I shall mention it to her.''

''Oh, I should be most grateful to you, Miss Hawkesworth. Oh, that is, Miss Harwood.''

''Mr. Burden, I do hope I can rely on your discretion in keeping my identity secret.''

''Indeed, ma'am, you may count on me to do so. Here at Hollingshead and Burden we are ever discreet.'' He smiled. ''There has been much speculation regarding Verrell Hawkesworth's identity. Only yesterday I received a most interesting letter from a gentleman from Plymouth. I must read it to you.'' Burden went to his desk and, setting the manuscript down, rummaged through his papers. ''Ah, here it is!'' The publisher put on a pair of spectacles and peered down at the letter. '' 'It is clear to me that Verrell Hawkesworth is not the author's true name. Only a military gentleman of great experience could have penned such vivid battle scenes. I suspect Verrell Hawkesworth is, in truth, a retired general.' ''

Valeria burst into laughter and Burden grinned. ''You do not look like a general, Miss Harwood, and certainly not a retired general.''

''How disillusioning it would be for that gentleman to find out the truth.''

''Well, there is no chance of that, I assure you.''

''I shall not take any more of your time, Mr. Burden.''

Burden escorted Valeria to the door. "Miss Harwood?"
"Yes?"

"When might I hope to expect another work by Verrell Hawkesworth?"

Valeria groaned. "Have pity on poor Mr. Hawkesworth, sir. He is in need of rest."

"Yes, of course," said Burden hastily. "A lady must have time to enjoy herself."

Valeria smiled and took her leave. Returning home, she had luncheon with Maria. The princess was highly amused at the suggestion that she write her memoirs, but informed Valeria that that task would be reserved for her dotage.

Following luncheon, Valeria set out for her brother's house. There she found her sister-in-law Fanny in the drawing room. The two women embraced.

"Valeria, do sit down. Kitty is getting ready and she will be down shortly."

"Won't you come with us, Fanny?"

"Oh, I do wish I could do so, but I am expected at Lady Claridge's house this afternoon. It is good of you to take Kitty shopping."

"Oh, I shall enjoy it. Indeed, there are many things I must buy. I have great hopes of finding a new hat."

"I so love buying hats," said Fanny, "but I always have a difficult time deciding which to purchase. You must go to Mrs. Rigby's shop. It is the very best milliner's establishment in town."

"We will do so," replied Valeria. Then, directing the discussion away from hats, she continued, "Maria is having all her guests again today."

Fanny smiled. "I do wish I could go. It was so amusing being there last week with all those interesting people. Of course, Julian was not very happy about us going. He is so unreasonable where Maria is concerned. At least dear Julian was quite pleased to hear that Kitty met Lord Merrymount there. The marquess is perhaps the greatest prize in town. If only Kitty could become interested in him and forget this dreadful Traverhurst."

"Well, Merrymount is a nice young man, but I fear Kitty is smitten with Traverhurst."

Fanny looked over at Valeria. "It must have been so trying for you meeting Traverhurst here that day."

"It was that."

"I thought it was very bold of him coming here, knowing how Julian feels about him. Of course, he does as he pleases with no concern for the opinions of others."

"He does appear to have an insolent nature."

"It is his French blood, I am sure. Indeed, I think he is scarcely English at all." Valeria smiled at this remark and Fanny continued, "I think there is much to commend English gentlemen. Sir Rupert is a very good example." Fanny directed a knowing glance at her sister-in-law. "I had not expected to find Rupert at Maria's. It appears you have made a conquest."

"That is perfect bosh," said Valeria.

Fanny laughed at her response. "It is not. Sir Rupert appeared quite smitten with you. Oh, Valeria, I think it wonderful. He would suit you very well. He lost his wife some years ago and it is time he remarried."

"Fanny! You have me married off after I have met the gentleman only twice?"

"I may be a trifle premature," admitted Fanny. "But you cannot fault me for caring about your happiness. It would be so splendid if you married a good and kind man."

Before Valeria could make a reply, Kitty appeared in the drawing room. As usual, that young lady looked stunningly beautiful in a cream-colored spencer and matching dress, a charming cottage bonnet atop her golden curls. "Aunt Valeria, I do hope you were not waiting long."

"Not long at all, Kitty. I can see you are ready to go."

Kitty nodded. "We have so many shops to visit. There is the linen drapers and the glove maker, and then I must find a new fan. I saw the most charming painted Japanese creations at Wimbleford's."

"And your aunt wants to buy a hat. You must take her to see Mrs. Rigby."

"Oh, how famous! I shall help you find the perfect hat." Kitty was suddenly impatient. "Then we must go at once. There is so little time to do so much!"

Valeria rose from her chair and, after exchanging an amused glance with her sister-in-law, allowed herself to be led off by her exuberant niece.

Mrs. Rigby's elegant shop was patronized by some of the most fashionable ladies in London. The proprietress prided herself in setting the styles of the day.

When Kitty and Valeria entered the establishment, they were immediately greeted by Mrs. Rigby herself. She was well acquainted with Miss Kitty Harwood, who was one of her best customers. "Miss Harwood!" she exclaimed. "What an honor it is to see you here again."

"Hello, Mrs. Rigby. My aunt, Miss Harwood, is here to buy a hat."

"Oh, we have many hats that would suit you splendidly, ma'am. Do allow me to show you the latest French designs." Mrs. Rigby led the two ladies from the shop's main area into a more private room in back and bade Valeria be seated in a chair that faced a mirror.

The milliner left them and returned a few moments later. In her hand was a lavish creation featuring an assortment of colorful wax fruit. "This style is the talk of Paris."

"I do not doubt it," said Valeria, eyeing the hat with amusement, "but I do not think it would suit me."

"Oh, Aunt Valeria," urged Kitty, "do try it on."

Valeria removed her own bonnet and then tried on the elaborate headdress that the milliner handed to her.

"Oh, I do like it," Kitty cried.

Valeria regarded herself skeptically in the mirror. "Oh, I don't know."

"Do not be hasty, aunt. Look at it a while." Kitty glanced over at Mrs. Rigby. "Perhaps there are a trifle too many grapes."

"Well, I have many more that I can show you," said the milliner. "I shall return with some of them."

"Do let me come with you, Mrs. Rigby," said Kitty. "I know what would suit my aunt."

"Very well, miss." The two left Valeria sitting before the glass. She continued to regard herself and the hat. So this hat is the talk of Paris, she thought. "Indeed, I should be the talk of London if I wore it," said Valeria aloud. She smiled at her reflection.

"Those grapes would make an admirable burgundy."

Valeria spun around at the sound of a masculine voice. Standing before her, an amused smile on his face, was the Earl of Traverhurst. She regarded him in astonishment and Traverhurst continued. "It really does not suit you, you know."

"What are you doing here?"

"What does one do at a milliner's shop? I am here to buy a hat."

"Indeed? Then perhaps you would like to try this one on."

Traverhurst laughed. "I think not. No, I am looking for something more flattering. The lady who shall receive the hat is most particular."

"So you are buying a present for a lady? Doubtless your sister or an elderly great-aunt?"

The earl grinned. "My sisters prefer to choose their own hats."

"I thought all ladies did so."

"Some prefer to rely on the taste of others. I am accorded a good judge of hats and I would be most happy to assist you. I would think, Madame Oracle, that you would be glad of a gentleman's opinion."

"A gentleman's, perhaps, but decidedly not yours."

Traverhurst threw back his head and laughed heartily. At that moment, Kitty, followed by Mrs. Rigby, entered the room. "Traverhurst!"

"Kitty," said the earl. "So your venerable aunt is chaperoning you?"

Kitty looked at him in surprise. "I did not know you were acquainted with my aunt."

"I fear only slightly acquainted. We were just now having a very pleasant conversation." He cast an ironical glance at Valeria.

"Lord Traverhurst is buying a hat, Kitty."

"For my great-aunt," said Traverhurst with a smile.

"What a kind thing to do," said Kitty. "Is she quite elderly?"

"Ancient," returned Traverhurst. The earl noted the hats that Kitty and Mrs. Rigby were carrying. "Ah, that one looks very suitable for my great-aunt, and I think it would also do very well for Miss Harwood."

Valeria directed a warning look at him and he grinned. "Oh, on second thought, Aunt Honoria prefers something with a bit more flair. You may have it, Miss Harwood." He took the hat from the milliner and handed it to Valeria, who quickly tossed it back at Mrs. Rigby.

"I think not," said Valeria. "Indeed, it appears his lordship is a better judge of wine than bonnets."

"But I think that hat is charming," said Kitty. "I fancy I shall try it on." She removed her own bonnet and then took the hat from Mrs. Rigby and placed it on her head. "Oh, I do like it."

"On you, my dear Kitty," said Traverhurst, "any bonnet would look charming."

Kitty smiled conquettishly at the earl. "Thank you, my lord." She turned to Mrs. Rigby. "I shall take it. Indeed, I think I shall wear it home."

"Very good, miss."

"But Aunt Valeria, you have not chosen yours."

"I shall buy one another time, Kitty. I think we should go."

"Allow me to escort you to your carriage," said Traverhurst.

"That will not be necessary," said Valeria coolly. "You must find your Aunt Honoria the proper bonnet." Taking her niece firmly by the arm, Valeria led her from the milliner's shop.

Once they were in the carriage, Kitty's face took on a dreamy look. "Now that you know him, aunt, you must understand how I feel about him."

"Indeed, I do not," said Valeria, frowning.

Kitty looked at her in surprise. "You cannot mean that you do not like him?"

"That is precisely what I mean. I am very sorry, Kitty, but I cannot approve of him."

"But he is so very charming."

"His charm is not apparent to me." But as Valeria said

these words, she realized they were not altogether true. It was useless to deny that Traverhurst possessed an unmistakeable appeal. She could well understand how more susceptible women could fall prey to him.

Valeria looked over and noticed the pout that had appeared on her niece's lovely face. "Do not be in the sullens, Kitty."

"You cannot think I would be happy that you so dislike Traverhurst."

Realizing that it was unwise to provoke her niece, Valeria tried to smooth things over. "Although I do not think so, there is a chance that I am being too hasty in my judgment of the earl. I am not very well acquainted with him, after all."

Kitty brightened. "Yes, I am certain that after you know him better you will realize what a wonderful man he is."

Thinking this highly unlikely, Valeria prudently made no response.

6

SINCE THEY had visited so many shops that afternoon, it was rather late when Kitty and Valeria returned to the Harwood townhouse. They found Fanny and Julian at home.

"Oh, Mama, Papa! You must see what I bought! Do you like my new bonnet?"

"It is very elegant," said Fanny.

Julian, who was never overly concerned with such things, voiced his agreement.

"I thought it would have been perfect for Aunt Valeria, but she did not want it."

"Then did you not buy a hat, Valeria?" said Fanny.

"No, but I shall return to Mrs. Rigby's establishment another time."

"You must see my fan," said Kitty, taking a small parcel and unwrapping the tissue paper that surrounded it. With a deft motion of her wrist, she flung the fan open. "Is it not beautiful?"

It was a striking creation, a delicate landscape painted on silk, and Fanny proclaimed it very lovely.

"I cannot wait until the Claridge ball," said Kitty, putting the fan up to her face in a flirtatious gesture. She glanced over at Valeria. "It is scarcely more than a week away. You are going, aren't you, Aunt Valeria?"

"I have no plans for attending any balls at present."

"But you must go to this ball, Valeria," said Fanny.

"It is a very important event. Lady Claridge is giving it. Indeed, I discussed the plans for it with her this very afternoon. It sounds quite splendid."

"I havè not been invited, Fanny," said Valeria.

"Oh, Minerva was not aware that you were in town. She sent your invitation today." She looked over at Julian. "She also invited Maria."

Julian hid his displeasure. "Then you will be attending the ball, Valeria?" he said.

"I expect so. I daresay Maria will wish to do so."

Fanny, encouraged by Julian's seemingly good temper, directed her attention to Valeria. "Will you dine with us tomorrow night?"

Valeria looked questioningly over at her brother.

"Maria may come if she is so inclined," said the viscount.

"Oh, I know she will be happy to accompany me."

A little bit surprised by her brother's amiability, Valeria smiled brightly at him. Then, realizing it was late, she left them and returned to Maria's.

The following evening, Maria's elegant carriage made its way through the darkened streets toward the Viscount Harwood's house. Inside the well-sprung vehicle, the Princess Lubetska sat talking to her stepdaughter. "I still cannot believe that your brother invited me. Perhaps he plans to poison my meat."

Valeria laughed. "Maria!"

The princess smiled and adjusted her diamond tiara. "I fear I should not have worn this."

"Oh, it looks lovely."

The Princess Lubetska did look very grand that evening, attired in a black silk gown trimmed with gray ribbons. The diamond tiara, a gift from her late husband, shone brilliantly in her bright red hair. Valeria also looked most attractive in her evening gown, a lace overdress worn atop a blue sarcenet slip.

"I do admit it is good of Julian to have me. It would be so nice if we could get along. When I was married to your father it was always such a source of pain to me that your brother disliked me so. Perhaps now he wishes to make amends.''

"I do hope so," replied Valeria.

The carriage stopped and the door was opened by a liveried servant. The princess and Valeria were shown into the house and met by Julian and Fanny.

"Valeria, Maria," said Fanny, "I am so glad you are here."

Maria placed a fond kiss on Fanny's cheek. "My darling Fanny," she said, and then, turning to her stepson, she regarded him expectantly.

Julian nodded coolly. "Maria, you look well."

"And so do you, Julian."

Her stepson made no further remark, causing an awkward silence that Valeria hastened to fill. "And where is Kitty?"

"She will be down in a minute," said Fanny.

"That girl spends far too much time getting ready," muttered Julian ill-humoredly.

"You are too impatient," said Fanny, laughing. "Come, let us go to the drawing room."

Fanny led her guests into the drawing room and they all sat down. The ladies talked in an animated fashion but Julian resisted attempts to draw him into the conversation. It was obvious that Lord Harwood had no intention of appearing amiable in the presence of his much disliked stepmother, a fact Valeria noted with some irritation.

A short time later, Kitty entered the room. "Oh, I am sorry I am late. Rose had such trouble with my hair."

"The result is lovely, my dear," said Maria, smiling at the girl.

"My dear Kitty," said Valeria with a smile, "I do wish you would not look so beautiful all the time. It is severely trying for the rest of us ladies."

Kitty laughed. "Oh, Aunt Valeria," she said, sitting down on the sofa beside her aunt. "What nonsense." She looked over at the princess. "Oh, Maria, what a lovely tiara!"

"Thank you. My dear Stanislaw gave it to me. It was part of the Lubetsky family jewels. According to legend, it came from ancient Byzantium. I fear my daughter-in-law, Sophia, was most unhappy that it was now in my possession.''

Julian frowned and regarded his stepmother with disapproval. Although he made no reply, it was clear from his expression that he thought the Princess Sophia had good reason to be upset.

At that moment the butler arrived and announced that dinner was ready. Fanny seemed very glad to hear this and rose quickly to usher them all into the dining room.

Once they took their places at the enormous cherry table, the servants began to serve the meal. "How nice it is to have such a small dinner party with only family present," said Fanny.

"Yes," said Julian. "I do prefer family dinners." His cool glance at Maria indicated that he did not include the princess in his definition of family.

Maria, seemingly unaware of Julian's intent, nodded. "It is so much like dinners at Melbury. So often it was just us and your dear father." She smiled. "He was such an entertaining and amusing gentleman that one did not need additional company."

This remark sparked numerous reminiscences over the pea soup and pidgeon pie. The ladies all spoke fondly of the late Lord Harwood, remembering many occasions that illustrated the fourth viscount's charming though decidedly strong personality. Julian, however, sat grimly, taking no part in the discussion.

As the table was cleared and the next course set out, Kitty turned the conversation to the present day. "It was such fun going to your house last week, Maria. I had never met such interesting people."

"Indeed," agreed Fanny. "Some were most unusual. But then, there was such a variety of persons in attendance. I had not expected to find Rupert there."

"Rupert?" Maria asked.

"Sir Rupert Netherton," said Fanny. "You must remember him."

Maria appeared thoughtful. "Not the odd young man

who insisted on speaking the most abominable German to me?''

"Most assuredly not," said Fanny. "Rupert is tall and most distinguished.''

"Ah, yes," said the princess. "The man who followed Valeria about.''

Fanny smiled at Valeria. "I think he has a *tendre* for you, my dear.''

"Don't be ridiculous," replied Valeria.

Kitty appeared very interested. "Aunt Valeria! How quickly you have found a suitor. But Sir Rupert? He is a prosy old fossil.'' Julian directed a warning look at his daughter, who only smiled. "Do you like him, Aunt Valeria?''

"I have only just met him," said Valeria.

"Well, I think he would suit you very well," said Fanny. "Perhaps he is a trifle too serious, but that is not a very grave fault. And he is such an important man. He often dines with the prime minister. Yes, I think Valeria and Rupert a very good idea.''

"But my dear Fanny," said Maria, "I am sorry to disagree, but I do not think them well matched. Sir Rupert is too humorless.''

"I suppose you think my sister would do better with one of your peculiar freinds?'' said Julian.

"Peculiar?'' said Maria, looking insulted.

Julian nodded. "Rupert told me all about the company he found at your house. It is my understanding that there were artists, poets, and all manner of other unacceptable persons. Why, Rupert and Merrymount were the only gentlemen there.''

"From his gabblemongering," said Valeria irritably, "it appears that Sir Rupert was the only man there who was not a gentleman.''

Julian frowned. "You cannot fault Rupert for reporting to me what he found at my stepmother's house.''

Fanny hurried into the conversation. "Please let us have no unpleasantness.''

"Yes," said Valeria, "and let us talk no more of my supposed suitor. Indeed, I want no matchmaking.''

"But, Aunt Valeria," protested Kitty, "don't you wish to marry?"

"I am too old and set in my ways for that," said Valeria.

Kitty persisted. "Have you not liked any gentlemen you've met? Mama has told me you had many suitors."

Valeria laughed. "Your mama has doubtlessly exaggerated. Indeed, in all my many years I have received but two offers."

"Oh, but why didn't you accept one of them?" asked Kitty.

Valeria smiled. "Neither gentlemen was to my liking. One was Mr. Tudberry."

Fanny appeared surprised. "Not Felix Tudberry! Valeria, you never told me."

"I didn't want you encouraging me to become Mrs. Tudberry," said Valeria, regarding her sister-in-law mischievously.

"Oh, I should never have done so! He was a dreadful vulgar man. I cannot believe his audacity at asking for your hand. What did your father say?"

Valeria smiled. "A lady could not repeat it. But I will say that Mr. Tudberry had not the courage to appear ever again at Melbury."

The ladies all laughed and even Julian looked amused. "But who was your other suitor, aunt?" said Kitty.

"A certain Mr. Hopewell."

"By God, I had forgotten him," said Julian.

"Forgotten Mr. Hopewell?" exclaimed Valeria. "Julian, you surprise me."

"Oh, the sad little man," said Maria, shaking her head. "I fear you broke his heart."

"I did no such thing, Maria."

"But who was he?" asked Kitty.

"He was Papa's librarian at Melbury when I was just a girl."

"He loved Valeria from afar," said Julian with a smile.

"You mean this librarian actually asked your papa for your hand?" said Kitty.

Valeria laughed. "He was far too hen-hearted for that.

But once, when I asked him where I might find one of Dr. Johnson's books, he made so bold as to declare himself.''

"And he must have been so disappointed when you refused him," said Kitty.

"In truth, I think he was relieved."

Julian burst into laughter. "The very idea of you˜and Hopewell! It was lucky that Father never learned of the fellow's presumption."

"Well, surely you will find someone you will like," said Fanny. "And now that you are in town you will have the opportunity."

"Yes, aunt, it is so wonderful that you are here," said Kitty. "There are so many exciting things happening. Why the Claridge ball is next week. You and Maria will have such fun."

"Although I cannot dance, being in mourning as I am, I shall very much like seeing everyone," said the princess.

Having now turned to the ball, the ladies began to discuss their dresses and whom they might see there. The conversation continued on that subject well into the gooseberry tart.

7

"I HAVE never liked myself in black," said the Princess Lubetska, eyeing herself critically in the mirror of the fashionable dressmaker's shop.

"Why, your new gown is splendid," said Valeria, who was sitting in a chair nearby.

"Indeed, *Madame la Princesse*, you look beautiful," said Madame Gauthier, a dignified looking woman of middle years. A modiste of the first stare, Madame Gauthier studied her creation carefully. "A few minor alterations and it will be perfect, no?"

"I suppose it will do," replied Maria unenthusiastically. "Now we must turn our attention to Miss Harwood's dress."

"Ah, I know you will be very pleased, *mademoiselle*," said the dressmaker.

A short time later, it was Valeria's turn to model her new gown. It was a beautiful dress of blue silk and showed her excellent figure to good advantage. Valeria noted the dress's low neckline with some skepticism. "Will there not be lace here, Madame Gauthier?"

"Lace? Certainly not. Why, this is the fashion, *mademoiselle*, and if I may be so bold, it suits you very well."

"Madame is right," said Maria. "It does no harm for a lady to display her charms."

Valeria laughed. "I daresay I would not wear such a dress in Melbury circles."

"But this is London," said Maria. "And there is the saying, 'When in Rome. . . .' "

"Very well," replied Valeria. "I do not wish to appear so very provincial, after all. But are you sure this is suitable for a spinster?"

Maria laughed. "Do not be a goose, my darling. The dress is excellent." She turned to the modiste. "When will the gowns be ready, madame?"

"In a few days, highness. Well before your ball."

Maria nodded and thanked the dressmaker. Two of Madame Gauthier's assistants helped Valeria undress, and soon she was once again attired in her walking outfit. She and her stepmother left the modiste's establishment and proceeded to a tiny restaurant to have tea.

Daintily nibbling on a buttered scone, Maria appeared well pleased with herself. "The ball dresses are very good. One could not expect any finer in Paris. How I love such affairs! I know I shall enjoy Lady Claridge's ball so much."

"I daresay, you will enjoy it more than last night's dinner with my brother."

Maria smiled. "Oh, it was not so bad. It was quite amusing. Fanny and Kitty are so very charming. And although your brother was very cold to me, at least he was civil."

"I think he might have been much more so."

"I am certain our talking about your papa and Melbury upset him. He so resented my marriage to Robert and thought I had no place at Melbury. Fortunately, the mention of poor Mr. Hopewell put him in a better humor."

Valeria smiled at the thought of the luckless librarian. "Of course, I think Julian would prefer a suitor like Mr. Hopewell for Kitty rather than Traverhurst."

Maria smiled. "I noticed there was no mention of *him* at your brother's house. You might have told Julian about meeting him at the milliner's shop."

"Do not even say such things in jest, Maria. What a hurly-burly it would have created."

"Oh, I wish I had been there to see Traverhurst," said Maria.

"And I wish I had not. There he was, buying a hat for

some high flyer and telling Kitty a Banbury story about its being for his great-aunt. Kitty has been so gulled by the man. I fear one day he will hurt her."

"Kitty is not such a ninnyhammer," said Maria. "Do not worry about her." She dabbed her lips with a linen napkin. "Well, I fear it is growing late. We must return home if we are to go to the opera tonight. Was it not kind of the count to invite us? His is the best box in the opera house."

Valeria nodded. "I am looking forward to it." Maria smiled and the two ladies rose from their chairs and left the restaurant.

The opera house, brilliantly lit by gas lights, was filled to capacity with eager opera-goers. Valeria shared the crowd's excitement as she and the princess entered the lavishly decorated box of Count Renzetti. That gentleman, attired in a splendid coat of claret-colored satin, escorted Valeria and Maria to their seats. "My dear ladies, I hope you will be comfortable."

"Indeed we shall," said Maria, gazing out into the crowd below. "What a crush of people."

"And how noisy they are," observed Valeria.

"But wait until my dear Teresa begins to sing," said the count. "Then there will be noise! The applause and bravos! They are thunderous!"

"I cannot wait to hear her again," said Maria. "She is a great artist."

The count nodded. "Yes, yes. She is that."

Valeria continued to scan the crowd and her eye fell upon a gentleman in a box across from theirs. She was rather surprised to recognize Sir Rupert Netherton, since he had expressed his disdain for opera. Netherton was talking to an elderly lady who was sitting beside him, and Valeria was glad that he did not look in her direction.

"Ah, here is my little Anna," said Count Renzetti.

Valeria turned and was surprised to see a girl of eight or nine years of age accompanied by a plainly dressed, gray-haired woman.

"Papa!" The girl, a diminutive sprite with dark hair and

enormous brown eyes, hurried over to the count, who leaned down to kiss her.

"Anna, my little one," said Count Renzetti. "You must meet our guests, the Princess Lubetska and Miss Harwood. This is my daughter, Anna, and her governess, Miss Quill."

Anna curtsied gracefully, first to Maria and then to Valeria. "I am happy to meet you, your highness, madame."

"And we are charmed to meet you, Anna," said Maria.

Valeria smiled at the girl. "What a pretty dress, Anna."

"Thank you, madame. My mama has one just like it."

"How sweet," said Maria. "Come, my dear, sit down."

Anna happily took a seat next to Valeria. Miss Quill nodded to the ladies and sat down behind them.

Valeria smiled at the child. "Do you often attend the opera, Anna?"

"Oh yes, madame. I do love to see Mama. She is always so wonderful when she sings. One day I shall be a great singer, too."

Valeria was somewhat startled to realize that the precocious child was the daughter of the count's mistress, Signora Borguesa. Certainly Julian would be scandalized at the little girl's presence.

"Yes, you will, *carissima*," said the count, regarding his daughter fondly. He looked over at Valeria. "Her singing teacher says she is doing very well."

"Do you enjoy your singing lessons, Anna?" asked Valeria.

"Yes, madame, now that I have a new teacher."

"Did you not like your former teacher?"

"No, madame. He was English, you see."

Valeria smiled. "That explains it then."

Anna looked sheepish. "Oh, but it was not that he was English. He was always cross and impatient."

"I do hope your new teacher is neither."

"No, indeed, madame," replied Anna. "He is Italian, you see." Valeria laughed. Anna smiled and then looked around the opera house. "Oh, look! There is the most beautiful lady!"

Following the child's gaze to a box some distance from

them, Valeria immediately spotted the cause of Anna's admiration. A stunning raven-haired woman in a revealing green dress stood looking out at the audience below. Glimpsing the gentleman beside her, Valeria caught her breath in surprise. There was the Earl of Traverhurst looking extremely handsome and slightly bored.

"Is she not lovely?" said Anna.

"What?" said Valeria, staring at Traverhurst.

"The lady in the green dress. Is she not lovely?"

"Oh, yes," replied Valeria absently. She continued to gaze at the earl. Suddenly he turned and looked in her direction. A flash of recognition came to his face as their eyes met, and then his lordship smiled at her. Valeria colored and looked away in some embarrassment.

"Oh, Papa," said Anna, "the gentleman is looking at us. Shall I wave?"

Count Renzetti looked toward Traverhurst. "Yes, dear girl. I know the gentleman. He is the Earl of Traverhurst."

Anna waved merrily at his lordship, who grinned and waved back.

"Traverhurst?" asked Maria, very much interested. "He is here?"

"Over there," said Anna, pointing.

Valeria feared she was turning very red and she dared not look at the earl's box. "Oh, I see him," said Maria. "But who is that lady with him?"

"That is Mrs. Edwards," said Count Renzetti. "She is an actress. What an enchanting creature. *Bellissima*!"

"Oh," said Anna, quite impressed. "I fancy I shall be a singer *and* an actress."

Her curiosity finally overwhelming her, Valeria cast a furtive glance toward the earl's box and was relieved to see that he was no longer looking at them. He and the lady had taken their seats and were engaged in conversation. Valeria took the opportunity to study Mrs. Edwards more closely. The actress was a beauty, she conceded. Valeria frowned and suspected that this was the lady for whom Traverhurst was buying the bonnet.

Without warning, the earl turned and looked directly at Valeria once again. Deeply mortified, Valeria fought her impulse to turn away and boldly returned his gaze. He smiled. At that moment, to Valeria's considerable relief, the lights dimmed and the curtain began to open.

It was soon apparent that the production was of high caliber. The singers were excellent and the audience responded enthusiastically, clapping and laughing as the musical farce proceeded. Valeria, however, was finding it difficult to concentrate on what was happening on the stage. She kept thinking about Traverhurst and glancing toward the darkened box where she knew he and Mrs. Edwards were sitting.

It was abominable, she thought, that he flaunted his mistress in public view. Of course, her fictional villain Morveau was similarly dissolute. How brazen of the earl to pay his attentions to Kitty while he was so obviously involved with an actress.

At the start of the second scene, the crowd erupted into loud applause at the appearance of Signora Borguesa. The singer acknowledged the tribute with a deep curtsy and began a duet. "It is my mama," whispered Anna excitedly.

Valeria turned her attention on the signora's performance. Her vibrant soprano voice filled the auditorium. Valeria, although acknowledging she was no judge of such things, decided that Signora Borguesa was very talented indeed.

At the end of the first act, the curtain went down to deafening applause and enthusiastic shouts. Then the house lights went on and the crowd began milling about. Since the fashionable ladies and gentlemen in attendance usually enjoyed the intermission as much or more than the performance, there was a flurry of activity. Many moved from box to box, greeting their acquaintances.

Valeria turned to Anna. "Your mother was simply splendid."

The little girl beamed. "She is wonderful."

"Indeed, yes," said Maria, fanning herself with a delicately painted Italian fan. "I do love *Cosi Fan Tutti*. It is so delightfuly amusing." The princess rose from her chair and the count jumped to his feet. "I should like to see the dowager Duchess of Westchester. Do you wish to come, Valeria?''

"Oh, no. I prefer to stay here."

"As you wish." Maria started out of the box.

The count smiled at his daughter. "Anna, you stay with Miss Quill."

Anna looked disappointed, but she nodded obediently. After the princess and the count had gone, Anna turned to the governess. "Oh, Miss Quill, I am so very thirsty. Could we not go and get something to drink?"

"I think you had best stay where you are, miss. There are so many people about." The governess looked hesitantly at Valeria. "If it would be agreeable to you, Miss Harwood, I shall go fetch Miss Anna a drink."

"Indeed, Miss Quill, I should be happy to watch Anna."

Miss Quill thanked Valeria and then left them. Anna rose from her chair and walked around the opera box. She then leaned out from the box and looked down at the moving throng below.

"Do be careful, Anna," said Valeria.

"Yes, madame," said the girl, coming back to her seat beside Valeria.

Valeria looked over at the box in which Traverhurst had been sitting. It was empty. Doubtlessly he and Mrs. Edwards were wandering about, greeting their fashionable and liberally minded friends.

"Madame Oracle!"

Valeria whirled around. There was the Earl of Traverhurst, looking infuriatingly handsome in his impeccable evening clothes. He smiled at her.

"Lord Traverhurst," said Valeria, trying to adopt an indifferent pose.

Anna got up from her chair and curtsied. He made an exaggerated bow in reply. "Good evening, young lady. I don't think I've ever had the pleasure of your acquaintance. Perhaps Miss Harwood would introduce us."

Valeria nodded. "Lord Traverhurst, may I present Anna. . ." Valeria stopped, uncertain what the girl's surname would be. "Anna, this is Lord Traverhurst."

Anna curtsied again and gave her hand to the earl, who

took it and bowed low. "I believe you know my papa, my lord. Count Renzetti."

"Indeed, I am well acquainted with him. And I know your mama as well. You look very much like her."

Anna smiled happily and Traverhurst sat down next to Valeria. Once again, she was irked by his careless disregard of propriety. Certainly a gentleman would have waited for leave to sit down.

"Are you enjoying the performance, Miss Harwood?"

"Very much," she replied coolly.

"And so am I."

"And is your Great-Aunt Honoria enjoying it as well?" inquired Valeria.

Traverhurst laughed. "I saw you were with the Princess Lubetska. Your stepmother is a charming lady. I had hoped to greet her."

"You may find her at the box of the Dowager Duchess of Westchester," replied Valeria.

Traverhurst smiled. "Is that a hint that I should leave, Madame Oracle?"

"I was trying to be subtle," said Valeria.

The earl laughed again and a trace of a smile appeared on Valeria's face. Anna, unhappy at being excluded from the conversation, remarked, "Lord Traverhurst, my papa and the princess should be back soon. I hope you will wait for them."

Traverhurst arched an eyebrow at Valeria. "You see, Miss Harwood, not every lady despises my company."

"That is apparent," said Valeria, directing a shrewd glance at him. "But not all women are as discerning as I."

The earl grinned. "And I am glad of it."

Anna was eager to reenter the conversation. "Do you like the opera, Lord Traverhurst?"

"Indeed, I adore it. It was once my secret wish that I would have a career on the stage." The earl smiled mischievously at Valeria. "I do not wish to appear immodest, but some account me a good tenor." Valeria regarded him skeptically and Traverhurst continued, "Oh, I see you doubt me, madam. I shall prove myself."

To Valeria's astonishment, he started singing a French

love ballad in a melodious voice. Valeria was very much embarrassed to find herself serenaded by the earl, and blushed, since the words of the song declared his lordship's undying devotion. "My lord, I pray you stop!" cried Valeria.

Traverhurst looked at her with a hurt expression. "Was it as bad as that?"

"It was wonderful!" exclaimed Anna, clapping her hands. "You might find a place in mama's company." The idea of the earl in a traveling opera troupe amused Valeria and she could not help but laugh.

Traverhurst appeared offended. "You don't think they would take me, Miss Harwood?"

"On the contrary, I am certain they would. And I think it a fine idea. I am told the company next travels to Budapest."

The earl laughed. Before he could reply, the sound of a man noisily clearing his throat made them all turn toward the door of the box. There stood Sir Rupert Netherton, regarding the earl with undisguised disapproval.

"Sir Rupert," said Valeria.

"Miss Harwood." Netherton entered the box.

Traverhurst rose from his chair and eyed Sir Rupert with disfavor. Valeria noted the earl's change in demeanor with interest. "Netherton," he said icily.

"Traverhurst," replied Sir Rupert.

Valeria looked from one man to the other and concluded that they were well acquainted. It was obvious from their expressions that they bore no love for each other. Indeed, the earl and Netherton seemed openly hostile.

To break the ensuing tension, Valeria said in a light tone, "Sir Rupert, I did not expect to find you here. You told me you did not like the opera."

"And I do not, Miss Harwood. I came only to humor my mother. I endure it for her sake."

Anna, offended by this remark, stared at Netherton in some indignation.

"What a dutiful son you are, Netherton," said Traverhurst.

Sir Rupert glared at the earl, but made no reply. Instead,

he directed his remark to Valeria. "I had hoped, Miss Harwood, that you might come with me to meet my mother. She would be so delighted to see you."

"Oh, how kind of you, Sir Rupert, but I cannot leave. I must watch Anna."

Netherton glanced questioningly at the girl.

"This is Anna," explained Valeria. "She is the daughter of Count Renzetti."

Sir Rupert frowned. "Indeed?" Valeria was rather irritated by his tone and the fact that he ignored the child completely. He turned to Valeria once again. "My mother will be very disappointed."

"Having you as a son, Netherton," interjected the earl, "your mother is doubtlessly accustomed to disappointment."

Sir Rupert's face turned red with indignation. "How dare you, sir?"

Traverhurst smiled contemptuously at him. Valeria, startled by the earl's rudeness, and fearing that the two might come to blows, rose from her chair. "Gentlemen, I pray you, calm yourselves."

"I think I had best go," said Netherton. "Good evening, Miss Harwood." He turned and hastened off.

Valeria looked at Traverhurst. "Whatever quarrel you have with him, my lord, I daresay, it would be better settled elsewhere."

The earl made no reply and continued to stare grimly after the departed Netherton. He seemed so different from his usual jocular self that Valeria was a trifle worried. A picture came to her mind of Traverhurst and Netherton locked in a violent struggle, swords in their hands and bloodlust in their hearts. She thought of the climactic fight scene in *The Villain of Versailles*.

"So he is courting you, Madame Oracle?"

She regarded him curiously. "I am too old to be courted."

His familiar smile returned to the earl's face. "If you are so very ancient, Miss Harwood, it appears that you must have found the Fountain of Youth."

"I an nearly seven and twenty!"

His gray eyes sparkled with amusement. "And you still walk without a cane!"

Valeria burst into laughter.

Traverhurst laughed too, but then he grew serious. "If I were you, Miss Harwood, I should beware of Netherton."

Valeria's eyes widened in surprise. "It is clear you have an antipathy for the gentleman, but he is my brother's dearest friend."

"It appears your brother is more fortunate in his sister than in his friend."

This unexpected remark disconcerted Valeria, and her hazel eyes met his questioningly.

"Oh, what good fortune! Traverhurst!" Count Renzetti's booming voice startled Valeria.

"Count!" Traverhurst extended his hand and the count shook it heartily. "I have met your charming little Anna."

Count Renzetti glowed with pride. "She is just like her mama."

"My dear Traverhurst!" The Princess Lubetska smiled at the earl. "How good it is to see you."

"Princess, you are as lovely as when I last saw you."

"Such flummery, sir! But I expect such talk from a charming rascal like yourself."

"But where is the beautiful Mrs. Edwards?" asked the count.

Valeria looked over at Traverhurst, very much interested in his reply.

"I fear the lady deserted me for more interesting company."

"I can scarcely believe that," said Maria.

The earl smiled. "Unfortunately, I must be getting back. The second act will be starting soon."

"Promise you will call on me, Traverhurst," said Maria. "I have taken a house on Chelmsford Square."

"I shall be very happy to do so," he replied, looking over at Valeria. "I shall be going now. Good evening, Anna. It was such an honor to meet you."

"And it was very nice to meet you, too, my lord," said the girl politely.

Traverhurst smiled once more and took his leave.

"Such a charming man," said Count Renzetti. "I am so very fond of him."

"Yes," agreed Anna. "And he is a very good tenor as well, Papa." The count regarded his daughter quizzically. "He sang a song to Miss Harwood."

Both Maria and Count Renzetti turned to direct curious glances at Valeria. "He seemed to want a part in the opera," said Valeria. She was spared further explanation by the appearance of the governess. Miss Quill entered the box with a glass in her hand. "I am sorry it took so long," she said. "There were so many people about. Here is your lemonade, Miss Anna."

"Thank you, Miss Quill," said the girl.

"I suggest we take our seats," said the count. "The second act is about to begin."

They were soon seated and once again watching the performance. After a short time, Valeria heard Anna whisper to her father, "Papa, Miss Harwood has two suitors. They were going to fight a duel over her!"

Valeria was barely able to refrain from laughing. She saw the count look over at her with newfound respect. A smile on her face, Valeria looked toward the stage and thought of Traverhurst.

❧ 8 ❧

It WAS late when the Earl of Traverhurst returned to his fashionable Georgian townhouse. He was met at the door to his rooms by his valet, Bouchot, a short, wiry young man with dark hair and eyes.

"Good evening, my lord," said the servant, speaking in French.

The earl replied in the same language, as was his custom in speaking to his valet. "Good evening, Bouchot."

"Did you enjoy the opera, my lord?"

"Very much so," said Traverhurst.

The valet was disappointed with the brevity of his master's reply. The earl was usually more talkative, especially after a night at the opera. Indeed, Bouchot never minded waiting up for his lordship, so eager was he to hear of his master's adventures amid London's glittering society.

"I expect it was very crowded, my lord," said Bouchot, assisting the earl with his coat.

"Quite crowded," said Traverhurst, knowing well his valet was fishing for information.

The earl sat down in a chair and Bouchot stooped down to take his shoes. He looked up at Traverhurst. "I imagine that many of my lord's acquaintances were there."

"A good many," said his lordship, purposely tight-lipped.

The servant got up and took the shoes away, and returned to take Traverhurst's waistcoat. "I am certain that my lord had a most interesting evening."

"Extremely interesting," replied the earl, glancing at his servant and noting with amusement that Bouchot was getting very frustrated. He grinned. "Oh, I shall not bore you with any details."

"But my lord never bores me!" cried Bouchot eagerly.

Traverhurst burst into laughter, and realizing that the earl had been quizzing him, the valet laughed too. "Very well, my inquisitive Bouchot," said the earl, "everyone was there, including the royal duke, Clarence. The singing was quite tolerable, especially Signora Borguesa's. I met her little daughter, a charming little girl. Her father is Count Renzetti."

"Ah, yes, Count Renzetti. We had him to dinner here last month."

Traverhurst nodded. "He was at the opera, as was the Princess Lubetska. You would not remember her, but she is a fascinating woman." A smile came to his face. "Her stepdaughter is a certain Miss Harwood. She is a formidable lady."

Bouchot regarded the earl with considerable interest. Was there a new woman in his life? Indeed, "formidable" was not usually a word his lordship used to describe females that struck his fancy. The valet was rather proud of his master's success with members of the fair sex. Among his inamoratas were some of the great beauties of society. Still, being very French and extremely romantic, Bouchot did not fail to note that the earl's affairs were never grand passions. Indeed, the servant wondered if his master had ever truly been in love.

"And I met our good friend Netherton, Bouchot."

The valet's face registered distaste. "That Englishman," he said.

The earl smiled. "Do not forget that I am English."

"Half-English," said the valet, correcting him. "That Netherton, he is a bad one, my lord."

"That he is. Fortunately, I had opportunity to insult him."

Bouchot grinned. "That is very good, my lord."

"Indeed, I did enjoy it. Well, my friend, I am very tired and it is late. I shall finish myself. You may go to bed."

The valet was rather surprised by this early dismissal, but he merely nodded and left. Alone, the earl paced across the room. He went to the window and stared out into the darkened London street. He reflected about Valeria Harwood and realized that he had thought of her with surprising frequency since first meeting her at her brother's house.

Remembering that meeting, he smiled. How protective she had been toward her niece Kitty. Indeed, she had had the temerity to ask if his intentions were honorable. The earl continued to look out the window. In truth, he had no intentions toward Kitty.

Of course, the arrival of his thirty-fifth birthday some months ago had caused Traverhurst to think seriously about marriage. Knowing very well that it was his duty to settle down and produce an heir, the earl had started to consider the various respectable and suitably high-born girls in the Marriage Mart. He had concluded that Kitty Harwood was a good prospect. She was very beautiful, and despite the fact that she was a bit of a featherhead, she was pleasant and good-natured.

He had paid much attention to the lovely young Miss Harwood, although admittedly, he enjoyed vexing her stuffy father perhaps more than he enjoyed her company. In truth, however, the idea of marrying Kitty did not especially appeal to him, though he sometimes thought she would make as good a wife as any.

Turning away from the window, he walked across the room and stood in front of the fireplace. Thinking once more of Valeria, Traverhurst smiled and continued his preparations for bed.

The morning after the opera, Valeria took a long walk. When she returned to the Princess Lubetska's house some two hours later, she found Maria reading a fashion magazine in the drawing room, the little dog Putti perched in her lap. "Such perfect weather for walking, Maria," said Valeria, taking off her bonnet as she entered the drawing room. "Brisk and exhilarating."

"I think it chilly," said Maria, pulling her shawl around

her. "I sometimes think a warmer climate more beneficial. Perhaps Italy. That is an idea! Why don't we go there?"

Valeria laughed. "I have only just got to London, Maria!"

"But after the Season, we might consider it. We could visit the count. He has a lovely villa in Naples. You would love it, my dear."

"I do like the count," said Valeria, sitting down across from her stepmother. "And his little Anna is a dear."

"She is very sweet and so well mannered."

"Anna certainly seemed to enjoy the opera."

"As did I," said Maria. "It was quite wonderful. And I was so glad to see Traverhurst."

Valeria feigned indifference. "He is not so well mannered."

"Oh, he is perfectly charming."

"But I told you, Maria, how he insulted Sir Rupert Netherton."

"I am sure he had cause," said Maria. "I do not like that gentleman. There is something about him . . . I do not know what it is exactly. What folly for dear Fanny to think of him for your husband. You deserve better. What of Traverhurst?"

"Traverhurst!"

"He would be a good husband."

"My dear Maria, the earl may be many things, but I very much doubt he would make anyone a good husband. Where did you get such a cork-brained notion?"

"Why, I saw the two of you last night. He seemed very interested in you."

"Maria, that is bosh."

"But Anna told me how he serenaded you. I thought it very romantic."

Valeria laughed. "Oh, Maria! You have my word that Anna is very much mistaken."

Maria looked disappointed. "Well, I know you will meet someone else soon."

Valeria sighed, but knowing it was useless to convince her stepmother that she did not need a husband, she turned the conversation to another topic.

9

THE NEXT several days passed eventfully for Valeria. Maria's house was filled with visitors, many of them interesting and unconventional. The poet Kingsley-Dunnett and his disciple Lord Merrymount had come every day and Count Renzetti and Signora Borguesa had appeared with regularity.

Valeria had also received a call from her publisher, Mr. Burden. That gentleman was very enthusiastic about *The Villain of Versailles* and extravagant in his praise of it, hinting broadly about another sequel. Although Valeria had protested that it was too soon to talk of that, after the publisher had gone, she had begun to think about the future adventures of Captain Wolfe and the despicable Marquis de Morveau.

As she sat at her desk the morning following Burden's visit, Valeria made notes about possible plot ideas. Perhaps, she thought, Morveau would come to England as an ambassador from the French court. There he would cause all kinds of mischief for the noble captain.

The thought of her villainous marquis caused Valeria to think of Traverhurst. Although she would not have admitted it, she was disappointed that that gentleman had not called. Of course, Valeria cynically told herself, the earl was probably too busy with the lovely Mrs. Edwards. Undoubtedly, he had not given her a thought.

Valeria chided herself for thinking about the earl. Frowning, she wondered if she had succumbed to his undeniable charm. Valeria put down her pen. "Am I a schoolgirl to swoon over a handsome face?" she said aloud. Indeed, it was quite ridiculous. She had thought Kitty a goose for losing her head over the man. At least Kitty's youth was an excuse for such foolishness.

Turning her thoughts to Kitty, Valeria decided she must pay a call at her brother's house that day. After luncheon with Maria, Valeria announced her plans to go to Harwood House and asked the princess to accompany her. Maria declined, saying she expected several guests.

Arriving at Julian's residence later that afternoon, Valeria was escorted to the empty drawing room by the butler. A moment later Julian entered. "Valeria," he said, greeting her with a kiss on the cheek. "What a pity that Fanny and Kitty are out. Let us sit down. You will stay until they return?"

"Of course. I would like to see them." Valeria sat down on Julian's elegant Grecian sofa. She untied the strings of her bonnet and, taking off the fashionable head-dress, laid it aside. "I had hoped you would have called upon me at Maria's, Julian. Oh, I know very well you will not do so. You are too stubborn, just like Papa."

Julian frowned slightly. "One does not know who one may meet at my stepmother's house. Much of her company is quite unacceptable."

"Really, Julian, you have such medieval notions. Most of Maria's guests are quite delightful. They are certainly not at all dull."

Her brother regarded her disapprovingly. "I do not think Maria would be a good influence on Kitty. I daresay she has not been a good influence on you."

Valeria's dark eyebrows arched in surprise. "What do you mean by that?"

"I mean that you have been seen in the company of certain unacceptable persons. If you do not take care, your name will be bandied about."

"What hum is this, Julian? What unacceptable persons?"

"I refer to the opera you attended some days ago. I heard all about it."

"I cannot imagine what you could have heard."

"That you and Maria sat in Count Renzetti's box."

"And what harm is there in that?"

"Good God, Valeria, the man is a notorious debauchee. And not only that, you entertained his illegitimate daughter!"

"Oh, Julian, there is no call to be on the high ropes. It is hardly so scandalous."

"Indeed? And is it not scandalous to entertain the Earl of Traverhurst alone in an opera box?"

Valeria reddened. "Who told you this?"

"It does not signify who told me."

"But indeed it does. I daresay it was Netherton." Since her brother did not deny it, Valeria continued, "How dare he carry tales! It seems your friend is an incorrigible tattlemonger."

"Rupert thought it was his duty to inform me. I must say, he was quite shocked to find you alone with Traverhurst and seemingly enjoying his company."

"I was not alone. Anna was there."

"Anna?"

"The count's daughter."

"I'll warrant she is a fit chaperone. What the devil has got into you, Valeria? First my daughter makes a fool of herself over the man, and now you!"

Valeria looked indignant. "I am not making a fool of myself! And I very much resent you and your friend Netherton talking about me in this way."

The brother and sister were interrupted by the appearance of Julian's butler. "Excuse me, my lord. Sir Rupert Netherton is here."

"Tell Sir Rupert I am engaged, Eliot. I shall return his call."

"No, Eliot," said Valeria. She turned to Julian. "I would very much like to see Sir Rupert. Indeed, I insist upon it."

Eliot looked questioningly at his master. "Oh, very well," said the viscount. "Bring him in." The butler nodded and retreated. When he had gone, Julian turned to his sister. "I caution you, Valeria . . ."

She made no reply, but regarded her brother coolly.

Moments later, Eliot returned with Netherton. Seeing Valeria, that gentleman smiled and made a polite bow. "Miss Harwood, I had not expected the pleasure of your company."

"And I had not expected the dubious pleasure of yours, Sir Rupert."

"Valeria!" Her brother directed a warning glance at her, and Netherton looked startled.

"Whatever is the matter, Miss Harwood?" said Sir Rupert innocently.

"My brother informs me that you have been telling tales about me, sir. I would not have expected it of a gentleman. I think it reprehensible."

"I assure you I meant no harm, Miss Harwood. I simply thought that your brother, as head of his family, should know of the company his sister keeps. He is responsible for you."

"I am responsible for myself."

"I am glad Rupert told me. If you are seen with unacceptable company, I have a right to know about it." Julian looked sanctimonious as he continued, "The earl's reputation with females is justifiably odious, but that is not the only reason why you should avoid him."

Valeria appeared intrigued. "What do you mean, Julian?"

"I mean that I do not think he is a true Englishman. You know his mother is French."

Valeria laughed. "Being French is hardly a crime."

"I'm not so sure of that," replied her brother. "With Bonaparte back in France, one must be on one's guard."

Valeria regarded him with incredulity. "You are ridiculous, Julian. You talk as if everyone with French blood is an enemy of England."

Her brother hesitated. "You may think it ridiculous, but I have heard that there are Bonapartist sympathizers in London. Why, Major Talbot told me just yesterday that it is believed that someone in the highest circles of society is passing secrets to Bonaparte."

"And you probably think it's Traverhurst," said Valeria sarcastically. "That is preposterous. I daresay, a man of the earl's cut would scarcely know any secrets."

"Oh, wouldn't he?" said Julian. "Why, he is intimately acquainted with many highly placed government officials. Indeed, I should think few would be in a better position to ferret out information and pass it on to the French."

Seeing that her brother was totally unreasonable, Valeria looked over at Netherton. "Sir Rupert, will you please tell Julian how absurd he sounds?"

Netherton looked uncomfortable. "I really cannot comment on such matters."

Julian looked triumphant. "You see, Valeria, Rupert does not think it unlikely."

Valeria eyed Netherton in surprise. Surely he did not think there was merit in Julian's nonsensical remarks. "I know you do not like Traverhurst, sir, but you cannot suspect him of treachery."

Netherton remained resolutely silent and Julian jumped into the conversation. "Do not badger Rupert, Valeria. If he thinks Traverhurst is a spy, he certainly can't tell you so. These are dangerous times and there are probably spies about everywhere."

Valeria looked disgusted. "Oh, I am sure you are right, Julian. From now on, I shall watch what I say when I am in the presence of my French dressmaker. Indeed, now that I think about it, she does look rather suspicious."

Julian frowned and Netherton, who appeared uneasy with the conversation, was suddenly eager to leave. "I really should be going. I only meant to stop for a moment to inquire if you were dining at the club tonight, Julian."

"Yes, I am."

"Then I shall see you there." Netherton turned to Valeria and, after uttering a few polite words, departed.

When he had gone, Julian nodded gravely. "By my faith, there must be something in this about Traverhurst. Rupert was acting deuced odd. He's probably off to see some military chaps. Talbot will probably get a dressing down for his indiscretion. Good lord! And to think Traverhurst has been playing up to Kitty! It will be the most awful scandal when he is revealed as a traitor."

"That is the greatest bosh!" cried Valeria. "I did not

think you such a cupboard-head to give credence to such fustian. The Earl of Traverhurst a French spy! The very idea!''

Julian regarded his sister with some irritation. ''Of course, you will not believe such a thing of a man who has obviously charmed you.''

Valeria colored, but before she could reply, Kitty and Fanny burst into the room.

''Aunt Valeria! What good luck finding you here!''

''Kitty, Fanny!''

Fanny kissed her sister-in-law. ''Valeria, how nice to see you.'' Upon entering the room, she had not failed to note her husband's and Valeria's expressions. Suspecting that they had been quarreling again, Fanny tried to appear especially cheerful. ''We are just returned from the dress-makers. Kitty's dress for the ball is quite marvelous!''

''Oh, yes,'' cried Kitty. ''I cannot wait until you see it. But it will not be long, since the ball is tomorrow night. Oh, my dress is so lovely. And Mama's is beautiful, too. What is your gown like, aunt?''

''My gown is quite nice, although I know the two of you will eclipse me.''

''Oh, stuff,'' said Fanny. ''I am so looking forward to tomorrow evening. I hope you are, too, Valeria.'' Valeria nodded and Fanny continued to talk excitedly about the upcoming ball.

⚜ 10 ⚜

THE SPACIOUS ballroom at Claridge House was filled with the cream of London society. The Claridge ball was one of the major events of the Season, and there was an air of excitement as all the splendidly dressed company arrived.

The Earl of Traverhurst, attired in a well-fitting double-breasted coat of black superfine, a white marcella waistcoat, and black florentine silk breeches, stood noting the arrival of the various guests. He looked very dashing and numerous ladies in the assembly were directing appreciative looks in his direction.

"Traverhurst." The earl turned to face a tall, bulky man in ill-fitting evening dress.

The earl nodded. "Is it here?"

The other man looked warily about him and then smiled. "It is. I left it in Claridge's library. It is in the bookcase inside Caesar's *Gallic Wars*."

Traverhurst grinned. "I warrant it will be undisturbed there."

"Take care that no one sees you," said the man, moving away from the earl. Traverhurst looked toward the main entrance of the ballroom just as the herald announced the newest arrival.

"Her highness, the Princess Lubetska, and Miss Valeria Harwood."

Traverhurst eyed the ladies who now entered the ballroom with great interest. Although he noted that Maria looked very well in her black dress, the earl's attention was focused on Valeria. She looked stunning in her blue silk gown with its high waist and daring décolletage. About her neck was a diamond necklace that glittered brilliantly, and her dark hair was dressed in tiny ringlets about her face and ornamented with blue flowers.

Traverhurst found himself staring at her. How beautiful she looked, he thought. His observation of Valeria was cut short by a feminine voice calling to him. "Rohan, there you are!" An attractive lady of perhaps forty years hurried over to him.

"Clarise, what a beautiful dress."

"Thank you, dearest brother," replied the lady, who was the earl's eldest sister, the Marchioness of Wynbrook. "Winny sent me to fetch you. You must come and see Lady Beaumont."

The earl groaned. "Have pity on me."

"Do not be horrid, Rohan." She took his arm. "Come with me."

Traverhurst grinned. "I see I have no choice."

"None," laughed his sister, and the two of them walked off.

Valeria felt somewhat out of place in the grand ballroom. It had been a long time since she had participated in such a lavish event. During her years at Melbury, her social activity had been confined mostly to small country parties. Of course, one of the local squires did give an annual ball before hunting season began, but it could hardly be compared to the magnificent affair given by Lady Claridge.

"Oh, everyone is here," said Maria, looking about excitedly.

Valeria nodded. "There certainly are a great many here. I wonder if Kitty and Fanny have arrived yet."

As if in answer to her question, she spotted her niece in the throng. Kitty looked dazzling in a gown of ivory satin, and as might be expected, she was surrounded by attentive gentlemen. Valeria looked at the eager swains and noted Traverhurst's absence. She found herself wondering where the earl might be. Thinking of him, Valeria remembered Julian's words. She smiled at the preposterous notion of Traverhurst being a French agent.

"Oh, Valeria! Maria!" Lady Harwood rushed up to her sister-in-law and the princess. Fanny looked splendid in a rose-colored silk gown with matching feathers decorating her elegantly coiffed blond hair. "I was beginning to think you weren't coming."

"Oh, I am always late," said Maria. "I enjoy being late."

"Well, I am glad you are here now," said Fanny. "It is such a wonderful ball."

"It appears Kitty is enjoying herself," observed Valeria.

Fanny looked in her daughter's direction. "She has been surrounded by gentlemen all evening. I do think she is a trifle disappointed that Traverhurst has not been more attentive."

"Where is Traverhurst?" said Maria.

"He is about somewhere," said Fanny. "In truth, I am glad he is not hanging about Kitty. It so upsets Julian. I do hope we see less of him."

"Less of him?" A masculine voice caused the three ladies to turn quickly around. There stood the Earl of Traverhurst, a broad grin on his handsome face. "Who is this unfortunate gentleman that you wish to see less of, Lady Harwood?"

Fanny appeared flustered.

"I do not wish to betray my sister-in-law's confidence, my lord," said Valeria, "but I may say that it appears her wish has been denied."

The earl threw back his head of dark curly hair and laughed. "I am happy to see you, too, Madame Oracle." He bowed to Maria. "Princess Lubetska, how radiant you look. Indeed, all three of you look astonishingly lovely. It would be like the judgment of Paris to decide which of you was the most beautiful."

Valeria regarded him in amusement. "I did not expect such fustian from even you, my lord."

He laughed again. "My dear Madame Oracle, would you permit me the honor of the next waltz?"

The request took Valeria by surprise, and she hesitated.

"That is, if you are not too ancient to dance, Miss Harwood."

Valeria smiled. "I could probably manage it."

The earl made an exaggerated bow and offered her his arm. Then, nodding to the other ladies, he led Valeria away. As the two of them proceeded to the dance floor, Maria and Fanny exchanged a questioning glance. Kitty, although some distance away, had seen the earl and her aunt. Her pretty face took on a frown as she watched them take their places among the dancers.

Valeria was unaware of her niece's displeasure. Indeed, she was unaware of anything but Traverhurst's presence.

As they joined the others, the earl smiled. "Let us hope the dance is not too lively. Perhaps I should ask the conductor to reduce the tempo."

"That may be wise," said Valeria. "But if I feel about to swoon, I shall inform you so you may assist me to the nearest chair."

His lordship grinned. The music started up and, taking her hand in his, Traverhurst placed a strong arm around Valeria's waist. Strangely thrilled at his touch, Valeria tried valiantly to appear unmoved as they began to whirl about the dance floor.

"You dance very well, Madame Oracle."

"I am trying very hard not to tread upon your feet, my lord."

Traverhurst laughed. "I am very much obliged to you, ma'am." He looked down into her hazel eyes. "I regret I have not had opportunity to call upon the Princess Lubetska. Her salon is becoming quite famous. They say the flower of London's artistic world is to be found there."

"Indeed so, Lord Traverhurst, although I do admit there are a good many weeds among the flowers."

His eyebrows arched with amusement. "I can see you are a harsh judge of artistic endeavor, Madame Oracle. But I knew that from your poor critique of my singing."

Valeria laughed. "I do hope you will come and sing for Maria's company. You could sing a duet with Signora Borguesa."

"I should like nothing better. But perhaps it could be a trio. You do sing, of course?"

"Of course, but badly."

"I cannot believe you do anything badly, Madame Oracle."

She looked up at him, expecting to find a mocking smile, and was disconcerted to find that he looked perfectly serious. She changed the subject a trifle awkwardly. "There are many interesting people who frequent Maria's house. Mr. Kingsley-Dunnett is one."

"You don't mean the awful poet?"

Valeria laughed. "You know him?"

"Good God, I had the misfortune to be at one of my sister's cultural afternoons some weeks ago when the fellow read a portion of the most ghastly poem. It was something about Sir Walter Raleigh."

" 'Gloriana, or the Divine Elizabeth,' " intoned Valeria, mimicking the poet's ponderous voice.

The earl laughed. "That is it exactly! By heaven, I shall think twice now about calling on Princess Lubetska, knowing he might be there." His eyes met hers again. "No, I shall come in any case."

Valeria's pulse quickened as his gray eyes gazed into hers. They continued waltzing, but after what seemed to Valeria a very short time, the music stopped and the dance was over. Traverhurst escorted her back to Maria and Fanny, and then he took his leave.

"What a lovely couple you make," enthused Maria.

Fanny looked questioningly at her sister-in-law. "Why, he seemed quite taken with you, Valeria."

"Bosh," said Valeria, hoping she was not blushing. "He is just amusing himself."

Fanny appeared unconvinced, but before she could say anything more, Kitty joined them. "Aunt Valeria," she said somewhat coolly.

"Kitty, how beautiful you look."

"And you look very well indeed, aunt," said Kitty in a tone that implied she was not altogether pleased with this fact. "I saw you dance with Traverhurst."

"Did they not look well together?" said Maria tactlessly.

A pout came to Kitty's lovely face. "I would not have thought it of you, Aunt Valeria."

Valeria regarded her niece quizzically. "Thought what of me, Kitty?"

"That you would try to steal Traverhurst from me."

"Kitty!" cried Fanny. "Do not be ridiculous."

"Is it so ridiculous? I saw how she was looking at him. I think it infamous that you come here and act in such a manner, knowing how I feel about him."

Not giving Valeria an opportunity to reply, Kitty flounced off. "Oh, dear," said Maria. "She was so upset. The poor girl."

Fanny looked apologetically at her sister-in-law. "I am sorry, Valeria. She is hopeless where Traverhurst is concerned. I pray she will get over this childish behavior. It is severely trying."

Valeria frowned. Certainly, Kitty was acting childishly, she thought. Upon reflection, however, she suspected that perhaps Kitty was not so very wrong. In truth, Valeria feared that she was growing dangerously fond of the earl. Of course, it was unlikely that a man like him could be interested in her, she decided.

Valeria's musings were cut short by the appearance of some distant relations of Fanny's. Valeria's sister-in-law made the introductions and they were all soon engaged in conversation.

As the evening progressed, Valeria found herself thinking more and more about Traverhurst and hoping he would appear again. She searched the crowded ballroom and finally caught a glimpse of him, standing by himself in the far corner of the room. Valeria saw him look about and then disappear into one of the doorways leading from the ballroom.

Now standing with a small group of ladies with whom she was only slightly acquainted, Valeria was beginning to grow bored. She was glad when Fanny appeared and took her away from the gathering "Valeria, have you seen Kitty?"

"Not since she left in a pique."

"Nor have I," said Fanny, looking slightly worried.

"Julian is convinced she has gone off with Traverhurst. He is looking for them in the garden."

"What a muddle-headed idea. Kitty is just pouting somewhere. Why, I saw Traverhurst just a few moments ago, and he was alone."

"Well, Julian saw them together not long ago. He lost them in the crowd. Oh, I fear dear Kitty is so besotted with the man that she cares nothing what people might say. If Kitty were to be found alone with Traverhurst, she would be hopelessly compromised. Do help me find her."

"Very well."

"Good," said Fanny. "I am going this way. Do search the other side of the room."

Valeria nodded, going in the direction she had last seen Traverhurst. Reaching the doorway through which he had vanished, Valeria hesitated and then entered the corridor. The long hallway was empty and Valeria's footsteps were the only sound on the cool marble floor. As she passed a door, Valeria thought she heard a noise. She stopped abruptly, listening, and then opened the door.

The room was evidently Lord Claridge's library. The faint light of a single oil lamp illuminated bookshelf-lined walls. Valeria looked about and her eyes suddenly grew wide. Thrown across the back of a leather sofa was a coat, and dangling from the end of the sofa was a man's stockinged foot. Valeria suddenly had a picture of her niece there, enfolded in the embrace of Lord Traverhurst.

Horrified, Valeria rushed to the other side of the sofa. Stretched out there was the sleeping figure of the Earl of Traverhurst. Valeria eyed him in embarrassment for a moment and then turned to retreat. In her haste, her arm bumped into an object sitting on a table beside the sofa. The object, a brass candlestick, clattered noisily as it hit the floor.

"What the devil!" Traverhurst's eyes snapped open and he sat up quickly. "Who is it?"

"It is Valeria Harwood."

"Good God, Madame Oracle. You startled me."

"I am sorry."

"What are you doing in here? Is the ball so dull that you have come in search of a book?"

"I was looking for Kitty," she said.

"Kitty?" He grinned. "And you thought you would find her here?"

"My brother thought she was with you."

"And is that what you thought?"

"The possibility did not seem so utterly fantastic."

"Well, as you can see, your bothersome niece is not here. And let me assure you, Miss Harwood, despite my reputation, I am not in the habit of seducing green girls. Indeed, I was but innocently napping."

"I did not think you did anything innocently, my lord." The earl laughed and Valeria continued, "And I did not take you for the sort of man who would steal away to take a nap in the middle of a ball."

"I admit it is not my usual habit. But after spending all night at Crockford's and most of the day at the O'Brien bout, I have scarce slept in more than twenty-four hours."

"In that case, I must apologize for disturbing you. I shall leave you." Valeria started to make her way past the sofa, but in the dim light, she failed to see Traverhurst's shoes in her path. Tripping over them, Valeria lost her balance and fell onto the sofa and into the earl's arms.

Precisely at that moment, the library doors were flung open wide. Both Traverhurst and Valeria turned toward the entryway in surprise. A stout gentleman was eyeing them in bewilderment. "Oh, Traverhurst. Dreadfully sorry, old man." The intruder stared at Valeria. "Carry on," he said, retreating hastily.

Valeria pulled herself away from the earl and jumped up. "Oh, no!" she cried. "Who was that man?"

Traverhurst smiled slightly. "I fear that was Colonel Baxter. What deuced bad luck. He is one of the worst gabblemongers in town."

"You cannot mean he will tell everyone . . ."

"I daresay he will, but I doubt he knows who you are."

Valeria was hardly consoled by this. "Oh, dear," she said.

"There is no need to worry. Come, I'll escort you back to the ball."

"Indeed, sir, I think that a very bad idea."

"Perhaps so. I shall allow a discreet time to elapse before I follow you." Traverhurst rose from the sofa and picked up his coat. As he did so, a paper fell to the ground. Valeria instinctively reached for it, but the earl snatched it up.

She regarded him in surprise. "A letter from your Great-Aunt Honoria, my lord?"

He smiled. "Precisely."

Valeria cast a curious glance at him and then turned and hurried back to the ballroom. What a muddle she had got herself into, she thought. To be found in such a compromising position with the notorious earl was horrible. Valeria tried to keep her composure. Perhaps this Baxter would say nothing. Indeed, she had never met the man, and he did not know her name. In addition to that, the room had been rather dark, and perhaps he had not got a good look at her.

Feeling somewhat better, she reentered the ballroom and made her way across the crowded room, trying to look unconcerned. Suddenly she caught sight of Colonel Baxter, surrounded by a group of ladies and gentleman. Hoping he would not notice her, Valeria held her head high and continued walking. However, to her dismay, Baxter looked directly at her, his face gleaming with recognition. She saw him make a remark to the others, and all heads turned toward her. Valeria hurried on, knowing very well that in a short time, everyone in society would think her Traverhurst's latest conquest.

❧ 11 ❧

VALERIA walked briskly past a row of townhouses as she made her way toward her brother's house. The April day was clear and pleasant, but she took little note of the fine weather. She was thinking of the previous night's ball. Indeed, since Valeria had awakened that morning, she had thought of little else.

Dominating her reflections was the Earl of Traverhurst and her disastrous encounter with him in the library. Worried about Colonel Baxter's spreading gossip, Valeria had wanted to tell Fanny about her unfortunate experience. However, she had no opportunity to do so because Kitty had reappeared and was standing with her mother. Valeria had found it prudent not to mention the incident. Throughout the rest of the evening, she had felt that people were watching her and was relieved when Maria had suggested that they depart for home.

Now on her way to visit Fanny, Valeria was eager to tell her sister-in-law about her unfortunate experience. When she arrived at the Harwood residence, Valeria rapped the brass door knocker firmly. Her brother's butler opened the door and quickly showed her to Fanny's sitting room.

Lady Harwood, attired in an attractive morning dress of striped muslin, was sitting in a comfortable stuffed chair. She looked up as Valeria entered. "Oh, Valeria, I am so glad you have come."

"Fanny, I must talk to you."

Valeria's sister-in-law directed a sympathetic look at her. "My poor Valeria. I have heard all about it."

Valeria regarded Fanny in surprise. "You have?"

Lady Harwood nodded. "Lady Biggerstaff and Mrs. Stanford-Weekes were here less than an hour ago. They told me everything!"

Valeria sat down in an Egyptian style chair across from her sister-in-law. "Good heavens! You cannot mean they are spreading gossip about so soon! What did they say?"

"Lady Biggerstaff told me Colonel Baxter found you with Traverhurst in a most compromising position. Lady Biggerstaff is the colonel's sister, you see, and they are both such dreadful rattles. Why did you not tell me last night what had occurred?"

"Nothing occurred, Fanny."

"My dear Valeria, to be found in a darkened library in the arms of a notorious rake is, in my mind, an occurrence of some significance. I must say, I was very much surprised, but then I did see how you danced with him. Indeed, everyone did."

Valeria colored. "I assure you, Fanny, it is all a dreadful mistake. It is very simply explained. You recall that last night after you told me Julian thought Kitty was with Traverhurst, I agreed to help find them?" Fanny nodded and Valeria continued, "I had seen Traverhurst leave the ballroom a short time earlier, so I went in search of him. I heard a noise in Lord Claridge's library, and so I went inside. I found Traverhurst asleep on the sofa."

Fanny regarded her somewhat skeptically. "Traverhurst asleep on the sofa?"

"I know it seems odd, but it is the truth. He awakened, and after we exchanged but a few words, I started to leave, but I had the misfortune to trip on his shoes and I fell upon the sofa. At that moment, Colonel Baxter opened the door and he drew an erroneous conclusion."

Fanny burst into laughter. "Oh, Valeria, that is too funny! And I fear that if I did not know you, I would think it the greatest humbug!"

"Fanny!" Valeria looked indignant for a moment and then she joined her sister-in-law's laughter. "Oh, very well, I know it sounds ridiculous, but it is the truth. Traverhurst can confirm it.''

Lady Harwood's face grew suddenly serious. "But, my poor Valeria, I fear that he does not deny that the two of you are . . . involved.''

Valeria's hazel eyes grew wide and she regarded Fanny with an expression of incredulity. "What do you mean?''

"Lady Biggerstaff said that her brother saw Traverhurst afterward and alluded to the incident, asking the earl if he had a new conquest. Not only did the earl not deny any impropriety, but—how did she put it?—Colonel Baxter said Traverhurst laughed and smiled slyly.''

"What! The colonel must have been foxed!''

"The colonel is known to never drink in excess. Indeed, his gossip is usually quite reliable. I cannot, for the life of me, understand Traverhurst. Even if it was true, one would have thought he would have at least had the decency to voice a denial.''

Valeria's incredulity changed to anger. "You mean that Traverhurst is going about acting as if he and I were . . .''

"Precisely," said Fanny. "It seems he cares nothing for your reputation. I am only glad that Julian does not know of this. Perhaps he will not hear of it.''

"And what about Kitty?''

"She knows nothing either. I am hopeful that the tattlemongers will be more reluctant to say such things to a girl of Kitty's tender years.''

Valeria frowned and shook her head. "This is dreadful. How can Traverhurst behave so abominably? I would not have thought him capable of this!''

Fanny regarded her sister-in-law shrewdly. "Then you do like him?''

"Certainly not!''

Thinking Valeria's reply a trifle too emphatic, Fanny frowned, fearing that her sister-in-law had, like Kitty, fallen under the earl's spell. "Well, perhaps it is not all that serious.''

"I think it quite serious that everyone in society will think I am involved in a dalliance with the Earl of Traverhurst. Would that I had stayed at Melbury.''

"Aunt Valeria."

Valeria turned to find that Kitty had entered the room. For a brief moment, she wondered if her niece had heard her remark but Kitty's expression convinced her that she had not. "Kitty."

Valeria's niece did not appear overly pleased to see her. "I imagine you and Mama were talking about the ball," said Kitty.

"Yes, we were," said Valeria.

"Indeed so," said Fanny. "It was such a lovely evening."

"I know you enjoyed it, Aunt Valeria," said Kitty accusingly. "Especially your dance with Traverhurst."

"Oh Kitty, you are not going to start that again," said Valeria. "It is utter nonsense to think I am scheming to take your earl from you."

Fanny nodded. "Kitty," she said severely, "I will have no more of this silly talk." There was an awkward silence that was broken when Julian appeared at the doorway.

"Valeria," said the viscount, regarding her coolly. "Eliot told me you were here."

Her brother's expression made Valeria suspect that he had heard the gossip regarding her and Traverhurst. "Hello, Julian," she replied warily.

"I did not expect you back from your club so soon," said Fanny.

"The discussion there was not to my liking." He directed a meaningful look at his sister.

Valeria rose from her chair. "Well, I must be going. I promised Maria I would not be gone long."

As usual, the mention of his stepmother's name caused a slight frown to appear on the viscount's face. "Well, if you must go, then I shall drive you home. I see you have no carriage."

"Yes, I walked here. It was such a lovely day."

"I do not think you should be walking about town alone," said Julian sternly.

"Oh, I am old enough to walk a few blocks without escort."

"I would be much happier if I drove you home,"

insisted Julian. "Besides, I've had no opportunity to talk with you."

Valeria and her brother exchanged a look and she knew that she could not escape. "Very well, Julian, but I think it needless bother."

She took her leave of Fanny and a rather sullen Kitty and then followed her brother outside. Julian helped Valeria up into his sporting new curricle and then jumped up beside her and took the reins. As they started off down the street, Valeria waited for her brother to speak. He remained silent an exasperatingly long time and Valeria finally grew impatient. "Don't you think it time that you started your lecture, Julian? It is not so awfully far to Maria's house."

The viscount frowned and looked sidelong at her. "If there is even a grain of truth in what I am told, I fear you deserve a lecture."

"There is no truth whatsoever in it."

"Then you weren't alone with Traverhurst in Claridge's library? And the fellow wasn't in his shirtsleeves with his arms about you on the sofa?"

"It was not what it appeared!"

Julian looked at her. "I don't know what else it could be." He shook his head. "I damned near thrashed that buffoon Huntley for bandying your name about the club."

"I am touched that you would defend my honor."

"I defend the honor of the family, and, by God, you seem to have little regard for it."

"You must believe there was nothing between Traverhurst and me. I explained it all to Fanny. It was all a dreadful mix-up. You must have trust in me."

"It is Traverhurst I cannot trust, and a girl like you is no match for him. Maybe it would be best if you returned to Melbury."

"Return to Melbury? Surely, that would be the worst thing I could do to set tongues wagging."

"Perhaps you are right," said Julian. "But this is a devilish bad business. The scandalmongers are having a heyday."

"I do not care what they think."

"Well, you should, miss. To have your name linked with Traverhurst is quite unacceptable." Julian would have continued had he not spotted Sir Rupert Netherton walking along the street toward them. "Rupert!"

Valeria frowned, thinking there were few people she wanted to see less than that gentleman.

Julian pulled his vehicle up as he came alongside his friend. Espying them, Netherton smiled and raised his hat politely. "Miss Harwood, Julian. How lucky to see you. Such glorious weather, don't you think?"

"Indeed yes," said Julian. "And where are you going, Rupert?"

"I have to meet with the prime minister," said Netherton smugly. "Affairs of state call me, I fear."

"We should not detain you then, Sir Rupert," said Valeria, ignoring the look of irritation her brother directed toward her.

"Oh, I am quite early. I wanted to walk in such fine weather."

"My sister shares your love of walking, Rupert."

"Do you, Miss Harwood?" replied Netherton, smiling at her. "I find it most efficacious."

Before Valeria could reply to this remark, a high-perch phaeton came careening around the corner. "What the deuce?" cried Julian.

Valeria looked at the fashionable vehicle that was coming toward them at a pace far too fast for town. She was startled to see that at the reins of the four splendid black horses was the Earl of Traverhurst. Sitting beside him was a lady whom Valeria recognized as Mrs. Edwards. Holding her fashionable bonnet in place, the actress was laughing and obviously enjoying the ride very much.

The earl urged his horses on, and as he passed Julian's curricle, Traverhurst looked straight at Valeria, grinned, and agilely tipped his hat. The fast-moving vehicle continued on and soon vanished from sight.

"The effrontery of the man!" cried Julian.

Netherton looked grim. "He is a nuisance. And that female with him! Any woman who would be seen alone with him is a disgrace!"

Julian looked over at his sister. Valeria avoided his glance and eyed Sir Rupert disapprovingly. Obviously, Netherton had not heard the latest *on-dit*. Sir Rupert continued, ''The man is an unprincipled knave.''

''That he is,'' said Julian.

Although unhappy with Traverhurst after learning he had not denied they were having an affair, Valeria was irritated with her brother and Netherton. ''Oh, yes, Julian, I know you think Traverhurst the greatest villain in the kingdom and one of Boney's spies to boot.''

Julian frowned. ''Go ahead, make light of it, my girl. You will sing a different tune when his treachery is revealed.'' He glanced over at Sir Rupert to corroborate his remark, but Netherton did not reply. Instead, that gentleman changed the subject, talking about an upcoming horse race. After a time, Sir Rupert took his leave and continued down the street.

After his friend had gone, Julian eased his curricle back into the street. ''Rupert is a dashed fine fellow. Of course, you would not notice that since you are evidently enamoured of Traverhurst. Why that is so is beyond my comprehension. And it doesn't signify if the fellow is a spy for the Frenchies. I would think his sullying your reputation is proof enough of his bad character.''

Valeria frowned, but made no reply and sat pondering her brother's words. As she thought of how the earl and Mrs. Edwards had driven past them, Valeria's frown deepened. Certainly, his morals were appalling, and it appeared to be true that he had no scruples about implicating her in a scandal. The more she reflected about Traverhurst, the angrier Valeria became.

Valeria thought about Julian's ridiculous suspicions about the earl's being involved in espionage. The idea was laughable. She smiled to herself, but suddenly her smile vanished as she remembered the paper that had fallen out of his coat in the library. Valeria knitted her brows in concentration, recalling how the earl had snatched it up. He had behaved in a very peculiar fashion. Could the paper have been a secret document instead of a *billet-doux*?

"Is something wrong, Valeria?"

Valeria looked over at her brother. "No, nothing," she said, managing to smile. Then, turning away from Julian, Valeria frowned once again as the curricle proceeded on.

❧ 12 ❧

THE FOLLOWING afternoon, Valeria entered the drawing room and found her stepmother sitting on the sofa, her little dog Putti beside her. Maria was engaged in tying red satin ribbons in the dog's long topknot.

"Oh, Valeria, does not Putti look adorable?"

The dog looked over at Valeria as if interested in her reply, and Valeria laughed. Although, in truth, she thought Putti looked rather silly, Valeria agreed readily with her stepmother, proclaiming the dog very pretty indeed.

Maria put the dog down on the floor. "Then you are ready, my darling one. Go on and play." The dog curled up on the floor and closed her eyes.

Valeria smiled. "Having one's hair done can be rather exhausting."

Maria laughed and patted the sofa. "Come and sit down beside me, my dear. We have a few moments before the guests arrive." Valeria sat down obediently and the princess regarded her with concern. "I do hope you are no longer upset over that little matter with Traverhurst."

"It is hardly a little matter, Maria. Certainly, Julian does not think it so."

"Oh, Julian. Your brother flies up into the boughs over the merest trifles. What is so terrible about it? Even if it were true, why would it be so dreadful?"

"Maria!"

"But my dear, the English are so childish about such

matters. In Vienna, not one eyebrow would have been raised over such a thing. Indeed, I almost wish it was true."

"Maria! How can you say such a thing?"

The princess laughed. "My poor darling, I so want you to be in love, and I do not doubt that Traverhurst would be a marvelous lover." Valeria looked scandalized, and Maria laughed again. "I see I have shocked you."

"Indeed, you have."

"You cannot say that you do not find him somewhat appealing," said Maria mischievously.

"Oh, I suppose every woman in the kingdom finds him somewhat appealing. And apparently, a great many of their feelings are reciprocated."

"Ah, but one day he will find a woman and be faithful. I am a good judge of men, and I know this. Yes, I like Traverhurst," said Maria, nodding.

"Could we not talk of something else?" said Valeria.

"Very well. I did not tell you Mr. Kingsley-Dunnet's news. He is nearly finished with his 'Gloriana.' He has so kindly agreed to read his work here as soon as it is done."

"Maria, you know I think him a pudding-headed fellow."

"You are too cruel. Perhaps he is a pudding-head, but everyone seems to think him a genius. Look at Merrymount. He idolizes him."

"Poor Merrymount. I do wish he would come out from under Kingsley-Dunnet's thumb. I think he is a nice young man."

Maria nodded. "And you know he has a *tendre* for Kitty."

"Yes, I did see how he looked at her, but then my niece inspires such looks from young gentlemen."

"Oh, yes," said the princess. "Kitty is such a beautiful girl. I do think Merrymount a good match for her. They are suited. I know such things, my dear. A man like Traverhurst is definitely not for her. But Merrymount, he is perfect. Indeed, even Julian could not object."

"Object? He would be elated at the match. Merrymount is the heir to a dukedom and fabulously wealthy. His lineage is impeccable. But I do not think Kitty even noticed him.''

Maria looked thoughtful. ''I have an idea.''

Valeria was uncertain whether she liked the look that had come into her stepmother's eyes. ''What do you mean?''

''Why, all we must do is bring them together. Kitty must fall in love with Merrymount and forget Traverhurst.''

Valeria laughed. ''And I suppose you think that will be very simple?''

''No, indeed. But I am not a stranger to matchmaking. Of course, I failed miserably with you.''

Valeria regarded her stepmother in surprise. ''Failed with me? You mean to say you played the matchmaker with me? I do not recall it.''

''My dear girl, I was constantly trying to throw suitable gentlemen in your path.''

''Such as?''

''You do not recall the Marquess of Epswitch? Or Sir Roland Weatherby? Then there was Mr. Danbridge—oh, he was such a nice man. And there were so many others whose names I cannot recall. But you would have none of them. So like your father you are, my dear. So stubborn! I soon gave up. But Kitty is not like you. We shall have much success.''

''We? My dear Maria, I want no part in your schemes, and, in truth, I do not know if you should become involved in such things.''

''But you do not want Kitty to continue to pine for Traverhurst?''

''No, but . . .''

''Then you cannot object.''

Before Valeria could reply, Maria's butler announced the arrival of two guests. Valeria and the princess were soon joined by the object of their discussion, Lord Merrymount, and Mr. Kingsley-Dunnett. Young Merrymount looked pale and soulful in his well-tailored clothes. Mr. Kingsley-Dunnett, as usual, looked quite unkempt in a bright blue rumpled coat and mud-spattered pantaloons. His hair looked even wilder than usual and Valeria found herself wondering how Mr. Kingsley-Dunnett managed to make it look that way.

"Princess," cried Kingsley-Dunnett, hurrying over to Maria and taking her hand. He kissed it noisily. "You are a lovely sight, water to a thirsty man!" He then turned to Valeria. "Miss Harwood, your beauty staggers me."

Before Valeria could prevent him, Mr. Kingsley-Dunnett took her hand and deposited a long and most unwelcome kiss upon it. Then, directing a bold look at her with his piercing blue eyes, he smiled with unmistakable lechery. Valeria was quite discomfitted by his look. "Mr. Kingsley-Dunnett," she managed to say.

Merrymount directed polite, well-bred bows to the ladies.

"Oh Lord Merrymount," said Maria, "I did want to see you. I have something to tell you." She rose from her chair. "Mr. Kingsley-Dunnett, you don't mind staying with Valeria for a few moments, do you?"

Mr. Kingsley-Dunnett assured her he did not and Maria quickly led the young marquess from the room. Valeria, who had not been enthusiastic about her stepmother's scheme, now was distinctly hostile to the idea, since it left her alone with Mr. Kingsley-Dunnett. "Do sit down, sir," said Valeria reluctantly.

That gentleman hurried to sit down beside her on the sofa. To her dismay, he leaned toward her and peered into her eyes. "Has anyone ever told you, my dear Miss Harwood, how beautiful you are?"

Valeria quickly pulled away and rose from the sofa. "Really, sir, I do not appreciate such flummery."

"Flummery?" The poet leaped up. "By my faith, madam, it is not mere flummery. You have dazzled this poor poet's eyes. Since first I saw you, Miss Harwood, I have not been able to sleep. You have entered my very soul! I hurry to finish my 'Gloriana' so I might immortalize you in verse. I shall call it 'Valeria, or the Rapturous Maiden'!"

Valeria did not know whether to laugh or express horror. Mr. Kingsley-Dunnett took advantage of her confusion and grasped her hand again. "My divine Muse!" he cried, kissing her hand passionately.

"*Herr* Kingsley-Dunnett!" A thunderous feminine voice

caused both Valeria and Kingsley-Dunnett to jump. Valeria recognized the Baroness von Mecklenberg. That formidable lady approached them, angry and bearlike. "What is the meaning of this!"

Kingsley-Dunnett quailed under the wrathful Prussian woman's gaze. "Dear baroness! I did not hear the butler announce you."

"I did not give the fool a chance to do so," returned the baroness. She glared at Valeria, who momentarily feared for her safety. Luckily, just then Maria and Merrymount returned. "Ah, my darling Baroness von Mecklenberg! Such a pleasure to see you."

"Princess," said the baroness, still frowning at Valeria.

"You have been too long absent," said Maria.

"I have been working," muttered Baroness von Mecklenberg.

"You artists are always working," said the princess. "You must bring some of your delightful sculptures in, baroness. You know, Count Renzetti has proclaimed you one of the greatest sculptors of our era. He compares you to Michelangelo."

Valeria found it hard to keep from laughing at this outrageous flattery, but the baroness seemed to think the comparison apt. "*Danke*," she said. "I will bring sculptures in. Next week perhaps."

"That is wonderful!" cried Maria. "Oh, Valeria, I cannot wait to see them. I shall tell everyone to come." The princess engaged the baroness in conversation and that lady took Mr. Kingsley-Dunnett's arm and held it firmly.

Valeria took the opportunity to escape. She joined Lord Merrymount, who looked a trifle melancholy. "Lord Merrymount, I do hope nothing is wrong."

"Oh, no, nothing."

"But you look troubled."

The young man sighed. "There is something, Miss Harwood. I feel I can confide in you. The Princess Lubetska and I were talking about your niece." He blushed. "I know that Miss Harwood is very fond of Lord Traverhurst. Her highness has told me it is but a passing infatuation."

Merrymount looked earnestly at her. "Do you think that is so, Miss Harwood, or is she truly in love with him?"

"I cannot speak for her, but it is my opinion that Kitty's feelings will change."

The marquess looked hopeful. "I pray you are right. I do not think Traverhurst worthy of her. Indeed, the idea of such a man as that capturing her heart is agony for me."

"My poor Merrymount, you are in love with her."

"I adore her," said the young man.

"But you do not even know her," protested Valeria.

"I do not need to know her," replied Merrymount ardently. "I had only to look at her once and know that she is the woman of my dreams."

"I do wish you would be more sensible," said Valeria.

"One cannot be sensible in love," replied the young man.

Valeria, who was beginning to feel that this was indeed an unfortunate fact, did not know how to reply. She changed the subject. "Have you been writing more poems, sir?"

Merrymount nodded. "I have. But Mr. Kingsley-Dunnett calls my work negligible."

"Then he is not very encouraging."

"He is a great master," said Merrymount.

"Some call him that," said Valeria.

The marquess did not seem to notice her remark. "I hope to learn from him. Perhaps one day my work will meet his approval."

"But what do other people think of your work?"

"I have never shown it to anyone else, ma'am."

"But I think you should, Lord Merrymount. I am sure there are other knowledgeable persons whose opinions you would respect."

"I would appreciate your opinion, Miss Harwood."

This remark took Valeria by surprise. She had no desire to read the young man's poetry and cursed herself for suggesting he get another opinion. "Oh, I am no literary critic."

"But Kitty, that is, Miss Harwood, told me you are the cleverest of women. I can tell by your conversation that you are so intelligent. I would be so grateful for your evaluation of my poems."

Valeria hesitated and then reluctantly accepted. "Very well, Lord Merrymount, I shall be happy to read your poetry."

The young man seemed very pleased and expressed his gratitude profusely, telling Valeria he would bring his poems to her at the first opportunity. Hoping desperately that they would not be as dreadful as Kingsley-Dunnett's, she tried to disguise her dismay at the task thrust upon her.

Valeria and Merrymount then embarked on a discussion of Mr. Coleridge's works. Some time later, Maria's butler entered the drawing room once again. "Count Renzetti, Signora Borguesa, and Mrs. Edwards."

Valeria, who had been only half listening to the servant's announcement, snapped to attention. Turning her head toward the door, she watched the three arrivals come in. Barely noting the count and Signora Borguesa, she studied Mrs. Edwards intently. That lady presented a stunning picture in a dress of apricot-colored silk. Mrs. Edwards was indeed a beautiful woman, thought Valeria glumly.

The princess hurried over to her new guests. "Teresa! My dear count!"

"Maria," cried the opera singer, "I have brought someone new. This is Mrs. Edwards. My dear Liza, this is the Princess Lubetska."

Mrs. Edwards directed a dazzling smile at Maria and took her hand. "The signora has told me of your splendid society. I was so eager to come and meet you and your company."

The princess beamed. "Come, you must meet the others." Leading her latest acquisition across the room, Maria first introduced Mrs. Edwards to Mr. Kingsley-Dunnett and the baroness, and then led her to Merrymount and Valeria. During the introduction, Valeria had the unsettling sensation that the actress was scrutinizing her intently. After they had exchanged a few pleasantries, additional guests arrived and the princess rushed off to greet them. To Valeria's dismay, Mr. Kingsley-Dunnett called to Merrymount, and that young gentleman begged to be excused to join the great poet.

Finding herself alone with Mrs. Edwards, Valeria felt decidedly uncomfortable. "I was very curious to meet you, Miss Harwood," said Mrs. Edwards, smiling sweetly at her. "I wondered who Rohan would next take up."

Valeria blushed. "I fear you are mistaken, Mrs. Edwards."

"My dear girl, there is no need to play the coy maiden with me. News of Traverhurst's newest amour is all about town. Do not take offense, my dear, but you are not quite what I expected. You are so decidedly . . . respectable-looking." The actress said the word respectable-looking as if it were a most undesirable quality.

Valeria was rather insulted by her tone. "I assure you, Mrs. Edwards, the gossip is wrong. You have no cause to fear that I shall take Lord Traverhurst from you."

"My dear girl, you are welcome to him."

Valeria looked startled. "Then you do not love him?"

The actress laughed. "Love him? Do not be such a goose. Of course, I do not love him. I admit that he is sweet and so charming and we have had some very amusing times together. But a certain foreign prince has looked my way and I fear Rohan cannot compete."

"And you care nothing if Lord Traverhurst is heartbroken?"

Mrs. Edwards broke into shrill laughter. "You are too amusing, my dear. So you think Rohan is in love with me? Good heavens! And do not mistake that he is in love with you either. I daresay he has never been 'in love' with anyone. My poor naive one, I fear you will only be hurt."

Valeria tried to maintain her composure. "I have said you are wrong, Mrs. Edwards. There is nothing between the earl and me."

"As you wish," said the actress with a smile. "I do hope you will enjoy yourself. He is generous, and no doubt you will have some lovely trinkets to remember him by. Then perhaps you, too, will move on to a prince."

Burning with indignation, Valeria glared at Mrs. Edwards. That lady only appeared amused and, without another word, walked off. Valeria frowned unhappily as she watched her go.

❧ 13 ❧

VALERIA sat alone in the Princess Lubetska's drawing room. Maria had gone to visit the Signora Borguesa, and, not in a mood for making calls, Valeria had rejected her stepmother's pleas to accompany her. Indeed, since seeing Mrs. Edwards the day before, Valeria had no wish for society. Instead, she had decided to spend the afternoon reading.

Looking down at her book, Valeria sighed. Then, closing the volume, she set it on the table. It was not that the book was uninteresting. Indeed, the memoirs of the Comtesse de Pompignan, a lady of the court of Louis the Fourteenth, were quite fascinating, and they provided admirable background for the sequel to *The Villain of Versailles*. However, reading of the intrigues of the French court made Valeria think of Traverhurst.

Since she had firmly resolved to keep the earl from her thoughts, Valeria decided it would be best to stay away from things that were French. Perhaps, she reflected, it would be better if her hero, Captain Hannibal Wolfe, went to an exotic land for his next adventure. Then the villainous Morveau would not even appear.

She began to picture her fearless captain in various far-flung settings. India and Persia came first to mind, and then the wilds of North America. Yes, Wolfe roaming the dangerous forests of the new world amid the threat of savages would be an excellent idea, Valeria decided.

Her imagination wandered to the vast Canadian wilderness. While enduring fearful weather and great hardship, Wolfe would gallantly struggle for the English cause during the French and Indian Wars. After a violent battle, he would be captured by Indian warriors.

Valeria formulated the scene in her mind. Wolfe would look defiant as the Indians led him into their camp and tied him to a stake. Bravely awaiting the horrible fate that his captors had in store for him, the captain would be startled to see a Frenchman appear. Valeria had a sudden image of the Frenchman now facing Wolfe. Standing there with a contemptuous sneer on his face was the villanous Morveau looking exactly like the Earl of Traverhurst.

"Good heavens!" cried Valeria. She stood up and paced across the room. It was quite disturbing that she could not keep the man from her thoughts.

The butler then appeared and Valeria was glad of the interruption. "Excuse me, Miss Harwood. The post has arrived." The servant deposited the mail on the desk.

"Thank you, Reynolds," said Valeria. He nodded and left, and Valeria went over to examine the pile of letters. Finding a bulky packet addressed to her, she opened it and took out a folded paper. It was a brief letter from her publisher, Mr. Burden. That gentleman informed her that all was well with *The Villain of Versailles* and enclosed a number of letters addressed to Mr. Verrell Hawkesworth.

Smiling, Valeria sat down at the desk and began to read her correspondence. She had barely got through the first letter when the butler once again entered the room. "There is a gentleman to see you, Miss Harwood."

Ther servant extended a salver to Valeria and she picked up the calling card that was upon it. She raised her eyebrows as she read the name engraved on the card. "The Earl of Traverhurst? Did you not tell his lordship that the Princess Lubetska was out?"

"He expressly wished to see you, miss."

Valeria frowned. How dare he call upon her knowing very well what everyone would think to see him at Maria's doorstep. "Tell the earl that I am indisposed, Reynolds."

"Very good, miss," said the butler, turning to go.

"Wait, Reynolds."

"Miss?"

"I shall see him. Show him in."

The servant nodded and left the room. Valeria rose from her chair at the desk. She found herself wondering about her appearance. Why had she worn her old gray dress and prim lace cap? She was sure the outfit made her look like a schoolmistress. Chiding herself for such thoughts, Valeria told herself that certainly this was the best way to appear to the earl.

"Madame Oracle."

Valeria looked over at Traverhurst as he entered the room. As expected, he was dressed at the height of fashion and looked deplorably handsome. He smiled at her and Valeria tried hard to repress the feelings that his presence engendered within her.

"Lord Traverhurst." Valeria hoped her voice sounded icily indifferent.

"Oh dear, it appears I have displeased you. You look precisely the way my old nanny did whenever I got into mischief."

"Then I daresay the poor woman looked this way all of the time."

Traverhurst grinned. "Most of the time, in any case." The earl walked over to Valeria. "Aren't you going to ask me to sit down?"

"You cannot mean you need to be asked? You never did before."

"But you never reminded me of my nanny before. I was always very polite to Nanny."

Despite her resolve to remain cool toward him, a slight smile appeared on Valeria's face. "Oh, very well, sit down." She sat down in an elegant French chair and the earl took the seat beside her.

"If I did not know better, Madame Oracle, I would think you were not pleased to see me," said Traverhurst.

"Indeed, I am not at all pleased that you are here."

The earl grinned. "I am devastated, Miss Harwood. What is it that I have done? Oh, I know. You are vexed that I drove my horses past you on the street and did not stop."

Valeria was indignant. "I am certainly not vexed about that. I am most grateful you did not stop. In any case, you were driving so fast you could not have stopped if you had wanted to."

Traverhurst looked insulted. "My dear madam, I could stop on a penny if I had a mind to do so."

"Oh yes," said Valeria with a rather bored expression. "You are *reputed* to be a great whip."

"Take care, madam. Do not belittle the skill of which a man is most proud."

"I did not think that was the skill of which you were most proud, Lord Traverhurst."

The earl looked at her in surprise and then he roared with laughter. "You amaze me, Miss Harwood. Now do tell me what has set you back up."

"And you don't know?"

"I am not prophetic like you, Madame Oracle."

"I am sure you know very well."

"And I assure you, I do not."

Valeria paused. "I suggest you think about the Claridge ball."

"The Claridge ball? Of course, you are vexed that I only danced one dance with you."

"You are the most odious and conceited man!" cried Valeria.

The earl laughed. "Then it was not that?"

"You are impossible. You know very well that I refer to what happened in the library."

"My dear madam, did something happen that I am not aware of?"

"Do not be so thick-skulled. Colonel Baxter has been spreading the most horrid tales, and I am dreadfully compromised."

"*You* are compromised? What about me? After all, I was the one in my shirtsleeves and stockinged feet."

"How can you make light of the situation? Now everyone in society thinks that I am your . . . that you and I are. . ."

"Are what?" Valeria reddened and Traverhurst grinned. "You cannot mean . . . ? Why, I am shocked!"

Valeria regarded him in angry frustration. "This may be a very good joke to you, but I do not find it at all amusing. Why have you not denied it? Why didn't you explain what happened?"

"I don't see why I should explain anything to gossips," said the earl.

"And you do not care that everyone thinks . . . ?"

"I never care about society's opinion, and I don't see why you should either. You make too much of this. Ignore it and soon it will be forgotten."

Valeria frowned. "It is easy for you to disregard society's opinion. A gentleman can do that much more easily than a lady. If you had but heard my brother Julian—"

"I am heartily glad I did not. I fear your brother bears no love for me. Of course, I must admit I am not so very fond of him, or his friend Netherton."

"I do not know why you would dislike Sir Rupert Netherton so much."

"And I suppose you think him a paragon of virtue?"

"In comparison with certain others, perhaps."

The earl, who, up until this point, had been so jovial, seemed to have an abrupt change in mood. He frowned. "You cannot like him?"

Valeria was surprised at the seriousness of his expression. "Well, he is a very important man. At least he has told me so many times."

The earl laughed, his good humor restored, and Valeria smiled in spite of herself. They were interrupted by the butler. "I beg your pardon, Miss Harwood. There is another gentlemen to see you. Lord Merrymount."

"Oh, do show him in, Reynolds." When the servant had gone, Valeria turned to Traverhurst. "Do you know Merrymount, my lord?"

"Westbridge's son? I've never met the cub."

"He is very nice, but he is rather shy. I pray you do not intimidate him."

"How could I intimidate anyone, my dear Madame Oracle?" replied Traverhurst. "I am as meek as a lamb."

Valeria cast a warning look at the earl, but before she could make a reply, the young man joined them. The impeccably dressed Merrymount looked very serious. Under his arm he carried a neatly wrapped bundle. The marquess smiled at Valeria, but he frowned upon catching sight of Traverhurst.

"Lord Merrymount, how good of you to come," said Valeria. "I do not believe you have met Lord Traverhurst."

The earl rose to his feet and extended his hand to the younger man. The marquess seemed almost reluctant to take it, but finally he shook Traverhurst's hand.

"Merrymount, I know your father," said the earl affably.

"Indeed," replied Merrymount stiffly.

Knowing how the marquess felt about Traverhurst, Valeria hastened to enter the conversation. "Do sit down, gentlemen."

"I cannot stay, Miss Harwood," said Merrymount. "I brought you this." He held up the paper-wrapped bundle.

"Oh, how nice," said Valeria, realizing that inside the parcel was Merrymount's poetry.

"That looks rather intriguing, Merrymount," said Traverhurst, eyeing the package with interest. He looked expectantly over at the young man.

Merrymount blushed and appeared most uncomfortable. He handed the parcel to Valeria. "I really must go, Miss Harwood."

Suspecting that the marquess wanted to say something to her in private, Valeria quickly rose. "I shall see you to the door, Lord Merrymount." She turned to Traverhurst. "Do excuse me, I shall be but a moment." Then taking Merrymount's arm, she propelled the young poet out the door.

The earl raised his eyebrows slightly, wondering about the relationship between Merrymount and Valeria. He walked across the room and looked curiously out into the corridor, where he saw Valeria and the marquess talking together. Merrymount had a very earnest expression on his face and Valeria was directing an encouraging smile at him.

Traverhurst frowned. Could the cub be Valeria's suitor? Surely she would not take him seriously. Of course, considered the earl, Merrymount was the heir to a dukedom and, as such, appealed to a great many females.

Feeling an uncommon twinge of jealousy, Traverhurst frowned again. Rather surprised at himself, the earl turned away and walked over to the window. After looking out for a moment, he glanced about the room. Beside him was a desk and upon it was a number of papers. His eyes fell upon a envelope and the name he saw inscribed on it caused him to regard it more closely. "Mr. Verrell Hawkesworth, Esq."

The earl was very familiar with the author. Although decidedly not a bookish man, Traverhurst had read Hawkesworth's novels and he had enjoyed them immensely. He saw several other missives similarly addressed and regarded them with a perplexed expression. Seeing a letter lying open on the desktop, Traverhurst picked it up. "My dear Miss Harwood," it said. "I am pleased to inform you that Hollingshead and Burden are proceeding on schedule with *The Villain of Versailles*. I know it will be as well received as *The Queen's Champion* and I anticipate excellent sales. I have enclosed some letters for you that were sent to this office. I do not doubt that they are from your admiring readers. Your obedient servant, Jeremiah Burden."

"Well, I'm damned!" said the earl with a grin. "Madame Oracle is none other than Verrell Hawkesworth!" Hearing Valeria at the door, Traverhurst quickly threw down the letter and hurried away from the desk.

Valeria returned to the room to find the earl standing by the chair in a languid pose with a slightly bored expression on his face. "I am sorry that I was so long, Lord Traverhurst. Do sit down."

"Oh, it is quite all right, Miss Harwood," said the earl, taking his chair. "I well understand a lady wishing to spend time alone with an ardent suitor, especially such an eligible one as Merrymount."

Suspecting that he was quizzing her, Valeria looked solemn. "I had hoped he would make me an offer today." She shook her head in disappointment. "Perhaps tomorrow."

Traverhurst regarded her in surprise, having the uncomfortable feeling that she was serious. "You would marry the cub?"

Amused at his reaction, Valeria tried hard to keep a straight face. "And what lady would not? How grand it would be to be Duchess of Westbridge!" She sighed melo-dramatically. "But how much easier if one might acquire a title without acquiring a husband as well!"

They looked at each other and both burst into laughter. "By God, Madame Oracle," said Traverhurst, "I thought you were serious. Poor Merrymount. You will break his heart. He is clearly enamoured of you."

"He is certainly not."

"But the way he looked at you, and he did bring you a gift."

Valeria laughed. "Hardly a gift. He brought me his poems."

"His poems?"

Valeria nodded. "He wants my opinion of them. I do hope they are not so awful. I have no wish to hurt his feelings."

"So the lad is a poet?"

"He is, and I do not doubt a man like you despises poets."

"You wrong me, Miss Harwood!" cried Traverhurst in mock indignation. "Do you think me a Phillistine? I have nothing but respect for literary endeavors, and I adore poetry. I shall recite some." The earl cleared his throat and proclaimed in a stage voice,

"Barber, barber, shave a pig?
How many hairs will make a wig?
Four and twenty, that's enough.
Give the barber a pinch of snuff."

He looked over at her. "How was that?"

"You amaze me, Lord Traverhurst. You are quite ridic-ulous." Valeria burst into laughter and he grinned.

"You do not appreciate any of my talents, Madame Oracle," said the earl. "First my singing and now my poetry recitation. You are a harsh critic. I pity Merrymount."

"I shall be as kind as I can be. I do like him."

"He certainly didn't appear to like me," said Traverhurst.

"That is because you are his rival."

Traverhurst raised his eyebrows. "But I understood he was not your suitor. If he is, I shall thrash him soundly."

"Don't be absurd. He is your rival for Kitty's affections."

"Kitty? She has never mentioned him."

"They have only met once. Poor Lord Merrymount fell in love with my niece the first time he saw her. Of course, that is not unusual for Kitty. Her beauty often inspires such feelings." She looked over at the earl, very much interested in his reaction.

He appeared rather indifferent. "She is a dashed pretty girl. What does she think of Merrymount?"

Valeria directed a meaningful look at the earl. "I fear her feelings are engaged elsewhere. It is a pity she could not be interested in someone like Merrymount."

"Someone respectable, you mean?"

"Precisely."

At that moment they were interrupted by the appearance of the Princess Lubetska. "My darling Valeria! And Traverhurst, what a wonderful surprise!" Maria smiled happily at them both as she entered the room.

The earl rose from his chair. "Princess."

"I do hope you do not say you have to leave soon," said Maria.

He glanced over at Valeria. "Indeed not."

"Good," said the princess, sitting down on the sofa. Traverhurst returned to his seat and Maria began conversing with him.

Valeria sat silently, a thoughtful expession on her face. She had hoped to pursue the matter of Traverhurst's feelings for Kitty, but her stepmother's arrival had prevented her from doing so. It was strange how hard it was for her to be angry with him for long.

"And Valeria, you must tell Traverhurst about your father's collection of sundials at Melbury. Really, it is quite extraordinary." Maria's remark to her brought Valeria from her reverie and, smiling, she entered the conversation.

✣ 14 ✣

AFTER THE earl had left, Maria announced that she wished to take a nap and retreated to her room. Valeria found she was glad to have Merrymount's poems to keep her mind off Traverhurst. Taking up the bundle the marquess had brought her, she went to her sitting room. Since she was familiar with Henry Kingsley-Dunnett's lamentable verse, Valeria was prepared for the worst. Fearing that Merry-mount's poetry would be dreadful, she read the first poem with some trepidation. Valeria was surprised and very relieved to find it quite good. Continuing her reading, she concluded that the marquess was quite talented. She suspected that Kingsley-Dunnett's criticism of his disciple's work stemmed from jealousy. Indeed, it appeared that the elder poet was even more reprehensible than she had thought.

She had just finished the last poem when there was a knock at her half-opened door and it was swung open. Valeria looked up in surprise to find Fanny and Kitty standing there. "Perhaps it is bold of us, but I told Reynolds you would not mind us coming up unannounced," said Fanny. "He said Maria was resting." Fanny noted for the first time the stack of papers in front of her sister-in-law. "Oh dear, I fear you are busy. I hope it is not household accounts. I cannot abide them. Julian is always scolding me because the figures never add up correctly."

"Oh, no, this is nothing like that. I am reading poetry."

Kitty, although still unhappy with her aunt, was interested. "Poetry, Aunt Valeria?"

"Yes, a young poet asked if I would read his work and tell him what I thought of it."

"How nice," said Fanny. "It does not surprise me that a poet would seek your opinion. You are so very clever and know all about such things."

"I wish someone would ask me to judge his poems," said Kitty with a trace of envy.

"I am sure the gentleman would be glad to know what you think, Kitty," said Valeria. She picked up one of the papers and handed it to her niece, who studied it.

"I suppose there are many poets visiting Maria," said Fanny. "I do remember meeting that particular gentleman— oh dear, what was his name? He was talking with a giantess all the time I was here. I do wish I could remember his name."

"I believe you mean Mr. Kingsley-Dunnett," said Valeria.

"Yes, that is it. What an odd-looking man. Are they his poems you are reading, Valeria?"

"Fortunately not," replied Valeria. "No, these are by a very young and unknown poet."

Kitty looked up. "And an excellent one! Oh, this poem is lovely!" She took up another of Merrymount's poems and read it avidly.

Fanny smiled over at her sister-in-law. "Kitty so loves poetry. I do not like it overmuch myself. Do you think the poems are good, Valeria?"

Valeria nodded. "Very good. I shall be very glad to inform the author how much I like them."

"Who is it, aunt?" said Kitty, seeminly having forgotten her animosity toward Valeria. "I would like to meet him."

"You have met him, Kitty."

"I have?"

"Indeed so. It is young Merrymount."

Kitty's blue eyes opened wide in surprise. "Merrymount?"

"The Duke of Westbridge's son?" asked Fanny.

"The same," replied Valeria. "He appears to be quite talented."

"Well, when I next see Lord Merrymount," said Kitty, "I shall tell him I think him a wonderful poet. Of course, I know my opinion will not be as welcome as yours, aunt."

"Do not be so sure of that, Kitty," said Valeria knowingly. "Indeed, I fancy that Merrymount will be delighted that you like his poetry."

"Yes," agreed Fanny, "Valeria is right. I am certain young Merrymount would be most grateful for your opinion. I'm sure it is a good thing to be a poet, although hardly necessary when one is going to be a duke. Of course, Julian thinks poets chowderheads."

"I fear," said Valeria, "that Merrymount's father shares my brother's views."

"Poor Merrymount," said Kitty. "I know what it is to have a father who is not understanding."

"Kitty!" Fanny frowned at her daughter. "I pray you cease complaining about your father." Not wishing to get into any family arguments, she hastily changed the subject. "I brought you something, Valeria. Vouchers for Almack's." Lady Harwood smiled triumphantly. "I wrangled them from my dear friend Lady Jersey. You and Maria must go tomorrow night."

"I cannot believe Lady Jersey would want me at Almack's. She must have heard of the scandal."

"Oh, I told Lady Jersey that was utter nonsense. Do say you will come."

"Oh, I don't know," said Valeria, not at all eager to go to the exclusive assembly rooms. However, at Fanny's downcast expression, she nodded. "Why yes, Fanny. I do think it would be great fun to go. I daresay, many girls in the country dream of going."

"Good. We will all go together." Fanny started to enthuse about going to Almack's and Valeria, who did not wish to go at all, suppressed a sigh.

Valeria stared absently into the mirror as her maid Sally, whom she had brought with her from Melbury, adjusted the satin ribbon that adorned her dark curls. "There, miss," said the maid, viewing her handiwork with satisfaction. "I am finished."

"Thank you, Sally," said Valeria. "It looks very nice. That will be all."

The maid smiled, bobbed a curtsy, and left. Valeria cast another look at her reflection. She was wearing a new evening dress, a lovely creation of lace and white satin, the skirt of which was decorated with bouquets of satin roses and bluebells. Although she looked very well, Valeria was not eager to go to Almack's. After all, it was not very long since the disastrous Claridge ball, and no doubt her appearance at the assembly rooms would provoke much talk.

At least, reflected Valeria, it was unlikely that Traverhurst would be there. She was certain the earl would think Almack's very dull. No, he was probably spending the evening gaming or dining with another beautiful high flyer.

"Valeria, you are ready. And how lovely you look." Valeria turned to see Maria come into the room, followed by Putti.

"Oh, your dress is exquisite, Maria! You look beautiful."

The Princess Lubetska smiled. "I am so looking forward to this evening."

Valeria looked puzzled. "But, Maria, I thought you considered Almack's a dead bore."

"I do," replied the princess matter-of-factly.

"Then why do you look forward to it?"

"My darling Valeria, although Almack's is so often dull, I fancy tonight it will prove quite interesting. Merrymount will be there."

"Merrymount? But how do you know that?"

Maria smiled conspiratorially. "I sent him a note, telling him to come."

"Whyever would you do that?"

"To give Kitty the opportunity to see him. Why, it was a stroke of genius, your showing Kitty his poems."

"Good heavens, you act as if I had some purpose in doing so."

"But of course you did, my dear. You knew Kitty is fond of poetry. Now that she likes the young man's poems, it is a small thing to have her like the young man himself.

Indeed, all is going very well. Yes, I am most eager to see them together this evening.''

"I do hope you will not be disappointed, Maria. Do not forget that Kitty is still infatuated with Traverhurst.''

"Oh, that,'' said Maria, dismissing it lightly. "That will pass quickly. Now, come along, my dear. Your brother will be here very soon and we both know he is not a patient man.''

Valeria smiled and rose from her dressing table. Picking up her fan and gloves, she followed Maria from the room.

Attendance at Almack's was essential for a young lady's success in society. Entry to the elite assembly was closely guarded by its formidable patronesses, who dispensed the vouchers for admission as if they were royal charters. However, as she entered the select company, Valeria did not seem in the least overcome by the honor of appearing there. She glanced about the large room, not recognizing anyone, and decided it would probably be a tedious evening.

Kitty seemed to share her aunt's lack of enthusiasm, a fact Valeria noted during the carriage ride. Valeria attributed her niece's attitude to the likelihood that Traverhurst would be absent. Unlike her niece, Valeria was glad the earl would not attend. In addition to not wishing to be seen with him, she found his presence most unsettling.

They all stood surveying the scene and then Fanny and Julian left to visit with one of Fanny's cousins. It was not long before the Marquess of Merrymount joined Valeria, Kitty, and Maria. Valeria smiled at the young man, noting that he looked rather handsome dressed in his well-fitting black evening clothes.

"Lord Merrymount,'' said Maria. "What a surprise to see you.''

Observing the wink her stepmother gave the marquess, Valeria suppressed a smile. "I am so glad to find you here, Lord Merrymount,'' said Valeria. "I wished to tell you how much I liked your poems. They are really very good. Indeed, although I know it is heresy to say so, I think they surpass the work of Mr. Kingsley-Dunnett.''

Merrymount reddened. "Surely you are gammoning me, Miss Harwood."

"She is not, Lord Merrymount," interjected Kitty. "I read them, too, and thought them wonderful. My favorite was 'To Aurelia.' I thought it was so very lovely."

Kitty's praise completely flustered the marquess for, in truth, that young lady had been the inspiration for the poem. To know that the object of his devotion so appreciated his tribute to her was overwhelming. "Thank you, Miss Harwood," he finally managed to reply.

"I certainly hope," continued Kitty, "that I may very soon see a book of your poems."

"I do not think that likely," said Merrymount modestly. "They are poor efforts."

"They are not, Lord Merrymount," said Valeria. "It would not at all surprise me if you had them published."

"Oh, yes," said Kitty, "you must share your gift with the world."

This remark so disconcerted the young marquess that he could not reply. He was spared that necessity by the appearance of Lord Traverhurst.

Intent upon the discussion, Valeria had not noticed the earl's approach. She viewed him in surprise. "Lord Traverhurst," she said.

"Madame Oracle," returned the earl, smiling at her. Her then greeted the others.

Valeria noticed that Merrymount was eyeing Traverhurst with obvious displeasure due to Kitty's happiness at seeing him. "I did not expect to see you," said Kitty, smiling at the earl. "You said you detested Almack's."

"How could I detest a place where I could find three such lovely ladies?" replied Traverhurst, looking at Valeria. That lady raised her eyebrows at his flummery and he grinned. Indeed, it was unusual for the earl to attend the assembly. However, earlier that day, one of the patronesses had informed him that the Princess Lubetska and Valeria would be attending. Wishing to see Valeria, Traverhurst easily overcame his aversion to Almack's. "I hope you are enjoying the evening," he said.

"We are," said Maria. "We were just discussing Lord

Merrymount's excellent poetry. You must hear all about it.''

The marquess looked embarrassed. "Let us change the subject, princess. I do not wish to bore Lord Traverhurst about poetry.''

"I fear you misjudge his lordship," said Valeria, casting an impish glance at the earl. "Traverhurst loves poetry and is fond of reciting it.''

Kitty looked surprised. "I did not know that. I have never heard you recite any.''

"Do recite something now, Traverhurst," said Maria.

Valeria smiled. "Yes, do," she said.

"Well, if you insist." The earl met Valeria's gaze, his eyes sparkling.

To Valeria's considerable astonishment, Traverhurst launched into a flawless recitation of a poem she recognized as the work of Lord Byron. When he had finished, the earl looked over at her, a mischievous expression on his face.

"How wonderful!" cried Maria. "My dear Traverhurst, you have a wonderful voice. Such a stirring rendition! Did you write the poem yourself?''

Valeria and Traverhurst exchanged a glance. "I fear not, ma'am," said the earl. "I must give Byron credit for it.''

"Your recitation was good, Traverhurst," said Kitty. "Of course, I must admit I do not like Byron overmuch.''

"Nor do I," said Merrymount. "He is so undisciplined.''

"I daresay," said Valeria, "that is why he appeals to Lord Traverhurst.''

"Exactly so," said the earl, grinning at her. "And I suspect that is why you also like his work.''

"I did not say I liked it," said Valeria.

"Well, don't you?''

Valeria hesitated. "Oh, very well, I do like it.''

"I knew it," said Traverhurst. "I shall tell Byron when next I see him.''

"Do so. I'm sure he has been awaiting my approval.''

Maria, a very perceptive lady, listened to this exchange with interest and she did not fail to note the way Valeria and the earl were looking at each other. The princess smiled knowingly, thinking her stepdaughter had made a conquest.

Kitty, too, noticed the earl's interest in her aunt, and she frowned petulantly at them both. Kitty was beginning to become irritated with Traverhurst. How dare he ignore her and flirt with Valeria, she thought.

Kitty was even more irked with the earl at his next remark. He looked at Valeria. "Would you do me the honor of dancing with me, Miss Harwood?"

Valeria hesitated, knowing very well it was folly to be seen with him. A sensible woman would have declined at once, hoping to avoid causing any further talk. However, looking up at the earl, Valeria wanted very much to be in his arms again. She nodded and allowed him to lead her away.

As they approached the other dancers, Traverhurst grinned wickedly at Valeria. "You are very brave, Madame Oracle."

"Yes, I know. Dancing with you is certainly the most dangerous thing I have ever done. After all, my brother Julian is here."

"And the loquacious Colonel Baxter."

"Oh, dear."

"Do not fear. The colonel seems so occupied with his bread and butter that he will not notice."

When the orchestra began to play a waltz, Traverhurst took her into his arms and they began to dance. Once again Valeria found his closeness exciting and she was suddenly oblivious to what society would think.

She looked up at him. "You did surprise me with that poem."

"You thought Mother Goose rhymes were the extent of my literary knowledge?"

"I admit I did not think literature your element."

"But I am quite knowledgeable about the subject. Indeed, I can talk for hours about literature, especially my favorite author's works."

"And who is your favorite author?"

He smiled down at her. "Verrell Hawkesworth."

This pronouncement so startled Valeria that she misstepped

and trod upon the earl's foot. She blushed. "Oh, I am sorry."

"It was nothing. But is something wrong, Madame Oracle? Perhaps you do not like Verrell Hawkesworth."

She appeared flushed. "It is not that."

"Good, because I own that I find disliking Verrell Hawkesworth a serious fault. Have you read *The Queen's Champion*?" Valeria nodded and he continued, "It is a devilish good book. Why I gave up gaming for three days to read it."

Valeria looked at him and his amused expression disconcerted her. The terrible suspicion that he knew her secret came to her. Surely he could not know the truth, she thought.

Traverhurst was enjoying her dismayed reaction. "Has Mr. Hawkesworth ever come to the Princess Lubetska's salon? I know many literary gentlemen do so."

"No," said Valeria, trying to regain her composure. "He has not done so."

"A pity," said Traverhurst. "I would very much like to meet him." His knowing smile made her certain that he had discovered her secret.

"Oh, look, there is Kitty and Merrymount," said Valeria, glad for the opportunity to change the subject. She saw her niece and Merrymount among the dancers.

"So you read the cub's poems?"

Valeria nodded. "Yes, they were quite good. How relieved I was to find them so. Kitty liked them, too."

The earl glanced over at Kitty and Merrymount. "They look well together. I hope he is not a die-away ninny like that Kingsley-Dunnett fellow."

"I assure you he is not."

"Thank God," said Traverhurst. Valeria smiled and the music came to a stop. "Dance with me again," said the earl.

"No, I think it best that I return to Maria." Traverhurst looked disappointed, but he nodded and escorted her back to the princess. Unfortunately, Maria was now standing with Julian and Fanny. As Valeria approached them, she could see by her brother's stern expression that he was most unhappy.

Traverhurst greeted Julian and Fanny with his usual aplomb, ignoring Lord Harwood's icy look. However, the earl had scarcely had an opportunity to exchange a few words when a very agitated gentleman appeared before them.

"Your pardon," said the man, speaking with a thick French accent. "I must speak to you, Lord Traverhurst."

The earl, who did not seem altogether happy to see the man, nevertheless made his excuses and left them. When he had gone, Julian turned to his sister. "Are you mad, Valeria? How could you dance with him here?"

"Oh, Julian," said Maria, "there is no harm in a little dance."

"*You* would not think so," said the viscount, regarding his stepmother with disapproval. "I do not like my sister to be the talk of society."

"Come, come, Julian" said Fanny, "do not get into the high fidgets. Surely, it was not so terrible. But who was that man who took Traverhurst away?"

"I don't know," said Julian, a disgruntled expression on his face. "But I am grateful to him."

"You are so unkind, Julian," said Maria. She looked over at Fanny. "That is the Comte de Tournefort."

"De Tournefort?" said Julian. "Was he not one of Bonaparte's advisors?"

The princess nodded. "I believe so. Of course, now he is loyal to the restoration."

Julian looked skeptical. "I do not trust men who shift their loyalties so quickly. How could such a fellow be admitted here? And what business could he have with Traverhurst?" He directed a meaningful look at Valeria.

"He did seem very anxious to see the earl," said Fanny. "The way they are talking together, it must be a matter of some importance."

Valeria directed her gaze toward Traverhurst and the Frenchman. The Comte de Tournefort appeared to be speaking earnestly to the earl, who looked very serious. Remembering Julian's suspicions about Traverhurst's Bonapartist sympathies, she frowned. She thought once again of the paper he had dropped in the library at the Claridge ball. Now he was talking with a person who had once been one of Napoleon's men. Although still thinking the idea that Traverhurst was in league with Bonapartists quite fantastic, Valeria continued to watch the earl closely.

❧ 15 ❧

THE FOLLOWING afternoon Sir Rupert Netherton called at
the Princess Lubetska's house. "Princess, Miss Harwood,"
he said, entering the drawing room and smiling at Maria
and Valeria. The little dog Putti, who had been asleep at
her mistress's feet, looking at Sir Rupert and, apparently
taking an instant dislike to that gentleman, growled
menacingly.

"Putti," cried the princess, reaching down and picking
up the dog. "You are a very bad girl. Do hush, darling."
Netherton eyed Putti with disfavor and the little dog growled
again. "I am sorry," said the princess. "Putti appears to
be out of sorts. Do sit down, sir."

Sir Rupert bowed to the ladies and lowered his stocky
frame into an armchair beside Valeria. "I am fortunate to
find you ladies alone. I know you are always surrounded
by company."

"Oh, I do anticipate other callers, Sir Rupert," said
Maria. "Indeed, I expect several others to join us soon."

Knowing the type of guests that frequented the Princess
Lubetska's establishment, Sir Rupert was none too pleased
with this information. However, he smiled. "How nice."

"It is good of you to call," said Maria. "We have not
seen you for a time. But then I know how busy your duties
keep you."

Netherton nodded. "I fear so, ma'am."

"How splendid to do such important work," said Maria. "Is it not so, Valeria?"

"Oh, yes," said Valeria. "I know Sir Rupert's work is very important."

Netherton made no attempt to deny the significance of his duties. "Yes, sometimes it is a burden. Especially in these trying times."

"Is there more news of Bonaparte?" asked Valeria.

"It appears we shall have to defeat him again on the field."

"How wearisome of him!" cried Maria. "If he were a gentleman, he would not cause so much mischief."

Valeria smiled at that remark. "Can you tell us any more details about the current situation, Sir Rupert?"

Netherton shook his head. "There are so many conflicting reports. I fear we do not know what is going to happen."

Maria frowned. "This Bonaparte! I have never been able to understand how such a little nobody could become an emperor."

Valeria smiled again. "It seems he is a very talented nobody."

"But not at all well-bred," said Maria disapprovingly.

Netherton nodded. "You are very right, princess. But do not forget he came to power amid chaos, and was supported by ruffians and knaves. Nonetheless, he has many admirers."

"But none of them in England," said Maria.

"Not according to my brother," said Valeria. "He thinks Napoleon's spies are everywhere. Last night Julian thought the Comte de Tournefort most suspicious."

"The Comte de Tournefort? Where was he?" Netherton appeared interested.

"At Almack's," said Valeria. "He was talking to Lord Traverhurst. Julian thought the worst of him since De Tournefort was once one of Napoleon's advisors."

"You said he was talking to Traverhurst?" said Sir Rupert.

Valeria frowned at the question. Did Netherton share Julian's suspicions about the earl?

Before she could reply, the butler interrupted them. "Pardon me, your highness, but the Baroness von Mecklenberg is here."

"Do show her in, Reynolds," said Maria.

"The baroness said she wishes to speak to you alone, your highness," said the butler. "I left her in the parlor."

The princess seemed a trifle impatient. "Oh, that woman is impossible. Ever since she has agreed to display her work here, she has badgered me incessantly. Oh, very well, I shall see her. Do excuse me." Maria rose and left the room.

Netherton seemed quite happy at being left alone with Valeria. "Did you enjoy Almack's last night, Miss Harwood?"

Valeria nodded. "It was a pleasant evening."

Sir Rupert smiled at her. "If I may be so bold, Miss Harwood, you look lovely today." The remark startled Valeria, who realized with some dismay that he was starting to sound like a suitor. "Julian has always talked about you," continued Netherton, "and I have long hoped to meet you. I have been a widower for many years, you know." Alarmed at the direction of the conversation, Valeria was glad when the butler once more appeared.

"Excuse me, Miss Harwood, Lord Traverhurst is here. Her highness is engaged with the baroness. Shall I show his lordship in?"

"Yes, Reynolds, please do," said Valeria, knowing well that Sir Rupert would be very unhappy to see the earl.

When the butler had left, Netherton turned to her. "Truly, Miss Harwood, I do not think it wise to admit such a man. You know his reputation."

"But you are here to protect me, sir," said Valeria ironically.

Netherton frowned but before he could reply, the Earl of Traverhurst entered the room. Seeing Netherton, the earl eyed that gentleman with disapproval. "I did not know you had company, Miss Harwood."

Sir Rupert looked daggers at Traverhurst but said nothing. "Do come in, Lord Traverhurst," said Valeria. "Won't you sit down?"

Netherton rose abruptly. "I cannot stay, Miss Harwood. I hope you will excuse me." He bowed quickly and, after casting one more hostile look at Traverhurst, left the room.

The earl sat down across from Valeria and regarded her questioningly. "So the fellow has the audacity to court you? I would have thought you would have sent him on his way."

"I think my guests are my own business, my lord."

Traverhurst frowned. "Do not tell me you can actually tolerate the fellow?"

"I would very much like to know why you despise him," said Valeria.

"You may trust that I have good reason," said the earl.

"And I would like to hear it."

"I fear it is between Netherton and myself."

"It sounds rather mysterious. Did the two of you quarrel over an actress?"

The earl smiled. "You may be assured it is nothing like that."

"Very well, if it is a secret, I shall not press you."

Maria reappeared, followed by the baroness, and the earl got quickly to his feet. "Oh, Lord Traverhurst!" said Maria. "I did not know you were here." She looked at Valeria. "Where is Sir Rupert?"

Valeria exchanged a glance with the earl. "I fear he had another appointment."

"Oh, that is too bad. It is going to be a very exciting afternoon. The baroness has brought her newest work. We shall have an unveiling." Maria looked at the baroness and found that the sculptress was eyeing Traverhurst with interest. "Oh, you two have not met. Baroness von Mecklenberg, may I present the Earl of Traverhurst?"

"Charmed," said the earl, taking the baroness's hand and bowing politely over it.

Valeria watched the sculptress scrutinize Traverhurst from head to toe and back again. "What a handsome man, you are," said the baroness appreciatively. "I must have a model for my next work. You would do very well." She turned to Maria. "It is my series of Greek gods. Next I do Adonis."

The earl raised his eyebrows ludicrously and exchanged a glance with Valeria, who tried valiantly to keep from laughing. The baroness studied Traverhurst again. "*Ja*, it would be *sehr gut*. You come tomorrow. Here is the address." The sculptress handed the earl a calling card. "I expect you at eight o'clock."

"I am flattered, baroness," said Traverhurst, looking down at the card. "However, I must decline."

The baroness frowned and looked as if she had not heard him correctly. "Decline? What? You have no wish to be immortalized?"

"I confess that was never my ambition, ma'am. I am certain that you will find many more worthy subjects than I."

The Baroness von Mecklenberg appeared very unhappy, and Valeria thought that it was very lucky that some other guests chose that moment to arrive. Since one of them was a good-looking young man, the sculptress turned her attention toward him.

Valeria then had the opportunity to speak to Traverhurst alone. "How could you disappoint her, my lord?" she said mischievously. "You know there is no other man in the kingdom who would make a better Adonis."

The earl laughed. "Have pity on me. The woman terrifies me! I could not bear the thought of being in the same room with her when she was wielding a hammer and chisel."

Valeria burst into laughter.

Other guests arrived and soon the drawing room was filled with ladies and gentlemen. Fanny and Kitty were among them. Valeria's niece seemed decidedly cool toward her and Traverhurst, and when Merrymount came in, Kitty hurried over to him. Fanny smiled at Valeria, but was prevented from joining her by two eccentric looking elderly ladies who latched on to her eagerly.

Mr. Kingsley-Dunnett was among the last guests to arrive. His appearance was greeted with much excitement. He bowed graciously to the admiring throng like a monarch moving among his subjects. Espying Valeria standing beside Traverhurst, the poet hastened to her side.

"My dear Miss Harwood," he cried. "I have counted the moments until I could see you again. How ravishing you look!" Valeria looked embarrassed and the earl regarded her with amusement. Kingsley-Dunnett viewed Traverhurst with suspicion. "And who are you?" he said rudely.

"Oh, I thought you had met Lord Traverhurst," said Valeria.

"Traverhurst? Oh, yes, perhaps I have met you." Mr. Kingsley-Dunnett seemed unimpressed. "But then I meet so many people," he said. Then, ignoring the earl, Kingsley-Dunnett turned to Valeria. "My poem is finished. 'Valeria, or the Rapturous Maiden.' I must recite it."

But before Kingsley-Dunnett could do so, Maria appeared beside him and grasped his arm. "Mr. Kingsley-Dunnett, we are about to have the unveiling. You must come with me. The baroness wants you to stand beside the statue." As the princess led the poet away, Kingsley-Dunnett cast a reluctant glance back at Valeria.

"I am glad to see, Madame Oracle, that at least one of us is going to be immortalized," said Traverhurst, grinning at her. "What deuced bad luck that he went away before he could recite 'Valeria, or the Rapturous Maiden.' "

"I should die with embarrassment if he did," said Valeria.

"He appears to be a most ardent suitor. The idea of being a great man's wife must be very tempting."

"Indeed, but being Mr. Kingsley-Dunnett's wife is not so tempting."

The earl laughed. At that moment, Maria called to all the guests, "It is time for the unveiling of Baroness von Mecklenberg's newest sculpture. Come, everyone, gather around."

The guests all came toward Maria. The princess was standing with the baroness and Mr. Kingsley-Dunnett. On a table beside them was a tall object covered with a cloth. After all the company had assembled there, the princess continued, "The baroness has entitled the sculpture, 'Hercules.' " Maria looked over at the sculptress. "Baroness, would you like to make some remarks about your work?''

''My work needs no remarks,'' replied the baroness. Then grasping the cloth, the sculptress snatched it quickly from atop the sculpture. For a moment there was a startled silence as the guests viewed the statue. It was a bronze image of a muscular nude and its head bore a distinct likeness to Kingsley-Dunnett. The figure had struck a faintly ridiculous pose, its arms poised to exhibit its hefty biceps. Although having viewed Greek statuary before, Valeria found the baroness's work somewhat immodest and wished there had been some drapery incorporated in the design.

Traverhurst looked from the athletic statue to Kingsley-Dunnett and then turned to Valeria. ''I daresay, I may reconsider that baroness's proposal.''

''I pray you do not make me laugh,'' whispered Valeria desperately. She was relieved when the crowd suddenly burst into applause. ''Oh, how can Kingsley-Dunnett stand there beside that . . . likeness?'' said Valeria.

''It is hardly a likeness,'' observed the earl wryly. ''Good lord, do you think that he actually posed for it?''

''I cannot bear to think of it,'' said Valeria, stifling her giggles. Fearing she was going to erupt into gales of laughter, Valeria hastily excused herself. ''I shall be right back.''

Once outside the drawing room and out of earshot, she laughed uncontrollably. After what seemed a long time, she was brought to her senses by the sound of voices in the entryway. She recognized the voice of Reynolds, the butler. ''I have told you, I shall see that the earl gets this.''

''But I wish to give it to him myself,'' replied another man, speaking with a pronounced French accent.

''I have said that is impossible,'' returned the butler. ''Now I suggest you leave or I shall have you thrown out!''

The other man exploded into an outburst of French. Although Reynolds could understand not a word of this, Valeria smiled at the string of colorful Gallic epithets. She hurried into the entryway to see if she could be of assistance. "What is the matter, Reynolds?"

"This French person has a note for the Earl of Traverhurst, and he insists on delivering it himself."

Valeria regarded the newcomer with interest. "Could I assist you, *Monsieur . . . ?*" she said in French.

"Bouchot, madame," replied the man, bowing. "I am Lord Traverhurst's valet. Your man will not allow me to give this note to my master. It is of grave importance that he sees it at once."

"Would you trust me to deliver it?" said Valeria.

The valet smiled. "Of course, madame." He handed her a folded piece of paper.

"Do wait, Bouchot, and you shall have your reply." The servant nodded.

Reynolds looked curiously at Valeria since the conversation had been in French. "I shall take care of this," said Valeria. "Lord Traverhurst's man will wait."

Valeria walked off, leaving the butler to eye the French servant disapprovingly. As Valeria neared the drawing room, she was filled with curiosity about the note in her hand. What could be so urgent? Julian would probably think it some secret communication. She stopped near the door and debated with herself. Then, feeling completely dishonorable, she unfolded the paper and read it. It was written in French and said, "My lord, the tide has turned. The Fox has finally agreed. If you act quickly, B's Favor will be yours. Bouchot."

Puzzled by this cryptic missive, Valeria read it over again. What in the world could it mean? Who was "the Fox" and what was "B's Favor"? Valeria knit her brows in concentration. "B's Favor," she repeated aloud. Bonaparte! No, surely, Traverhurst's servant would not be so careless about such an incriminating note. Still, he had been very adamant about delivering it to the earl in person. Well, she decided, she would give it to him and Traverhurst would explain everything.

Valeria reentered the drawing room and found the company buzzing with talk. She saw that Traverhurst was now speaking to Fanny and she hurried over to him. "Lord

Traverhurst," she said, handing him the note. "Your man Bouchot is here. He brought this for you."

The earl unfolded the paper and read the message. He grinned. "This is good news," he said.

"Good news?" said Valeria, hoping he would elaborate.

He folded the paper and put in in his pocket. "Yes, very good news. I fear it does mean I must hurry away. Lady Harwood, you must excuse me." He turned and smiled at Valeria. "And Madame Oracle, I shall see you again soon." He took her hand and then was gone.

Valeria frowned as she watched him go. "My dear Valeria," said Fanny, "I think the earl appears very interested in you." Looking over at her sister-in-law, Fanny noticed her perplexed expression. "What is the matter, Valeria?"

"Oh, nothing, Fanny."

"His interest in you will surely distress Julian. Of course, my dear husband will be very happy to know Kitty no longer seems so enamoured of the earl."

"She is not?"

Fanny nodded. "Kitty seems quite taken with young Merrymount. Of course, it is too soon to judge, but I do hope this may be serious."

"Indeed," said Valeria, barely attending. Fanny launched into more talk about her daughter and the marquess while Valeria continued to wonder about Traverhurst and his mysterious note.

◈ 16 ◈

"WE HAVE done it, Bouchot." The Earl of Traverhurst smiled at his valet, who was sitting across from him in the carriage.

The servant nodded. "That we have, my lord."

"I never thought the Fox would change his mind. What good fortune. I have wanted that horse for months!"

"Lord Foxworth was very reluctant to sell Beauty's Favor."

"And he drove a hard bargain."

"From what I observed," said Bouchot, "it was you who drove the hard bargain, my lord."

Traverhurst grinned. "Perhaps so. In truth, I would have paid much more. God, he's a beautiful horse! Prinny himself has no better in his stable. There is not a horse in England who can outrun him."

Since Bouchot shared his master's enthusiasm for the sport of kings, he was as excited as Traverhurst at the earl's acquisition of the new race horse. Beauty's Favor, a descendant of the incomparable Eclipse, was a proven winner and a prize indeed.

"It was lucky we arrived when we did," said the earl. "Poor Harcourt, appearing just as the agreement was reached."

Bouchot smiled. "Lord Harcourt was rather unhappy that Lord Foxworth had already sold Beauty's Favor to you."

"Rather unhappy?" The earl laughed. "He was furious! What a joy it was to best him. Yes, I am very glad you found me at Princess Lubetska's house." Traverhurst grew suddenly thoughtful. "Of course, I do admit I was not so eager to leave there."

"That Englishman there," muttered Bouchot, "what a detestable fellow."

"What Englishman is that?" said the earl, amused at his servant's expression.

"The princess's butler. Had the lady not come out and assisted me, I would have thrashed the insolent dog!"

"I shall have to tell Miss Harwood that she saved Princess Lubetska's butler from calamity. That wicked left of yours is to be feared."

Bouchot grinned at this reference to his pugilistic prowess. "Miss Harwood, my lord? Not the formidable lady you once mentioned?"

Traverhurst laughed. "Perhaps she does not look so formidable, but she is indeed."

The valet eyed his master with a shrewd look. "She is very pretty and her French is excellent."

"That does not surprise me. She is a lady of many accomplishments." Thinking of Verrell Hawkesworth, the earl smiled and adopted a reflective pose.

Bouchot made no reply. He glanced at his master and then turned to look out the carriage window, a knowing smile on his face.

Valeria entered the drawing room, but stopped abruptly upon noticing the Baroness von Mecklenberg's statue on display there. Valeria frowned at the bronze figurine, thinking the baroness's Hercules an abominable work. That it had Kingsley-Dunnett's face and seemed to be leering satyr-like at her was quite disturbing.

Suddenly she smiled, remembering Traverhurst's expression when the baroness asked him to pose for her. The thought of such a statue of the earl made Valeria blush.

"Would you be needing anything, miss?"

Valeria turned to see the butler standing at the doorway.

"No, Reynolds. Oh, wait, there is something. Do you think you could turn that statue the other way?"

Reynolds allowed a smile to appear on his usually solemn face. "Gladly, Miss Harwood." The servant walked to the table and twisted the bronze Hercules around.

"Oh, that is much better, Reynolds. Thank you."

The servant smiled again and took his leave. Valeria went over to the desk and pulled out some papers from a drawer. She had made some notes about her next novel, and sitting down at the desk, she started to peruse them.

Seeing the name of the villainous Morveau, Valeria thought again of Traverhurst. How dreadful that he had somehow discovered that she was Verrell Hawkesworth. She wondered how he had found out her secret. Valeria pondered this for a time. Perhaps he was a spy and, as such, was adept at ferreting out secrets.

Frowning, Valeria propped her elbows on the desktop and cradled her head in her hands. She reflected about the mysterious message Bouchot had brought to Traverhurst the day before. Valeria certainly knew what Julian would think. Indeed, her brother would have considered the note proof that the earl was a spy. Although disturbed by her thoughts, Valeria firmly rejected the idea that Traverhurst was capable of treachery.

"Valeria, darling," said Maria, entering the room. "I thought I would find you here." The princess noticed the statue. "What has happened to the baroness's Hercules? Someone has moved it!"

Valeria smiled. "I cannot bear to look at that face, Maria."

The princess laughed. "You are terrible! What if the baroness or Mr. Kingsley-Dunnett should come in? They would be offended."

"But I am offended by it, Maria. Why, it is a most unsettling work of art, though perhaps I am being generous saying it is art."

"You are too harsh, my dear," said Maria. "It is but a bit unusual."

"It is indeed. I find the head and body quite mismatched. It looks more like a monster than a Greek god."

Maria laughed again. "Well, the baroness is very pleased with it, as is Kingsley-Dunnett. Our sculptress is eager to begin her new work. She is sorely disappointed that Traverhurst would not pose for her Adonis."

"Oh, Maria, the very idea!"

The princess smiled. "I think I would rather like to see such a statue of Traverhurst."

"Maria!" Valeria reddened and Maria laughed heartily.

"Well, I must content myself with visiting the real Traverhurst," said the princess. "Come, you must get ready. I promised him yesterday that we would call on him this afternoon."

"Call on him? I could not! I don't want to cause any more gossip."

"You did not seem overly concerned about gossip when you danced with him at Almack's."

Valeria blushed, realizing the truth of her stepmother's words. Indeed, when she was with the earl, she forgot all about the unfortunate rumors about the two of them. "Perhaps I was foolish."

"Certainly not. After all, my dear, everyone already thinks the worst."

"Oh, Maria!"

Princess Lubetska laughed. "Why should you care a fig what anyone thinks? One cannot worry so much about the opinions of others. I assure you, your father never did. But, my dear Valeria, if you do not wish to accompany me, I shall understand. I shall go myself." Maria paused. "Of course, Traverhurst will be so disappointed if you do not come."

"Oh, bosh."

Maria smiled. "It is not bosh. After all, he is in love with you."

"What hum, Maria! He is not the sort of man to fall in love with someone like me."

"What do you mean, someone like you? My poor girl, you are so clever about some things and so bird-witted about others. I know about such matters and his feelings toward you are obvious to me. And do not deny that you are in love with him."

Valeria appeared flustered. "Maria, you are spouting pure fustian."

Her stepmother laughed. "I do not have time to argue with you. I must get ready to go see the earl. Are you coming?"

Valeria hesitated and then nodded. "Oh very well, I shall come with you, Maria," she said.

"Good," said Maria and the two ladies left to change their clothes.

A short time later, Valeria and her stepmother arrived at Traverhurst's Georgian townhouse. Although still unsure of the wisdom of visiting the earl, Valeria did want to see him again.

Traverhurst's butler led the ladies to the drawing room and said that his master would soon join them. Valeria glanced curiously around. The room was exactly as one would have expected, tastefully and expensively decorated. There was a decidedly French empire look to it and it crossed Valeria's mind that one of the Emperor Napoleon's rooms would have looked very much like it.

"What a lovely room," said Maria. "And look at this chair. I remember one exactly like it at the Palace of Versailles. And this picture! A Fragonard! Queen Marie Antoinette loved his work."

The earl's obvious preference for things French made Valeria slightly uneasy. She frowned as she looked at the painting.

"You don't like my painting, Madame Oracle?" Traverhurst strode into the room, a smile on his handsome face.

Somewhat startled, Valeria turned toward him. "Oh, I do like it, very much."

"Good, for if you did not approve of it, I would immediately cast it into the fire."

Valeria smiled, her misgivings suddenly swept away. "You are preposterous," she said.

He grinned in return and then looked at Maria. "Princess, how good of you to call. This is a happy surprise."

"A surprise? But, Traverhurst, I did promise we would come," said Maria.

The earl glanced over at Valeria. "But I didn't think

Madame Oracle would want to do anything so scandalous as to call upon me.''

"And you are quite right, my lord," said Valeria. "My boldness even now astonishes me."

The Princess Lubetska, who had been watching her stepdaughter and the earl with interest, noted the way their eyes met. She smiled to herself.

"Do sit down, ladies," said Traverhurst.

Maria nodded and did so, sitting down in a chair beside an elegant French sofa. This maneuver forced Valeria to sit upon the sofa and enabled the earl to sit beside her.

"Your house is exquisite," enthused the princess. "You have wonderful taste."

"You are kind, princess," said the earl.

"It appears you have a fondness for French styles, Lord Traverhurst," said Valeria.

"You do not like French decoration, Miss Harwood?"

"I do indeed, but even if I did not, I would not dare say so, since I would not wish you to throw all of your furniture into the fire."

The earl laughed. "I cannot help my inclination toward French decoration. You see, I spent most of my earliest days in France. One might say I was French before I was English."

This remark had an ominous sound to Valeria. "Your mother was French, I believe?" she asked.

Traverhurst nodded. "Her father was the Duc de Châteauroux. I spent much of my early boyhood on his estate. That was, of course, before the revolution."

"I once met your grandfather in Paris," said Maria. The princess looked nostalgic. "That was so many years ago. And I also remember your uncle Robert de Rohan du Plessis. I believe he became one of Bonaparte's most competent generals."

The earl laughed. "I do not like to mention that connection, princess. Of course, it was fortunate for my mother's family, since the emperor restored the family estates."

Valeria frowned at these remarks. So Traverhurst's uncle was one of Napoleon's generals! It seemed his family certainly had reason to be loyal to Bonaparte.

Noting Valeria's expression, Traverhurst regarded her curiously. "Is something the matter, Miss Harwood?"

"Oh, no." Valeria was glad when at that moment the valet Bouchot appeared.

"Your pardon, my lord," he said in French. "Someone is here. It is important."

Valeria looked over at Traverhurst, who was regarding his servant questioningly. The valet raised his eyebrows slightly and Traverhurst, seeming to understand this communication, rose to his feet. "Do excuse me, ladies. I shall be back shortly."

He then followed Bouchot out of the room and closed the door behind him. After he had gone, Valeria found herself wondering what had caused his abrupt departure. Finally unable to contain her curiosity, Valeria got up and went to the door. Opening it a crack, she peered out into the hallway.

Maria viewed this with surprise. "Whatever are you doing, Valeria?"

Valeria put her finger to her lips and Maria regarded her in bewilderment. Valeria took no note of her stepmother's expression, so intent was she on watching Traverhurst.

The earl was standing at the end of the corridor, engaged in a serious conversation with a most peculiar looking man. Bouchot stood beside the earl and looked very grave. The stranger was a rough-looking man, dressed in rude clothing. He seemed an odd acquaintance for Traverhurst, thought Valeria, straining to hear what the man was saying. The stranger seemed to be purposely keeping his voice low.

Valeria could only hear a few phrases. There was something about "danger increasing" and "the time would soon be at hand." Twice she distinctly heard the man say "the emperor." Finally, Traverhurst clapped the man on the back and the stranger went quickly away.

Valeria hurried back to her place on the sofa. "Whatever were you doing?" asked Maria.

"I cannot explain now," whispered Valeria as the door opened and Traverhurst entered.

"I am sorry about that interruption, ladies. I realize this

is most ramshackle of me, but there is a matter of some importance that I must attend to."

"I hope it is not a problem," said the princess.

"Nothing that cannot be settled easily. However, I must go. I do apologize." The earl looked over at Valeria and met her gaze. "I hope you will call upon me again."

Valeria, somewhat shaken by what had transpired, only nodded. The earl seemed puzzled by her reaction.

"We shall leave you then, Traverhurst," said Maria. "And I do expect you at the salon."

After assuring her he would be there, the earl escorted the ladies out. Once inside their carriage, Valeria sighed. "Valeria," said Maria, "I insist you tell me what is going on. You are acting very strangely."

"Oh, Maria, this is terrible!"

"What is terrible? My dear girl, you must tell me."

"I am not certain myself, Maria."

"It is not another woman?" Noting her stepdaughter's grim expression, the princess concluded that this was indeed the problem. "My poor darling," she said sympathetically, "but I had thought that he and Mrs. Edwards had parted."

Valeria did not seem to hear her and Maria decided it would be best not to say anything further. Valeria stared glumly out the carriage window as the vehicle made its way down the fashionable street.

When they arrived home, the princess tactfully retired to her rooms, leaving Valeria alone in the drawing room. Frowning, Valeria paced across the room. Surely there must be some other explanation, she thought. But as she sat down upon the sofa, she realized that the conclusion was inescapable. It appeared that Julian was right to suspect that Traverhurst was a French agent.

Indeed, she could no longer ignore the evidence. She thought of the paper that had dropped from the earl's coat in Lord Claridge's library. Then she recalled Traverhurst's talking to the Comte de Tournefort and later receiving Bouchot's mysterious note. Now, she had seen him talking with a rough-looking man who spoke about the emperor. Valeria suddenly remembered the earl's words about being

French before he was English. Yes, she concluded miserably, Traverhurst must be the highly placed source that
Major Talbot had told Julian about.

Her dismal reflections were interrupted by the appearance of the butler. "Lord Harwood is here, miss."

Valeria was very much surprised to hear that Julian was
there. Indeed, she had never expected him to call at Maria's. "Do show him in, Reynolds."

The butler nodded and left. Moments later, Julian entered the drawing room. He looked quite cheerful and
greeted his sister warmly. "Good afternoon, Valeria. And
where is Maria?"

"In her rooms," said Valeria, regarding her brother
strangely. "I don't expect that she will join us. I know that
will not distress you."

Lord Harwood smiled. "Even seeing my stepmother
could not dampen my mood today, Valeria."

"Good heavens, Julian. What has caused you to be in
such uncommonly high feather?"

Julian smiled again as he sat down across from his
sister. "Fanny has informed me that Kitty's silly infatuation with Traverhurst is over. She has transferred her
affections to young Merrymount. Upon my honor, it is a
miracle!"

"And you approve of Merrymount?"

"I would be daft if I did not. I do admit he is a bit of a
moonling, but he is young and will outgrow it. Yes, I am
very pleased about this. Of course, Merrymount has not
yet made an offer for Kitty. But even so, my daughter is
done with Traverhurst." Julian eyed Valeria closely. "And
I hope you are done with him too." Valeria looked down
and made no reply. "Good God! Don't tell me you are
smitten with him?"

"Don't be ridiculous," replied Valeria without much
conviction.

Julian shook his head. "I always thought you were far
too sensible for such folly, and I caution you, Valeria,
involvement with Traverhurst would be folly. And I refer
not only to his reputation with women."

Lord Harwood was surprised that his sister did not make

an angry retort. Instead, Valeria appeared dispirited. "Julian, I know that you have had suspicions that Traverhurst has Bonapartist sympathies, indeed, that he has been actively aiding the enemy cause. Do you really think there is truth in this?"

Julian shrugged. "I have no evidence to support such a view, although because of his family connections, I have not thought it impossible. Why, Claridge and I were just discussing the matter at the club yesterday."

Valeria appeared shocked. "You were discussing Traverhurst?"

"Yes, his name did come up. Claridge had heard that there was most definitely a spy among the first circles of society. At first he did not wish to mention Traverhurst, knowing that your name has been linked with his." Julian frowned and then continued, "When I voiced my concerns about the earl, Claridge agreed he was suspect.

"Truly, Valeria, you must avoid this man, for he may indeed be a traitor. Claridge told me that he has noted some suspicious behavior on Traverhurst's part."

"In what way suspicious?" said Valeria.

"Not long ago Traverhurst left town and went off to his estate Seahold. He returned a few days later."

"And what is so odd about that?" said Valeria.

"My dear girl, the day after Traverhurst left town was the Reilly bout. Why, the fellow had a hefty wager on the Irishman. There is not a gentleman in the kingdom who would have missed such a pugilistic exhibition."

"That is hardly damning evidence, Julian," said Valeria doubtfully.

"Well, it appears dashed peculiar to me. Why would he rush off to a country estate at such a time?" Lord Harwood directed a knowing look at his sister. "Claridge has told me Traverhurst's estate is not very far from Dover."

"Is that in some way significant, Julian?"

"I did not think you such a goosecap, Valeria," returned the viscount. "If one is a French spy, what better location could one pick than near Dover? Why, how convenient it is to send messages across the Channel from there. Claridge thought so too, and I intend to speak to

Rupert about it. He would know what to do. I daresay, if government troops would go out to this Seahold, they would doubtlessly find all manner of evidence against Traverhurst.''

Julian was once again surprised to find that his sister did not proclaim his words perposterous. She seemed unusually reserved. Satisfied that Valeria was taking his warning about the earl seriously, but not wishing to alarm her further, Julian changed the subject. Valeria barely heard her brother's words, but kept thinking about Traverhurst and her own suspicions about him.

❧ 17 ❧

AFTER TALKING to Julian, Valeria spent a sleepless night. Her mind was filled with Traverhurst and the possibility that he was an enemy of England. She lay awake, thinking about the recent events. She could not forget the suspicious man who had come to Traverhurst's house. What other explanation could there be than that they were part of some nefarious scheme?

She imagined a gathering of Bonapartist spies at his estate, Seahold. Seahold. Indeed, the very name conjured up intrigue. It was probably a perfect place for French ships to come in. But still, she had no irrefutable evidence of Traverhurst's involvement. If only she knew the truth.

Her suspicions gnawed at her and then suddenly she had an idea. She would go to this Seahold and try to discover the truth herself. If the estate was, as Julian suggested, the site of Traverhurst's treacherous activities, she might learn something there that would confirm her suspicions.

After resolving to go to Seahold, Valeria finally fell into a fitful sleep. That morning she got up early and began to make preparations for her journey. By the time Maria arose, Valeria was packed and ready to depart.

The princess was quite astonished when her stepdaughter, dressed in traveling clothes, entered her sitting room. "But what is this, Valeria? Where are you going?"

"To Melbury, Maria."

"Melbury?" Maria regarded her in amazement. "Now?"

Valeria nodded. "I shall not be gone long."

"My dear Valeria, you cannot be serious. You never said a word about it."

"Oh, I just decided to go."

"That is not like you, my dear. Is something wrong?"

"Oh, no. I just wish to go to the country."

Maria regarded her with a worried expression, fearing that Valeria was terribly upset over Traverhurst's inconstancy. "Why, then I shall go with you," she said.

"That is very kind of you, Maria, but I could not ask you to do so. You cannot leave now. Do not forget the salon."

"But you cannot go alone."

"Oh, Sally will accompany me. Now do not worry about me, Maria. I will be back very soon."

"You will take my carriage and grooms," said the princess.

"Oh, no. I have hired a postchaise. It should be arriving at any time. Truly, Maria, this is nothing to be concerned about."

Maria shook her head. Despite her stepdaughter's assurances, she thought it very odd that Valeria would dash off to the country.

"Well, I really must be going, Maria. I shall see you in a few days. Do tell Julian and Fanny for me. I expect you will see them soon."

Valeria kissed a very confused Maria and then turned and hurried out of the room.

The sun was bright and the weather remarkably fair as the postchaise made its way along the narrow road that followed the coast toward Dover. Valeria would have on most occasions enjoyed the fine weather and lovely sea views, but that day she was uncharacteristically glum.

The maid Sally looked out the carriage window and then glanced over at her mistress. The worthy servant was quite bewildered by Valeria's actions. Sally thought it very curious that, after informing the Princess Lubetska that they were going to Melbury, Valeria had announced to her maid that they were going in the opposite direction. Sally had been sworn to secrecy and, indeed, even now she was not sure of their destination.

Of course, the maid was quite happy to have a change of scenery and some adventure. It had been rather exciting racing off and spending the night in an inn that could be charitably termed colorful. Now that morning they were traveling along the coast toward Dover and Sally had to admit that the sea air was refreshing. The only negative aspect about the trip was that her mistress was so preoccupied that she said very little. That certainly wasn't like Miss Harwood, reflected the maid.

In the afternoon they stopped at a tiny fishing village where the postchaise driver asked directions. Then the vehicle proceeded on, arriving finally at a country estate. As the carriage pulled to a halt, Valeria looked out the window. "So this is Seahold," she said, studying the grand residence.

It was a magnificent house, perched high atop cliffs overlooking the sea. Valeria's practiced eye judged the house to be an excellent example of Elizabethan architecture.

"What a fine house, miss," said Sally.

"Yes," said Valeria.

"Will we be staying here, miss?"

"No, Sally, I only wish to have a look at this estate."

The maid looked rather confused as one of the drivers opened the door and helped Valeria and herself down. "You want to have a look at it, miss? You aren't thinking of buying it?"

Valeria laughed. "Heavens no, Sally. Although, by my faith, this is the sort of house I would like to have. No, I simply wish to see it. I daresay, many come here to visit it. It is in the guidebook."

Sally thought it most odd that her mistress would come this distance simply to visit a house. It did appear to be a fine residence, but there were many such places far closer. However, the maid said nothing, and followed her mistress to the door.

The butler, immediately taking Valeria for a lady of quality, was most gracious. "Good day, ma'am."

"My maid and I were traveling through the vicinity,"

said Valeria, smiling at him. "I noticed the listing for Seahold in the guidebook and if it would not be inconvenient, I would appreciate a tour."

The butler nodded. It was not uncommon for travelers to stop at the estate, wishing to see it. Proud of his master's house, the servant was always rather flattered at the interest it provoked. "Certainly, ma'am. I shall have the housekeeper, Mrs. Trotter, show you about. Do wait here."

A few minutes later, the butler returned with a gray-haired woman dressed in a plain brown dress. She wore a severe white cap, but her merry eyes belied her prim attire.

"This is Mrs. Trotter," said the butler.

Mrs. Trotter curtsied. "Good afternoon, ma'am. Mr. Keating tells me you wish to see the house. Glad I am to show it to you. Follow me please."

"Thank you, Mrs. Trotter," said Valeria. She and Sally then followed the housekeeper from the entry hall.

"I suppose your master is in London this time of year," said Valeria.

"Aye, ma'am, but his lordship comes and goes at a moment's notice. We never know when he may appear." This remark made Valeria a little uncomfortable, but she smiled. "I shall show you the drawing room first," continued the housekeeper. She led them into a large room, stylishly decorated. Again, Valeria was aware of a decidedly French influence in its decoration.

"This is a beautiful room," said Valeria. "The furniture is French, is it not?"

"Aye, most of it. His lordship's mother was French and she bought most of the furniture you see here."

"She was obviously a woman of taste," observed Valeria.

The housekeeper appeared pleased with this remark. "Aye, that she was, and a lovely person. It has been four years now since her death and I miss her still. Some might think it hard to serve a French mistress, but it was not. The countess was the kindest lady." Mrs. Trotter looked nostalgic. "Not that she didn't have a temper, mind you. That she did. My master is so much like her. Perhaps you know his lordship?"

"I have met Lord Traverhurst," said Valeria.

"What a fine man he is," said the housekeeper proudly.

"You have known his lordship long, Mrs. Trotter?"

"Aye, since he was in short coats. I've been with the Warrender family for nigh on fifty years, ma'am. I watched the present earl grow up. What a rascal he was! What trouble he gave us as a lad, but there was not a servant who did not love him."

Although very much interested in the housekeeper's remarks, Valeria wondered how she might obtain more useful information. "Mrs. Trotter, you said Lord Traverhurst comes often to Seahold. Does he have many guests?"

The servant looked thoughtful. "He often meets with gentlemen here."

"You mean local gentlemen?"

The housekeeper regarded Valeria strangely, obviously thinking the question unusual. "Just gentlemen," she said. "I do not know them. Come, let me show you the portrait gallery."

Valeria realized she must be more subtle in her questions. She followed the housekeeper in silence as they went up an impressive oak stairway and entered a long room lined with paintings. "This is splendid," said Valeria.

The housekeeper nodded. "All the Warrenders are here." She pointed to a picture of a man in Elizabethan costume. "That was the first earl, and that the first countess. He was a favorite of James I."

They progressed through the portraits, the housekeeper commenting on each one and providing Valeria with Traverhurst's family history. At the portraits of the sxith earl and countess, Valeria paused for some time. The earl's father was a very handsome man, although he appeared a trifle stern in the painting. Traverhurst's mother was strikingly beautiful. There was an obvious family resemblance, decided Valeria, noting how the late countess's eyes and smile were very much like the present earl's.

"And this is the master," said Mrs. Trotter. "A good likeness, I think."

Valeria stared at the portrait. Traverhurst looked very handsome and the artist had captured his roguish charm.

Seeing the earl looking down at her from the wall rather disconcerted her.

"Not a bad effort, but, I daresay, the Baroness von Mecklenberg would have done better."

Stunned at the sound of Traverhurst's voice, Valeria grew pale. Summoning her courage, she turned to face him. "Lord Traverhurst," she said weakly.

"Miss Harwood. By Jupiter, this is a surprise!"

"Yes, it is," said Valeria, fearing she was turning very red.

"My lord!" cried Mrs. Trotter. "We had no idea you were coming." She regarded him fondly. "I was just telling the lady that we never knew when you might appear."

"Yes, I keep my people in the high fidgets," said the earl, continuing to smile at Valeria. "But, Miss Harwood, I am most anxious to discover how you happen to be here."

Valeria tried to appear nonchalant. "My maid Sally and I were traveling in the vicinity. Your house is in the guide-book, you know."

"And your interest in architecture drew you here?"

Feeling like a complete idiot, Valeria nodded.

Traverhurst grinned and then he turned to his house-keeper. "Mrs. Trotter, please take Miss Harwood's maid to the kitchen. I'm sure she would appreciate some re-freshment. Miss Harwood and I will have tea in the draw-ing room."

"Very good, my lord," said Mrs. Trotter, leading Sally off.

"And now, my dear Madame Oracle, I am most inter-ested to hear what you are really doing here. And do not speak to me of guidebooks. I know a Banbury story when I hear one."

Valeria looked down in embarrassment. "I . . . that is . . . oh, I cannot tell you."

"Come now, Madame Oracle, there must be an expla-nation."

Her mind racing for a plausible tale, Valeria hesitated. "Oh, very well. I realize you know my secret."

"Your secret?"

"You know what I mean."

Traverhurst grinned. "Perhaps I do, Mr. Hawkesworth."

"However did you find out?"

"I saw the letters that were on your desk the day I called on you at Princess Lubetska's."

"Oh," said Valeria, "how careless of me."

"But my dear Madame Oracle, what does my knowing that you are Verrell Hawkesworth have to do with your coming here?"

"You see, I am doing a new book and since it is set near Dover and I have never been there before, I felt it necessary to visit it. This is most embarrassing. I did see your house listed in the guidebook and I confess I was curious. You must think me the greatest near-nose."

Traverhurst laughed. "And I confess that had I passed by your Melbury, I could not avoid stopping." Valeria smiled, very happy that the earl appeared to accept this explanation. He continued, "And now I shall escort you myself. Then we will have tea and later dinner. My chef is a great master and enjoys an opportunity to do his best."

"Oh, no, I could not stay," said Valeria. "Indeed, I think Sally and I must be going. I hope to arrive at Dover this evening and find a room at an inn there."

"My dear madame, I will not allow it. You will be my guest at Seahold tonight. You can go to Dover tomorrow."

"Truly, sir, that is out of the question. It would be best if we left shortly."

"Well, I can see you are a stubborn woman, Miss Harwood, and I must resort to other tactics to make you stay. Blackmail is my only recourse."

"Blackmail?" Valeria regarded him in surprise.

He nodded. "If you do not stay and have dinner with me, I shall reveal to the entire world that you are the esteemed Verrell Hawkesworth. Colonel Baxter will seem tight-lipped compared to me."

"You would not!" cried Valeria.

"I would indeed. I will resort to any measures to attain my ends. You must say you will stay."

"You are a ruthless villain, Lord Traverhurst," said

Valeria with a smile. "But surely you know I could not stay here."

"What harm is there in dinner, Madame Oracle? And afterward I shall escort you to a nearby inn myself."

"Oh, very well," said Valeria.

"Good," replied the earl. He then offered her his arm and they began the tour.

❧ 18 ❧

NOW THAT she was with Traverhurst, Valeria found it difficult to think about his alleged spying activities. As he led her around his house, Valeria thought only of how much she enjoyed being in his company. Soon they were laughing and joking.

"And this is the library," said Traverhurst, escorting her into a large room. "You may be interested in comparing it to Claridge's library."

She laughed. "Do not remind me of that."

He grinned. "Very well, I shall be a true gentleman and say nothing more about it. My father was very proud of his collection."

Valeria looked at the large number of books lining the walls. "It is very impressive."

"But my father was not the only book collector. You must see what I have added to the library." He led her over to a small bookshelf by a chair. "All my favorites are here." Traverhurst pointed to a shelf on which there were some thick leather-bound volumes.

Glancing at the books, Valeria opened her hazel eyes wide in surprise. There were all three of the published works of Verrell Hawkesworth.

The earl smiled at her reaction. "I was not gammoning you at Almack's, you know. Verrell Hawkesworth *is* my favorite author. And now that I have met him, I am an even greater admirerer."

She looked up at him and found him regarding her intently. Disconcerted by the feelings stirring within her, Valeria looked away quickly. "You are very kind, sir," she said. Feeling it prudent to leave the library, Valeria walked away from him. "Could we see the garden?"

The earl, who had come very close to yielding to his urge to take Valeria into his arms, nodded. "Anything you wish, Madame Oracle."

Valeria was glad to get out into the air. Leaning on the earl's arm, she walked out into the formal gardens that stretched out behind the house. A profusion of spring flowers greeted them. Beyond the garden was a magnificent view of the sea.

"It is so beautiful," said Valeria. "How you must love it here."

He nodded. "I do. I like no place better. Indeed, I prefer it to town."

Valeria smiled. "I did not take you for a country gentleman."

"That is my secret, Madame Oracle," said Traverhurst, smiling in return. "I shall rely on your discretion to keep it so."

"I shall do so," said Valeria, "on condition that you keep mine."

"Agreed, Mr. Hawkesworth. Although I daresay it will be sorely tempting to reveal your identity. Why, the last time I saw Prinny, he mentioned you, that is to say, Verrell Hawkesworth."

"The Prince mentioned me? What did he say?"

"Actually, it was a complaint."

Valeria looked startled. "A complaint? Oh, dear!"

The earl smiled. "He complained that your *Queen's Champion* kept him up all night. He was so eager to find out what happened to the diabolical Morveau that he couldn't stop reading."

Valeria laughed delightedly. "You are quizzing me!"

"Upon my honor, I am not," said Traverhurst. Smiling at each other, they continued to stroll about the garden. Some time later they went inside and had tea.

The afternoon passed quickly. No longer having any

desire to protest staying at Seahold for dinner. Valeria was
happy to retire to a room to change. She was glad to find
that the efficient Sally had packed one of her favorite
evening gowns. The admirable maid, although very curious about her mistress and Traverhurst, said nothing as she
helped Valeria to dress.

Gazing into the mirror as Sally fixed her hair, Valeria
grew suddenly thoughtful. It seemed that she had forgotten
her purpose in coming there. Valeria frowned and then she
cautioned herself not to let her feelings for Traverhurst blind
her. She must still endeavor to discover the truth about him.
Frowning again, Valeria wondered how she might do so.
Perhaps she had been foolish and impulsive, she reflected.

"Is that to your liking, miss?"

Sally's words brought Valeria out of her reverie. "What?
Oh, my hair. It is fine. Thank you so much, Sally. You
may go now." The servant turned to leave. "Oh, Sally?"
said Valeria, stopping her.

"Yes, miss?"

"Did you enjoy your tea in the servant's hall?"

"Indeed so, miss," said Sally. Then seeing that her
mistress wanted to hear about it, the talkative maid was
happy to oblige. "Oh, miss, what a fine hall it is. And the
kitchen! Why, it is so very modern. Wait 'til I tell them at
Melbury. Cook will be so envious."

"Did you find his lordship's servants friendly, Sally?"

"Aye, miss. All were very friendly. Even the foreigners."

"The foreigners?" Valeria regarded her maid with
interest.

Sally nodded. "Aye, miss, Frenchies, but still pleasant.
There was a Mr. Bouchot, his lordship's valet, and a Madame
Duclos, a very old woman who was maid to her ladyship."
The servant smiled. "Mr. Bouchot spoke the funniest
English, but I didn't mind. I thought him very handsome."
Sally paused to look over at her mistress. Since Valeria
made no objection, she continued. "Mr. Bouchot asked
about Melbury and then he told me all about France. I
think he is homesick. He said he wished his master would
live in France. Of course, I told him that was silly. Why
would his lordship go off and live in a foreign country,

especially being an earl and having such a house as this?
But Mr. Bouchot said his lordship loves France and he would
not be at all surprised if Lord Traverhurst did go to live there
someday. His grandfather was a French duke, you know.''

Valeria nodded absently, thinking about what Sally had
just said. Traverhurst's obvious love for France was rather
disturbing. Still, having a fondness for another country did
not necessarily make one disloyal.

''Mr. Bouchot talked on and on about the estate where
he was born. It was where Lord Traverhurst's grandfather
lived. Mr. Bouchot said it was like a fairy castle and very
grand.'' Sally smiled. ''Mr. Bouchot said he hoped one
day I might go to France to see it. Is that not ridiculous,
miss? I go to France? Not that I would not like it, of
course. But I told Mr. Bouchot it not likely that I would go
there. Indeed, I said that I would not wish to do so with
that Bonaparte on the loose. He laughed at that and said
that I should not worry about such things. I said that an
Englishwoman has every right to worry about Bonaparte,
but Mr. Bouchot seemed to think him a fine fellow.''

''He told you he approved of Napoleon?''

''Not exactly, miss, but from his words, I took it to be
his meaning. Indeed, if Bonaparte became emperor of the
French again, I should think Mr. Bouchot would not be at
all unhappy.''

Valeria looked thoughtful. Whatever the earl's sympathies, it was clear that he had a Bonapartist servant. ''That
will be all, Sally,'' she said. ''I must go. Lord Traverhurst
will be wondering where I am.''

After rising from her chair, Valeria went down to join
the earl. She found him in the drawing room. He smiled as
she entered the room and Valeria experienced an involun-
tary flutter of excitement. As always, Traverhurst looked
extremely handsome dressed in his modish evening clothes.

''Madame Oracle, your beauty overwhelms me.'' He
walked over to meet her and, taking her hand, he kissed it
gallantly.

Valeria hoped she was not blushing. ''Lord Traverhurst,
your flummery overwhelms me.''

He laughed. ''You do look beautiful. I hope you are

hungry. Thibodeaux has assured me he has created a masterpiece.''

''Your chef?''

''Yes, and he is a wonder. He was once employed by Josephine Beauharnais.''

''The Empress Josephine?''

''It was long before she was an empress. Poor Thibodeaux. Josephine dismissed him. I fear his sauces did not agree with General Bonaparte's delicate digestion. But Thibodeaux is a great artist. Prinny is always trying to steal him away from me. I would do much for Prince and country, but not that.'' The earl was surprised when Valeria did not laugh and instead, regarded him seriously. ''Madame Oracle, you do not think I should allow His Royal Highness to take my chef?''

She smiled. ''No, indeed. I fear our prince is stout enough without your excellent Thibodeaux.''

Traverhurst grinned and offered Valeria his arm. The two of them quit the drawing room and made their way to the dining hall, a splendid room illuminated by candlelight. Valeria noted the two place settings of fine gold plate upon the long cherry table. The idea of being alone with the earl at dinner seemed suddenly daunting. Valeria thought of her brother Julian, knowing how shocked that gentleman would be if he could see her now.

Traverhurst escorted Valeria to the table and then seated himself. Valeria looked down the long empty table and tried to put aside her misgivings. ''It is a pity that it is only the two of us here to sample Monsieur Thibodeaux's dinner.''

The earl directed a meaningful glance at her. ''I am glad of it, Madame Oracle. It is nice not having to share you with anyone.''

This remark and the way Traverhurst was looking at her disconcerted Valeria and she was relieved when the servants started to bring out the first course. She tried to concentrate on her food, pronouncing it excellent and the chef a great master.

''Thibodeaux will be very glad to hear you appreciate him,'' said Traverhurst. ''French chefs need to be appreciated. That is what they live for.''

"Then I daresay your chef was quite distressed when Josephine dismissed him."

"He was heartbroken, but he did not blame her. Indeed, Thibodeaux was ardent in his devotion to her. He was devastated by her death last year."

"But his devotion did not extend to the emperor?"

Traverhurst laughed. "Hardly. Thibodeaux never forgave Bonaparte. Oh, I do not mean that he was not a loyal subject, but I fear he could never be devoted to an emperor who did not like his béarnaise sauce."

Valeria laughed in spite of herself. She then grew serious. "But it appears that Bonaparte has many loyal supporters even now."

The earl nodded. "He is a man who inspires loyalty."

Valeria frowned at this remark and she regarded him questioningly. "Many think Napoleon a great man."

"And I daresay you do not share that opinion, Madame Oracle?" said Traverhurst.

"If one considers Alexander and Caesar to be great men, perhaps Bonaparte is one. However, I do not judge greatness by military conquest. A woman cannot but think of the death and suffering he has caused." She paused. "Julian calls Bonaparte a monster." She smiled. "And Maria says he is no gentleman."

Traverhurst laughed. "A grave fault, to be sure. Yet, despite all Napoleon must answer for, he has many accomplishments. One must respect his ability. Enemy or no, he is an extraordinary man." Valeria frowned, finding this remark too sympathetic to the former emperor of the French. "But let us not talk any more of Napoleon," said the earl. He adopted a lighthearted attitude. "Why, I'm dashed bored hearing about the fellow. I'd rather talk about you."

"If you think the Emperor Napoleon a dull subject, my lord, I can't imagine how I would be at all interesting."

"But you are an intriguing lady, Miss Harwood. You are, after all, an oracle and an authoress." Traverhurst leaned toward her. "And you have the most beautiful eyes I have ever seen."

Valeria reddened. "Really, Lord Traverhurst, I am no green girl to be taken in by such remarks. Save your flatteries for ladies who would better appreciate them, such as your Great-Aunt Honoria.''

The earl appeared amused. ''You are too hard on me, Madame Oracle. It is clear you think me a rogue.''

Valeria smiled. ''I admit there is something of the rogue about you.''

''I wish you might have a better opinion of me,'' said Traverhurst, rising suddenly from his chair and tossing his linen napkin melodramatically on the table. He took on a look of mock dismay. ''It is hard knowing you despise me.''

''Despise is perhaps too extreme a word, my lord,'' said Valeria, looking up at him with amusement.

To her surprise, he knelt down beside her. ''Then you do not despise me?''

Valeria laughed. ''Pray get up, my lord. You embarrass me.''

She expected him to rise laughingly to his feet, but he remained kneeling beside her. His face grew suddenly serious and he fixed his intent gray eyes upon her. ''Say you don't despise me, Valeria.'' Valeria became flustered and, taking advantage of her discomposure, the earl took her by the shoulders and pulled her toward him. Too stunned to resist, Valeria found the earl's mouth upon hers. He kissed her passionately and, her senses reeling, Valeria responded with surprising ardor.

''Traverhurst!'' The shout startled Valeria and she quickly pulled away from the earl. Turning toward the sound, she saw that a man had entered the dining room. Her eyes opened wide in surprise as she recognized the intruder as the rough-looking man she had seen at Traverhurst's London house.

The earl rose to his feet and scowled at the man. ''In God's name, Dorsey, you choose a fine time to appear.''

The man looked from Traverhurst to Valeria. ''I can see that, Traverhurst,'' he said, directing a grin at Valeria. ''My apologies, madam.'' He turned to the earl. ''I must see you, Traverhurst.''

His lordship did not look at all happy, but he nodded. ''I am sorry, Miss Harwood, I shall have to ask you to excuse me.'' Valeria made no reply as he left the room with the man.

Not quite recovered from the kiss, Valeria found herself in a state of confusion. She had never felt like this before. The memory of Traverhurst's lips upon hers made her blush violently. Valeria tried to calm herself. She must keep her wits about her, she told herself.

Valeria rose from her chair and, in agitation, paced across the room. Who was the rough-looking man and why would Traverhurst find it necessary to see him? Valeria frowned. The explanation was as disheartening as it was obvious. He was involved in some sort of plot. Julian was right. Traverhurst was a Bonapartist spy.

The earl chose that moment to reenter the room. "I am sorry, Valeria, but I must go."

"Go? Where?"

Traverhurst hesitated. "I am called back to town."

"Back to town? At this hour? What do you mean?" said Valeria.

He shrugged. "I fear it is difficult to explain but I assure you it cannot be avoided. By God, if I could avoid leaving you, I would. You must finish your dinner and you will stay the night. I have instructed my servants to be at your disposal."

"But I don't understand . . ." began Valeria, but before she could complete her sentence, the earl abruptly took her into his arms and kissed her once again.

Releasing her, he smiled. "I shall see you soon, my dear Madame Oracle." Not allowing her a chance to reply, he hurried off.

Valeria was confused and upset. Where was he going, she wondered. It was very mysterious. Valeria moved quickly to the window and peered out into the moonlit grounds. She was surprised to see a group of riders assembled there. She watched as Traverhurst and the man called Dorsey joined them. Her eyes followed the earl as he mounted a horse. He then rode quickly away, followed by the others. As the riders vanished into the night, Valeria turned away from the window, a troubled look on her fair countenance.

❧ 19 ❧

VALERIA sat in her sitting room at Maria's townhouse glumly reflecting about Traverhurst. Since she had last seen him at his estate Seahold three days ago, she had scarcely thought of anything else.

Valeria had returned to Maria's the previous afternoon and the princess had been surprised at the shortness of her trip. However, Maria, sensing her stepdaughter's reluctance to talk, had not pressed her for information about the journey. Instead, the Princess Lubetska had urged Valeria to rest in her room and retire early.

It was now late morning. From her chair near the window, Valeria looked out onto the street below. Rain was falling and the sky was dark and gloomy, matching her mood. A sigh escaped Valeria as she glanced down at the fashion magazine in her lap. She then turned her gaze once more to the window.

"This infernal rain!" Princess Lubetska entered the room and smiled at her stepdaughter. "It is the one thing I do not like about England. How I wish the sun would return."

Valeria smiled. "Good morning, Maria."

"Good morning, my darling. I hope I do not disturb you."

"I am glad of your company. Do sit with me."

The princess sat down in a chair beside Valeria. "My dear, it is very clear that you are—what is the expression?

—blue-deviled. Yes, that is it. Blue-deviled. Is something wrong? You did say that everyone was well at Melbury?''

Valeria seemed to hesitate for a moment. ''In truth, I did not go to Melbury.''

Maria's eyes widened. ''Not go to Melbury? Wherever did you go?''

Valeria hesitated again. ''I went to Traverhurst's estate, Seahold.''

''*Himmel*!'' cried Maria. ''You ran off with him!''

''Finally something has shocked you, Maria,'' said Valeria, smiling. ''No, I did not run off with Traverhurst. I went to see his house. I did not think he would be there.''

''And he was?''

Valeria nodded.

''But, my darling girl, what made you do such a thing?''

''I had hoped I might find out the truth about him.''

''Whatever do you mean?'' said Maria.

''I have reason to believe he is a spy in league with Bonapartists.''

The princess looked as if she had not heard correctly. ''A spy? Traverhurst? That is quite absurd. It is what you would call bosh of the worst sort. The very idea makes me laugh.''

''At first I, too, thought it was absurd, but now I know it is true. Oh, Maria, I cannot bear it! I am in love with him!''

''My dear child, I shall never believe such a thing of Traverhurst. You must be mistaken!''

Valeria shook her head sadly. ''I myself have witnessed enough that is incriminating. When I was at Seahold, a dreadful man came there, demanding that Traverhurst go with him. The earl did so at once. It was the same man I saw at his house here in town.''

''So that is why you listened at the door that day.''

''Yes,'' replied Valeria. ''Oh, I did not want to believe it, Maria.''

''Well, I think it nonsense,'' said the princess. ''Traverhurst is not the sort to be a spy. It is preposterous! You must forget all about this. How Traverhurst would laugh to know about it.''

''Maria, I pray you say nothing to anyone.''

''Of course not. I should not spread such a silly story.'' Maria would have continued trying to convince her step-daughter of the absurdity of the idea, but there was a knock at the door and a maid entered.

''Lord and Lady Harwood are here, your highness.''

''We will join them shortly. Show them to the drawing room.'' The servant nodded and hurried off. Maria turned to Valeria. ''We must talk more of Traverhurst later. Truly, I know it is some misunderstanding. But we had best not keep Julian and Fanny waiting. I fear your brother will be vexed with you. He was most unhappy at finding you had gone off without informing him. I pray you do not mention going to Traverhurst's estate, my dear.''

Valeria managed to smile. ''Do not fear, Maria, I am not so great a goose as that.'' The ladies got up and left the sitting room to join Julian and Fanny.

''Valeria!'' Fanny embraced her sister-in-law.

''Fanny, how nice to see you.'' Valeria looked over at her brother and found that Julian was regarding her disap-provingly. ''Julian,'' she said.

''I shall not pretend I am not upset with you, Valeria,'' said Lord Harwood sternly. ''What was I to think when I called upon you and found that you had run off. You might have sent me a note. I think it quite ramshackle for a lone female to behave in such a manner. I am only glad to find you are returned so quickly. I daresay, you scarcely had time to get to Melbury and back.''

''I didn't actually get to Melbery, Julian,'' said Valeria. Maria cast a warning look at her and Valeria smiled. ''You see, I went as far as Dunston, but then I realized it was rather foolish going, so I decided to return to town.''

''That was sensible,'' said Julian, ''but I wonder why you thought to go in the first place.''

''But surely that does not signify,'' said Fanny. ''Valeria is back now. There is no cause to speak any more about it.''

Maria nodded emphatically, eager to change the subject. "Let us all sit down."

Julian and the ladies took their seats. "Valeria, I must tell you about Kitty."

Valeria eyed her sister-in-law warily. "Kitty?"

"Yes, the most marvelous thing has happened. Merrymount has made an offer for Kitty, and she has accepted him. She has forgotten Traverhurst altogether. Indeed, Kitty told me that she found it incredible that she could have ever cared for him. Oh, we are so thrilled about the match."

"How splendid! I do hope Kitty and Merrymount will be happy!" Valeria looked over at the princess. "It seems your plan was successful, Maria."

"Plan?" said Julian. "What do you mean, Valeria?"

"It is nothing," said Maria.

"Do not be modest," said Valeria. "Good heavens, it was Maria's idea about Merrymount and Kitty. She acted the matchmaker."

"You did as much as I did, my dear," said Maria. She turned to Fanny and Julian. "Valeria had Kitty read Merrymount's poetry. Kitty adored it!"

"It was pure chance," protested Valeria.

"Well," said Julian, "if either of you had anything to do with this, I am heartily grateful. To keep Traverhurst out of my family is the greatest good fortune."

Valeria frowned, but she made no reply.

"And that is not the only interesting news," said Fanny. "My dear Valeria, this concerns you."

"Me?" Valeria regarded her in surprise.

"Yes, Rupert Netherton has asked Julian for your hand!"

"What!" cried Valeria, quite astonished.

"Fanny!" Julian frowned at his wife. "I think Rupert wished to inform Valeria of this himself."

"Oh, don't be silly," said Fanny. "It is best she knows beforehand. A lady must have time to collect her thoughts and decide how to reply."

"My dear Fanny," said Valeria, "I assure you, I need no time to collect my thoughts. I would never accept Sir Rupert Netherton."

Julian appeared surprised. "Why ever not, Valeria?"

"I could never have any affection for him."

"Affection?" said Julian. "You're talking like a girl not out of the schoolroom. Rupert is a good man and my best friend. His fortune is quite adequate. It would be a good match."

Fanny agreed with her husband. "Do not be hasty, Valeria. Do not toss aside a chance for happiness."

Valeria laughed. "Dearest Fanny, you must believe I am far happier without Sir Rupert than with him. We are not at all suited. Indeed, I would make him miserable. No, I am adamant. I would never accept Sir Rupert."

Julian was growing very irritated with his sister. "I did not think you could be so addlepated, Valeria. You are not a young girl any longer. There may not be any other offers. You would be a fool to refuse Rupert."

"Then I shall be a fool!" Valeria replied angrily. "But I am not so ninnyhammered to prefer a bad husband to no husband."

Julian glared at his sister and then stood up. "I see you are resolved to be unreasonable. Come, Fanny, I think we should go."

"But you have only just arrived," said Maria. A look at Lord Harwood's face told the princess it was useless to attempt to persuade him. She nodded and allowed them to take their leave.

When they had gone, Valeria frowned. "I hope that Julian informs Netherton of my response to his offer. It would be so much better if he dropped the matter."

Maria agreed with her stepdaughter. However, that afternoon, it became apparent that Julian had not done so. Valeria was quite dismayed when a servant announced that Sir Rupert was there to see her. She considered saying she was not in, but upon reflection, she decided it would be best to settle the matter at once.

Since the princess had gone out, Valeria received Netherton alone. He seemed overjoyed to see her. "Miss Harwood, how fortunate for me to find you in."

"Sir Rupert," said Valeria civilly but without enthusiasm. "Please sit down."

He bowed slightly and did so. "Your brother told me that you had gone to Melbury and I was very glad to hear of your return. Town is very dull without you, ma'am."

"I am sure that life is seldom dull for you, Sir Rupert. Your duties keep you so well occupied."

Netherton nodded. "True," he said, "I am very busy. But, dear lady, I do not wish to talk about my duties. Indeed, I have a very different subject in mind." Valeria braced herself for what she knew would follow. "I think, Miss Harwood, that you have probably sensed that I am not indifferent to you. Indeed, I esteem you highly. I have been for many years a widower, immune to the charms of the ladies I have met. However, I could not be immune to your charms, Miss Harwood. I am, therefore, here to beg the favor of your hand in marriage."

Grateful to her sister-in-law for preparing her for this announcement, Valeria replied without hesitation. "I am well aware of the honor you do me, Sir Rupert, but I fear that I must refuse you."

Netherton regarded her in some surprise. "I pray you take time to consider the matter, Miss Harwood."

"Indeed, sir, that is not necessary. My decision is firm. It is based on my conviction that we should not be happy together. We are not well suited."

"But, Miss Harwood—"

"Please, Sir Rupert, there is no point in any further discussion of the matter."

Netherton frowned. He had not expected the lady's refusal. Indeed, Sir Rupert had assumed Valeria would be happy to accept him, since Julian had informed him that no one had offered for her in many years. It was a crushing blow to his vanity, and, because Julian had assured Netherton of a most generous marriage settlement, that gentleman was severely disappointed.

Netherton glanced at Valeria and he could not fail to note the look of resolution on her face. "Very well, ma'am," he said, rising from his chair. "I shall trouble you no more." He nodded curtly and was gone, leaving Valeria very relieved at his departure.

❧ 20 ❧

AFTER THE disastrous visits of Julian and Sir Rupert Netherton that day, Valeria was in no mood for more company. She would have preferred to spend the evening quietly in her rooms, but the Princess Lubetska would not hear of it. Maria was having a soiree and she had invited all her numerous acquaintances. Arguing forcefully that her stepdaughter needed diversion, the princess finally convinced Valeria to attend her gala evening.

After reluctantly getting dressed, Valeria came downstairs. When she entered the drawing room, it was apparent that Maria's party was to be a great success. Already many guests had crowded into the room and they were talking excitedly.

Valeria smiled, trying to appear sociable. In truth, she was very much preoccupied with Traverhurst. She kept thinking about his abrupt departure from Seahold and wondering where he had gone. Her expression grew thoughtful and she frowned.

"My dear Valeria, how pensive you look," said a masculine voice.

Valeria looked up to see Count Renzetti and Signora Borguesa standing before her. "Oh, good evening," she said, smiling at them.

"That is much better," said the count. "I think a pretty woman should always be smiling."

"Such a squeeze," said Signora Borguesa. "But Maria

has so many friends. I do not see Mr. Kingsley-Dunnett. I do hope he will appear.''

Although Valeria did not share these sentiments, she assured the opera singer that the poet would very likely attend. This pleased the signora and the count, who then began to talk about Kingsley-Dunnett's genius. After enduring the poet's accolades for some time, Valeria was glad when Count Renzetti and the signora moved on to other company.

Scanning the crowd, Valeria saw Fanny and Kitty enter the drawing room. She made her way toward them. ''Fanny, Kitty!''

''Aunt Valeria.'' Kitty smiled, all traces of animosity seemingly gone. Valeria's niece looked lovely as ever, her ethereal beauty heightened by a dress of white lace and delicate flowers in her gold curls.

''I am so happy to see you,'' said Valeria. ''I didn't know that you were coming.''

''Oh, we could not miss it,'' said Kitty. ''John is reading one of his poems.''

''John?'' said Valeria, looking puzzled.

''Lord Merrymount,'' said Kitty.

Valeria smiled. ''Your mama has told me that you are to be married. I wish you every happiness.'' Valeria embraced her niece.

''Thank you, Aunt Valeria. Oh, I am so fortunate. John is the kindest and dearest man. And he is a great poet. I had only to read his poems to see the nobility of his soul.''

''It seems you are fond of him,'' said Valeria, amused at her niece's effusive remarks.

Kitty blushed prettily. ''More than fond. I love him. Oh, I know you must think me the most fickle creature to change my affections so quickly. But I was such a peagoose to fancy myself in love with someone like Traverhurst. How ridiculous.'' Valeria tried hard to appear indifferent and Kitty continued, ''Indeed, a man like that has nothing to commend him but the cut of his coat and the shine of his boots. How shallow I was to be concerned with such things.'' The girl looked suddenly embarrassed. ''Oh, dear. I am sorry, Aunt Valeria. Perhaps you still admire him.''

Valeria hoped she was not reddening. Her niece was regarding her sympathetically, as if she were an addlepated schoolgirl. "Certainly no sensible woman would form an attachment to the earl," said Valeria.

"How true," said Fanny, eyeing her sister-in-law with interest. "But he is so very handsome. And one must concede he is charming." Fanny smiled at her daughter. "But I am so glad you have recognized Merrymount's worth, Kitty. He will make you an excellent husband, and, I daresay, the prospect of one day being a duchess in the bargain is undeniably appealing."

"Oh, I do not care a fig for that," replied Kitty. "I should love John had he no rank at all."

At that moment the subject of the discussion appeared. Merrymount had been fortunate enough to have heard Kitty's remark and he gazed at her adoringly. "Kitty," He then addressed the other ladies a trace reluctantly. "Lady Harwood, Miss Harwood."

"Merrymount," said Fanny. "Is it not exciting that you are reading your poem tonight? You are the cleverest young man."

The marquess looked embarrassed at the praise. "You are too kind, ma'am."

"You are so modest," said Kitty fondly. She turned to her aunt. "Oh, you have not heard the news! It is quite marvelous. John is going to have his poems published."

Valeria smiled at the young man. "Merrymount, that is wonderful! Oh, I am so pleased for you."

"I must thank you for your encouragement, Miss Harwood," said Merrymount. "I fear if I had listened to Mr. Kingsley-Dunnett, I would never have been bold enough to attempt it."

"And what does Mr. Kingsley-Dunnett think of your success?" said Valeria.

Merrymount frowned. "He was most unkind. He said that it was obvious that a duke's son could get anything published."

"Oh, odious man!" cried Kitty.

Valeria laughed. "He is as ungracious as he is untalented."

The marquess nodded. "I certainly see him in a different light."

"Good," said Valeria, smiling at Merrymount. "I have heard that there is other cause to congratulate you, Lord Merrymount. I am so pleased that you and Kitty are to be married."

"Thank you, Miss Harwood," said Merrymount. "In addition to my joy at Kitty's agreeing to wed me, I feel I am most fortunate in my new relations."

Valeria smiled again at the compliment and, suspecting that the two young people wanted to be alone, suggested that Kitty and Merrymount go try Maria's punch. Happy for the excuse, they went off.

"Julian is simply ecstatic about the match," said Fanny. "I am sorry that he was so unpleasant this morning. You know that Rupert Netherton is his dearest friend. He was so enthused at the idea of your marrying him."

"But it was perfectly ridiculous," said Valeria. "I had hoped that Julian would have informed Sir Rupert of my feelings on the matter and that I would have been spared the necessity of refusing him."

"You saw him?"

"This afternoon. I think he was quite surprised that I did not accept him."

"Are you certain you have done the right thing, Valeria? I know Rupert is not at all dashing—"

"That has nothing to do with it, Fanny. I do not like the man. It is as simple as that."

"Then there is no need to discuss it further," said Fanny. "You have always been able to make decisions. I have always admired how sure you are of everything."

Valeria frowned, thinking her sister-in-law very much mistaken. Fanny did not take note of Valeria's reaction, because her attention was drawn toward a glamorous woman coming in their direction. "Look, it is Mrs. Edwards." The actress was wearing a daring gown of a startling red color. Around her neck was a magnificent ruby necklace, and even at a distance the great size and brilliance of the stones were evident.

Glancing over at her, Valeria reflected that there were

few people she wished to see less. Unfortunately, it appeared that Mrs. Edwards was planning to speak with them. "Lady Harwood, Miss Harwood. How wonderful to see you both."

Valeria regarded her coolly. "Mrs. Edwards," she said.

"Lady Harwood," said the actress, smiling at Fanny, "the Duchess of Windhaven was asking for you. I said I would fetch you."

Fanny did not want to leave, but she was reluctant to displease the elderly and very influential duchess. "Very well," said Fanny. "I shall return as soon as I can."

Mrs. Edwards seemed very happy to be alone with Valeria. "Well, my dear, do tell me all about it."

Valeria frowned. "About what?"

"Don't be coy, Miss Harwood. About you and Rohan. He is such a good lover, is he not?"

Valeria blushed. "I assure you, I would not know."

"My dear, you cannot still be denying that you are his new mistress?"

"I do deny it, Mrs. Edwards. Now, I suggest you take your absurd remarks elsewhere."

The actress laughed. "I must remember that you are obliged to be discreet. What would your respectable brother think if he knew? Very well, I shall not spread this about town, although I think it such a delightful story. How amusing for Traverhurst to take up with a spinster from the country. Although I do admit you are not altogether plain."

Valeria's color rose and she fought an urge to slap the actress's smug face. Pleased at the reaction she had provoked, Mrs. Edwards continued, "I do hope for your sake that he does not become bored too soon. It is so difficult to keep a man like that interested. Now, my Prince Oswald is very different. He is such a slow top and, I regret to say, not so very passionate. But then, there are compensations." She fingered the ruby necklace at her throat. "This is but one small token of his affection."

Not trusting herself to reply, Valeria glared at the actress. She then abruptly turned and, infuriated at the woman's insolence, stalked across the room. Why had she not given Mrs. Edwards the setdown she deserved, Valeria

asked herself. She frowned. Perhaps the actress had not
been so very wrong. Certainly, Valeria had not been far
from becoming his mistress. That night at Seahold she had
wanted nothing more than to be in his arms. Indeed, her
body had ached for him.

Yes, had the earl not been called away to his doubtlessly
nefarious purposes, he would have made another conquest.
In all likelihood she meant nothing to him, she thought
cynically. He was just trifling with her affections.

In the midst of this gloomy reflection, Valeria glanced
toward the doorway of the drawing room. To her great
consternation, she saw the Earl of Traverhurst stride into
the room. Suddenly filled with a horror of seeing him,
Valeria hurriedly sought a hiding place. Perhaps if he did
not notice her, she could manage to sneak out and retreat
to her rooms.

Valeria positioned herself behind two large potted palms
and from this strategic location, she watched Traverhurst's
progress. He was looking about the room and, seeing him
glace in her direction, she crouched behind the enormous
pots. Valeria was relieved when she saw him begin speaking with Maria and, since his attention was taken up with
the princess, she began to plot her escape. Just as Valeria
was about to venture forth from her sanctuary, Traverhurst
looked once again in her direction. Valeria saw him say a
few more words to Maria, and then he began to walk
toward her. "Oh, no," she said, panic-stricken. What was
she to do? It was obvious he had seen her crouching
behind the palms.

Knowing it was ridiculous to stay there, Valeria moved
out from behind the plants. She bravely tried to appear
nonchalant, and stood eyeing the plants with interest.

"There you are, Madame Oracle," said Traverhurst,
regarding her with some amusement. "Why are you hiding
back here?"

"Lord Traverhurst," she replied in embarrassment. "I
was not hiding. I was simply studying the plants."

The earl raised his eyebrows. "Indeed?"

"They are very interesting plants," said Valeria. "Na-
tives of Africa, I believe. Quite rare."

"Surely not so rare since there is one in almost every house in London." He grinned. "My dear Valeria, you are hiding from me. Do not pretend otherwise." Valeria looked down in confusion and he continued, "Indeed, I wish to know why. I think it most unusual after what happened at Seahold."

"Please, I do not want to talk about that."

"But I do. I have thought of nothing else since leaving you. Now tell me what is the matter."

"Nothing, I assure you."

He looked at her with a puzzled expression. "Come, I know something is wrong."

"You are mistaken, sir." Valeria forced herself to smile. "Oh, I do hope your business in town went well."

"My business in town?"

"You could not have forgotten whatever caused you to rush off."

Traverhurst regarded her curiously. "Yes, all went very well. It was an important matter." His gray eyes met hers. "If it had not been important, I would not have left you."

Valeria acted as if she had not heard the last remark. "Your friend seemed a most interesting man. You did not introduce him. I believe you called him Dorsey."

"The devil take Dorsey," said the earl in some frustration. "Dash it, Valeria, you are acting deuced odd. You behave as though nothing happened between us."

"Nothing did happen," replied Valeria. "Nothing of consequence, in any case."

Traverhurst eyed her incredulously. "Nothing of consequence?"

"Indeed, my lord, I suspect that for you such things are everyday occurrences."

The light of understanding came to the earl's eyes. "So that's it. You think I was just dallying with you?"

"It seems you are much addicted to dalliance." Valeria dirested a glance toward Mrs. Edwards, who was engaged in conversation with a rotund gentleman.

Traverhurst followed her gaze. "Liza Edwards? That is why you are upset with me. My dear Valeria, that was over some time ago. You have no cause to worry on that matter.''

"You flatter yourself, my lord, if you think I am jealous,'' said Valeria icily. "Gentlemen aren't the only ones who amuse themselves sometimes.''

The earl's handsome face expressed surprise and then anger. He grasped her wrist. "You mean you feel nothing for me?''

Valeria pulled her arm away. "I think we have said enough, Lord Traverhurst. I pray you excuse me.''

He looked at her for a moment, then replied, "Gladly, Miss Harwood. Please make my excuses to the princess.'' Traverhurst bowed and then abruptly departed.

As she watched him go, Valeria fought back tears. How amazed he had been at his reception, she thought, wondering if she had been too harsh. No, she concluded, she had acted correctly. The earl was only upset because of the blow to his vanity. Surely, it was good to be rid of him. After all, he was most certainly a rake and even worse than that, all evidence pointed to his being a traitor as well. Valeria started to walk across the room, reflecting as she did so that her prudent actions had made her completely miserable.

❧ 21 ❧

"MARIA," said Valeria, regarding her stepmother in surprise. It was nine o'clock in the morning, earlier than the Princess Lubetska was accustomed to rising. "I had not expected you up at this hour."

Maria entered Valeria's sitting room carrying her little white dog. "Oh, I could not sleep. I kept thinking about last evening. It was wonderful. I so enjoyed it." She sat down on the sofa beside Valeria. "And young Merrymount was such a triumph."

Valeria smiled. "Everyone but Kingsley-Dunnet thought so. I fear he is envious of his protégé."

"Perhaps you are right. He did seem ill-tempered. But didn't Kitty look radiant? She and Merrymount are perfect for each other. They will be very happy."

"I do hope so," said Valeria.

"Yes, it was a lovely evening." Maria directed a searching look at her stepdaughter. "But you have told me nothing about Traverhurst. He only stayed a few moments. Did you two quarrel?"

"I suppose we did."

"Not about that silly spy business?"

"Maria, it is not in the least silly. I only wish it were. But, no, it was nothing to do with that."

"Then what was it about, my dear?"

Valeria appeared reluctant to discuss the subject, but at her stepmother's imploring look, she finally nodded. "Oh, very well. I shall tell you. I do not believe that Traverhurst is serious in his intentions toward me.''

"Whatever do you mean?"

Valeria shrugged. "You know his reputation. He is just amusing himself.''

''That is not true! I can tell by how he looks at you. My darling girl, you must trust me in these matters. I know he is in love with you.''

"Bosh, Maria, but even if that were true, how can I overlook that he is involved in espionage? He is a traitor to England!''

"That is utter nonsense." Maria eyed her stepdaughter as if she were an unruly child. "I think you had best settle this matter with Traverhurst.''

"What do you mean?"

"I mean that you must see him immediately. You must ask him about this spy nonsense.''

"Ask him? You mean accuse him of it?"

"And why not? I know he must have a logical explanation for everything. How he will laugh at you when you tell him. You must go this very morning.''

"I could not," said Valeria. "Why, the idea is preposterous. I cannot call upon Traverhurst and ask him if he is a spy. If, indeed, he is a spy, he certainly will not say so to me.''

"But if he is, then he will know that his secret is out. He will have no recourse but to flee.''

Valeria looked thoughtful. She remembered Julian saying that he would talk to Sir Rupert Netherton about Traverhurst. Netherton would undoubtedly arrange for government agents to watch the earl and in time, he would most certainly be caught. Valeria suddenly imagined the earl in prison awaiting his punishment. The idea was horrible.

"Yes, you must go and see him," said Maria. "I shall have Fletcher ready the carriage.''

When Valeria made no further protest, her stepmother rose from the sofa and left the room. Yes, as difficult as it would be, she should see the earl. She must confront him and demand the truth. She would tell him her suspicions. Perhaps it would be unpatriotic to warn him, but she could not bear the idea of his being executed as a spy. Thus resolved, Valeria rose from the sofa and rang for her maid.

Since Maria's stylish phaeton was being repaired, Valeria set off in Maria's other vehicle, a lumbering closed carriage. The distance to Traverhurst's house was not great, and it was not long before the equipage turned onto the earl's fashionable street.

Looking out the window as the carriage neared the elegant townhouse, Valeria was startled to see the man called Dorsey standing at the earl's door. A moment later Dorsey was admitted. As the carriage slowed to a stop in front of Traverhurst's house, Valeria leaned out the window. "Fletcher," she shouted, "go on past the house and stop some distance away."

Doing as he was bid, Fletcher drove past the earl's residence. Valeria recognized Traverhurst's stylish phaeton and magnificent black horses waiting at the curb. Spying one of Traverhurst's servants standing with the horses, Valeria leaned back against the leather carriage seat.

Fletcher brought his horses to a halt a short distance down the street and Valeria peered back at the house. The servant leaned toward the carriage window. "Would you be wanting to get out here, miss?"

"No, Fletcher. I shall wait here for a time. Do try not to look suspicious."

The servant thought this remark most peculiar, but he nodded. "Very good, miss."

Valeria looked out the tiny window in the back of the carriage. She did not have to wait long, for Dorsey soon reappeared accompanied by Traverhurst and a servant carrying what appeared to be a very heavy box. The earl assisted the servant to deposit the box into the phaeton. Then he climbed up into the vehicle and took up the reins. Dorsey got up on the seat beside him and Traverhurst pulled his horses out into the street.

Valeria quickly ducked down as the phaeton passed by. She then leaned out the window. "Fletcher, you must follow that gentleman's phaeton."

"Follow it, miss?"

"Yes, Fletcher, but do not let him observe you." The servant, although thinking this a most unusual request, found it more diverting than his usual duties. After waiting for Traverhurst's phaeton to get sufficiently far ahead, he whipped his horses onto the street.

The coachman Fletcher had not expected such an interesting morning's work. Instead of depositing Miss Harwood after a short ride, he found himself following the earl's phaeton across town. It was not an easy task, since Traverhurst's horses were quick and the earl an excellent whip. His lordship easily maneuvered his vehicle through the traffic while Fletcher had more difficulty. Maria's carriage was heavier and harder to manage. It took all of the coachman's considerable skill to keep Traverhurst in sight.

After some time, Fletcher found himself out of the city on a main road heading south. Wondering if he should continue, he pulled the vehicle to a stop. Valeria peered out the window. "What's wrong, Fletcher?"

"We're going out of town, miss. This is the road to Dover. Do you wish me to go on?"

Valeria paused, wondering if the earl was going to his estate Seahold. Thinking of Dorsey and the box the servant had carried to the phaeton, she was sure there was mischief afoot. "Yes, Fletcher. Go on."

Enjoying the adventure, Fletcher needed little persuasion. He whipped his horses again and set off after the vanishing phaeton. Almost two hours later, the coachman stopped at an inn. Fletcher jumped down from the driver's seat and opened the carriage door. "I fear, miss, the horses are spent. We'd have to change them afore we could go on."

"What of the other carriage?"

"They must have passed her some time ago, miss. I can go inquire of the ostlers."

Valeria nodded and then she got down from the carriage to stretch her legs. The coaching inn was bustling with activity. Stablemen were busy unharnessing and harnessing horses to a variety of vehicles. A number of travelers milled about, waiting to depart.

Fletcher appeared a short time later. "They were here, miss. One of the ostlers said they were bound for Dover."

"Could he have meant his lordship's estate near Dover?"

"The man said Dover, miss. I fear, Miss Harwood, we must go back to town. Her highness will be worried. We'll have to rest the horses first, of course."

Valeria nodded absently. It had been folly to set off in pursuit of Traverhurst. What had she thought she might accomplish by doing so? Now it would be late before she returned to town and she would have to explain her impulsive behavior to Maria. Valeria was reminded of her other impulsive journey to Seahold.

Valeria thought of Traverhurst and wondered if he was, indeed, going to Dover. There was something odd about the entire affair and she wanted very much to know what was going on. "Very well, Fletcher, I shall go into the inn and obtain some refreshment. You, too, should have something to eat."

"Aye, miss. I'll see to the horses first."

Valeria entered the public room of the inn. She found it crowded with wayfarers and rather noisy. The innkeeper, seeing a lady of quality, hurried over to her. "Might I be of service, ma'am?"

"I should like some luncheon," said Valeria.

"And the others in your party, ma'am?"

"I am alone," replied Valeria.

The inn's proprietor, although surprised at this admission, showed no sign of it. He ushered her to a table and, with an obsequious bow and assurances of a speedy meal, left her. True to his word, he appeared a short time later with a plate of cold mutton, bread, and cheese.

"You're bound for London, ma'am?" said the innkeeper.

Valeria nodded and looked about the room. "The inn is rather crowded today."

"Aye, ma'am. Business is good. Many coaches stop this way, I'm glad to say. Why, the mail coach to Dover is due at any minute."

"The mail coach?" said Valeria, suddenly interested.

"Aye, ma'am, and a good fast one it is."

An idea occurred to Valeria. "Might a person obtain a seat on the coach?"

"Why, yes, miss," said the innkeeper. "But you did say you were going to London."

"I have changed my mind. I should very much like to see Dover."

The innkeeper, who had always thought the ways of the upper classes very strange, had his opinion confirmed. "I could see that your luggage is taken to the coach, ma'am."

"Oh, I have no luggage," said Valeria matter-of-factly. "But I should be most grateful if you would inform me when the coach arrives."

"Very well, ma'am," replied the perplexed proprietor, starting to turn away.

"Oh, and would you have a piece of paper and a pen? I must inform certain people in London of my change of plans."

The man nodded and soon did as she requested. Valeria scribbled a hasty note to Maria. She then hesitated. Finally she made up her mind and began another note to Sir Rupert Netherton.

❧ 22 ❧

THE CROWDED mail coach arrived at Dover and quickly deposited its passengers. Among the weary travelers was Valeria, who was very much relieved to finally come to the end of a long and uncomfortable ride. She had been squeezed between two loquacious merchants, who had seemed especially pleased at her company.

Now free of the coach, she eluded the merchants and hurried down the street. Once safely away from her fellow travelers, Valeria stopped and began to assess her situation. Here she was in Dover, tired, friendless, and almost penniless.

More than eight hours had passed since she had left Maria's house that morning. Valeria knew that her stepmother would be beside herself with worry after receiving the note she had sent with the driver. Valeria knitted her brows in concentration. Whatever had possessed her to do such a thing, she asked herself. Why had she felt compelled to follow Traverhurst?

Valeria frowned. She had to know what he was about. He was undoubtedly part of some plot and she could not put aside her fear that what he was doing was endangering England. She hoped that Sir Rupert Netherton, upon receiving her note, would know what to do. Surely, Traverhurst must be stopped. Valeria's frown deepened. Even though she knew the earl was a spy, she could not help feeling treacherous herself for betraying him.

Looking around the street, Valeria wondered what to do next. She had no idea where Traverhurst and his confederate Dorsey might be, if, indeed they were even in Dover. She had been mad to come here, she told herself. Valeria started to walk down the street. Noting that the sun was low in the sky, she realized that it would soon be dark. The thought of being in a strange town with no place to spend the night was rather daunting. Shaking aside her misgivings, Valeria tried to fix her attention upon finding Traverhurst.

After walking down several streets and beginning to think it was hopeless, Valeria stopped short. There ahead on a narrow side street, she spied the earl's phaeton. Standing beside it was the man Dorsey. Valeria retreated a few steps, hiding herself in the shadow of a building. Dorsey seemed impatient and ill-humored. After some time, Traverhurst appeared. Valeria saw the two men exchange a few words and then they got into the carriage and drove away.

Valeria hurried to follow them, almost running down the street. Seeing the vehicle turn and head toward the harbor, she hastened after it. She stopped breathlessly as she saw the phaeton draw up beside a ship at the water's edge.

Positioning herself at the side of a building, Valeria watched Traverhurst and Dorsey as they unloaded the box from the carriage and carried it onto the vessel. A few moments later, another man came off the ship, jumped up into the phaeton, and drove it away. It appeared, thought Valeria, that Traverhurst and his companion intended to sail for France.

Standing there in the misty twilight, Valeria wondered what was in the box. It must be of importance, she concluded, and she wanted desperately to know what was inside. Suddenly, her fictional hero Hannibal Wolfe came to mind. What would the heroic captain have done at such a time as this? Valeria knew he would not stand there meekly hiding at the dock. Certainly, he would attempt to discover the plans of the enemy.

Chastened by this realization, Valeria began to make her way toward the ship. It was fairly dark by now and she could see but two crewmen on the sleek craft. They were talking loudly on the far side of the ship and her approach was unobserved. Valeria hesitated for a brief moment at the gangplank and then hurried aboard.

The wooden deck creaked as she stepped across it and, terrified that the men would hear her, Valeria froze. They continued to talk, however, so she made her way stealthily to the ship's cabin area, creeping down the stairs to a partially opened door. Pausing there, Valeria heard Traverhurst's voice. She peered inside, finding a narrow corridor leading to the captain's quarters and other rooms.

Suddenly the voices of the two crewmen caught her attention. They appeared to be coming in her direction, so she ducked inside the door. Now inside the enclosed area, she could hear Traverhurst's voice more clearly. She crept silently toward the entrance to the main cabin and peered inside. There was the earl sitting in a chair, a glass of wine in his hand. Dorsey was standing beside a table, upon which was the box they had brought from London.

"God, you're a cool one, Traverhurst."

"There is nothing to be in a lather about, Dorsey," said the earl, taking a sip of wine.

"Oh, no?" Dorsey reached over and flipped open the lid to the box. Valeria's hazel eyes widened at the sight of the box's contents. It was filled with shiny gold coins. Dorsey reached in and grabbed a handful, allowing them to slide through his fingers. "You have no qualms at the idea of carting this about the French countryside?"

"Not particularly," replied Traverhurst. "I don't expect any trouble."

"I hope to God you are right," said Dorsey, closing the box. "Our friend will be very happy to see this. I hope he will carry out his part of the bargain." Traverhurst made no reply, but looked gloomily at his wine glass. Dorsey looked over at the earl. "You're not attending, Traverhurst. I'll wager you're thinking of your bit of fluff."

His lordship glanced at at Dorsey. "What?"

A grin appeared on Dorsey's swarthy face. "Your bit of fluff, the one I saw you with at Seahold. Aye, she was a pretty piece. I'll wager the wench would give a man a fair ride.''

Traverhurst jumped to his feet and, to Dorsey's astonishment, grabbed him angrily by the coat. "Damn you, Dorsey! Speak one more word about the lady at your peril!" Traverhurst released him roughly.

"God, you are touchy," cried Dorsey. "I didn't know she was a lady." At Traverhurst's threatening look, he quailed. "Not another word. Since you are in such a foul mood, I'll go. It is time we weighed anchor." Dorsey started to leave.

Valeria turned in dismay and, seeing another door, quickly opened it and fled inside. Finding herself now inside a tiny cubicle with one porthole, Valeria stood very still as Dorsey passed by. She breathed a sigh of relief as she heard him go up the stairs and bark a few words to the other men. Valeria peered out the small window that faced the dock and her relief quickly turned to horror as she saw the gangplank being drawn into the ship.

They were setting sail! Valeria stood debating what to do. She considered rushing in to see Traverhurst. Indeed, the idea of throwing herself into his arms was not without appeal. Yet, he was most assuredly a villain, an enemy of England and, therefore, her enemy.

She turned away from the porthole and looked about the cramped room. The light was so dim she could barely discern its contents. Supressing a sigh, Valeria sat down on the floor, hugging her knees. Whatever was she to do now, she asked herself. Then, listening to the noises of the ship, Valeria thought of Traverhurst.

23

VALERIA was jolted awake by the movement of the ship and the sound of voices. She opened her eyes, for a moment totally disoriented. It was still dark, although upon rising stiffly to her feet and looking out the porthole, Valeria could see the faint light of early dawn. The ship was docked and despite the early hour, there was activity on the wharf. Men were loading and unloading ships, speaking to each other in French.

Valeria suspected they were in Calais, and reasoning that the ship must have docked there for most of the night, she wondered if Traverhurst was still aboard. She was rather irritated with herself for falling asleep. Valeria found it hard to believe she had slept so long in such an uncomfortable position, but she realized that she had never before been so exhausted.

Her attention was drawn to an approaching wagon, which pulled up alongside the ship. The driver, who was dressed like a French peasant, jumped agilely down from the wagon and then turned toward the gangplank. Seeing the man's face for the first time, Valeria was very much surprised to find that it was Traverhurst.

He was soon out of sight, but moments later, he reappeared with Dorsey. The two men carried the box to the wagon and after glancing from side to side as if to make sure that no one was watching, Traverhurst reached down into the wagon and pulled up what appeared to be some

sort of door. They then hurriedly hefted the box into
the wagon and closed the door upon it. Dorsey shouted
toward the ship and a number of crewmen came from the
vessel carrying bulky bags, which they plopped into the
wagon.

"Well, Traverhurst," said Dorsey, "you're on your
own. Damned if I know why I couldn't come with you."

"With your abominable French, Dorsey," said the earl,
"you'd only be a hindrance."

"Perhaps you're right. You'll have to make your way to
the inn at Pontvieux by yourself."

"Damn it, Dorsey, keep quiet about that!"

"And I thought you weren't nervous about this mission,
Traverhurst."

"There is no point in being foolhardy," muttered the
earl irritably. Traverhurst jumped up into the wagon.

Dorsey grinned up at him. "Not your lordship's usual
conveyance, is it?"

A slight smile appeared on the earl's face. "Farewell,
Dorsey, and I warn you, there had best be some wine left
when I return."

Dorsey laughed and Traverhurst urged the horses on
away from the water's edge. Valeria watched the earl
vanish from sight. She frowned, thinking that she must
somehow get off the ship and follow him. Luckily, she
knew his destination, Pontvieux. However, where or how
far this might be, she had no idea.

She heard voices in the hallway outside her tiny room,
but fortunately the men passed by, evidently going into the
cabin beyond her. Hearing the sound of a door closing,
Valeria grew bold enough to open her own door a crack
and peer out. Finding no one in the hallway, she quietly
ventured out and headed toward the entranceway. Her luck
held as she went up the stairs and glanced about the ship's
deck. Some crew members were working some distance
away, but they were so engrossed in what they were doing
that they did not see Valeria slip across to the gangplank
and hurry down it.

Hardly believing her good fortune, Valeria walked hastily across the dock. The sky was brightening and the village

was becoming more active. "Might I assist you, mademoiselle?" said a voice, speaking in French.

Valeria was startled at being addressed. She turned to see an elderly fishwife, eyeing her with interest. "Perhaps you could, madame," said Valeria in her impeccable French. "Could you tell me how far the village of Pontvieux is from here and how one might get there?"

"Pontvieux, mademoiselle?" replied the woman, who obviously thought it a strange question. " 'Tis many miles distant, due south of the village. A good day's journey, it is. The main road goes there."

Valeria was dismayed to hear that the village was so far away. How would she get there? She had almost no money. Looking over at the woman, Valeria saw that she was eyeing her with suspicion. Certainly, it must appear very odd that an Englishwoman would be wandering about alone. She thanked the woman and quickly left her.

Walking down the village street, Valeria tried to develop a plan of action. Indeed, her position seemed hopeless. She realized that a sensible woman would have thought only of returning to England. Valeria smiled wryly, thinking she was not at all a sensible woman. After a time she reached the edge of the town and stood by the road that stretched southward. Looking down it, Valeria tried to see Traverhurst, but there was no sign of him.

She frowned and then looked the other way. A lone cart was approaching. It was an unpromising looking vehicle, pulled by a mule. As it neared her, Valeria saw that the cart's driver was a middle-aged woman dressed in rude clothing. She was wearing a shapeless hat and in her mouth was a pipe. Although she was not encouraged by the woman's expression, Valeria walked into the road and waved her arms at the vehicle. "Please stop, madame!"

The woman pulled her mule up and grabbed the pipe out of her mouth. "Get out of my way! Do you wish to be killed, you fool!"

Although shocked at the woman's rudeness, Valeria continued in a civil tone. "Are you going toward Pontvieux?"

"Everyone on this road is going toward Pontvieux," replied the woman scornfully.

"Then perhaps I shall be fortunate enough to find some-one going there who is less rude than you, madame," said Valeria angrily.

To her surprise the woman grinned. "I doubt that, mademoiselle. I am the most well-mannered person you are likely to meet."

"Then it is clear I shall have to walk the entire way." Valeria stepped aside. "Do not let me detain you."

"So you want a ride?"

Valeria eyed the woman hopefully. "Yes, I do need a ride to Pontvieux."

"Then get in," said the woman gruffly, sticking the pipe back into her mouth.

"Thank you," said Valeria, quickly getting into the cart beside the woman.

They drove a short distance in silence. Finally, the Frenchwoman spoke. "So what is an English lady doing alone on the road to Pontvieux?"

Valeria hesitated. "I am looking for someone."

The woman turned and regarded her knowingly. "A man, no?"

"Yes, it is a man."

"I might have known. He has left you, has he? It is a familiar tale. But you are better off without such a man. You'll soon find another. Forget him. Oh, you will say that that is impossible. I know how these things are. I was once young myself. Tell me all about the scoundrel."

Valeria suppressed a smile and then launched into a suitably tragic tale.

24

THE Earl of Traverhurst pulled his horses to a stop in front of an unprosperous looking inn at Pontvieux. Darkness was rapidly descending upon the quiet village and Traverhurst was glad to have finally reached his destination. His trip had been uneventful and tedious. Throughout the day's travel, he had had more than ample time to think about Valeria, and his thoughts had not put him in a very good humor.

Since the unpleasantness at the Princess Lubetska's house, the earl had been perplexed and unhappy. He was so much in love with Valeria that her behavior that night had deeply disturbed him. Traverhurst had been certain that she loved him and the thought that he had been wrong was unbearable.

The earl drove his wagon to the stable behind the inn and was met by a lethargic stableman. "I am here to see a man about selling my goods," said Traverhurst.

The stableman appeared indifferent. "A gentleman did mention he was waiting for someone. You must be the man."

"Where is he?" asked Traverhurst.

The other man shrugged. "In the inn, I suppose."

"Could you fetch him for me?"

The stableman appeared insulted. "Look, fellow, fetch him yourself."

"I would be grateful if you would do so," said Traverhurst, producing a coin and tossing it to the surly man, whose personality seemed to alter magically at the sight of money. He nodded and hurried off.

The earl waited in the near darkness for a short time, and then a tall man appeared. "You have my goods?" he asked Traverhurst.

His lordship nodded. "And you have mine?"

"Of course."

Traverhurst eyed him warily and then climbed down from the wagon. The other man gestured toward the stable. "I think we can talk privately in there." The earl nodded again and the two of them walked inside. Once in the dimly lit stable, the man continued. "It is all there and in gold?"

"To the last sou. There is a false bottom in the wagon. It is hidden there."

Traverhurst was surprised when the man called out into the darkness. "Jacques, go and see." Noting the earl's expression, he smiled. "I am a cautious man, but I suspect that you, too, are a cautious man." He pulled a leather pouch from his coat and handed it to Traverhurst. "They are there."

The earl opened the pouch and extracted some papers. After glancing at them quickly, he put them back, and then he placed the pouch in his coat. "It appears to be in order."

"Monsieur, it is as he said," came a voice from the doorway. "I have taken the box."

The man nodded at Traverhurst. "Then our business is settled. We each have what we want. I have a fortune in gold and you have the honor of knowing you have played a part in foiling Napoleon."

Traverhurst smiled. "I am told you once supported him."

The other man smiled in return. "I am a practical man. I know which way the wind is blowing. You English will defeat Bonaparte again. This will just make it a little easier. Good evening, monsieur." He bowed slightly and left. Traverhurst stood for a moment and then he went to see to his horses and wagon.

*   *   *

"This is Pontvieux?" asked Valeria.

Her companion nodded. "That it is, and I am glad to see it."

"So you can be rid of me."

The other woman grinned. "So I can get something to eat."

Valeria smiled in return. Although their relationship had started so unpromisingly, the day's ride had made Valeria and the Frenchwoman fast friends. The woman, whose name was Madame Boudreaux, had commiserated with Valeria on the perfidy of the male sex and, as if in illustration, had recounted the story of her own life. This had occupied a good part of the journey and, far from being bored, Valeria had been glad of the distraction.

Madame Boudreaux pulled her mule up to the stable and when the stableman was lackadaisical about attending to her, the Frenchwoman upbraided him harshly. Then the two women approached the inn. At the entrance, Valeria hesitated, wondering if Traverhurst might be inside. Madame Boudreaux seemed to understand. "Is he in here?" she asked.

Standing at the doorway, Valeria scanned the inn's customers. Traverhurst was not among them. She shook her head. "No, he is not here."

"It is for the best, Mademoiselle *Anglaise*," said Valeria's companion. "Come, let us get something to eat. But do not expect much from this place. I have eaten here before." The older woman led Valeria to a table and the two of them sat down.

The waiter, noting the contrast between Valeria's fashionable attire and Madame Boudreaux' sorry clothing, thought them an incongruous pair. Nonetheless, he attended them politely, hurrying off to see to their food.

A short time later a young man appeared before them. He was dressed like a gentleman, although rather slovenly, and he was obviously inebriated. "God's blood," he cried, looking at Valeria, "a beautiful lady!" He looked over at Madame Boudreaux. "And with an old crone!"

"Watch your tongue, you insolent puppy," said the Frenchwoman, shaking her fist at him.

He ignored her and turned back to Valeria. "You are a pretty wench," he said. "Give me a kiss."

Valeria looked startled and Madame Boudreaux fixed a look of disgust at the interloper. "I pray you leave, monsieur," said Valeria. "I find you insulting."

"And I find you intoxicating."

To Valeria's horror, the young man grabbed her, pulling her to her feet and attempting to kiss her.

Valeria struggled to extricate herself. "Release me!" she cried.

The Earl of Traverhurst chose that moment to enter the main room of the inn. A woman whose back was toward him was struggling with a man. Traverhurst's chivalrous instincts came instantly to the fore. He rushed up to them. "See here, monsieur. Let her go!"

Startled, the man released Valeria and she turned to face her rescuer. Traverhurst was stunned. "Valeria! What the deuce!"

The young man, taking advantage of the earl's bewilderment, hit him squarely in the midsection. "Now you will learn to mind your own business, fellow," he said, eyeing Traverhurst contemptuously.

The blow had taken the earl by surprise and he doubled over in pain.

"Traverhurst!" cried Valeria, horror-stricken.

However, it did not take his lordship long to recover. He righted himself and then with two neat blows, dispatched his young opponent.

"Well done!" said Madame Boudreaux, nodding approvingly at Traverhurst. "So this is your man, is it? I can see now why you did not want him to get away." The earl looked at the Frenchwoman with a puzzled expression. Madame Boudreaux continued, "Why did you leave her, monsieur? A man should not abandon his lover so coolly. You must take her back and be good to her."

Traverhurst turned to Valeria and spoke in English. "What in God's name are you doing here, Valeria, and what the devil is that woman talking about?"

Valeria blushed. "I can explain."

"I think you'd better." He glanced around and noted

that all eyes in the crowded inn were upon them. "Come outside." Traverhurst took her arm and started to lead her out. Valeria cast a glance at Madame Boudreaux, who grinned and winked at her.

Once outside, the earl again demanded an explanation. "How did you get here and why are you here?"

Valeria looked up at him and then she burst into tears. "Oh, Traverhurst," she finally managed to say, "I had to find out about you."

"What do you mean?" he said more gently, handing her his handkerchief.

Valeria dabbed at her eyes. "I did not want to believe it. Truly I didn't. Oh, how could you do it!"

"Do what?"

"Betray your country!"

Traverhurst regarded her incredulously. "Betray my country?"

"Do not deny it. I know everything. I followed you to Dover and was on the ship. I saw the gold and heard you talk to that dreadful man, Dorsey. You're a Bonapartist spy!"

"A Bonapartist spy?" The earl shook his head in disbelief. "You think me a traitor and you followed me all the way from London here? Upon my honor, Valeria, this is the most crack-brained thing I have ever heard."

"I've told you, it is useless to deny it. And not far from London I sent word to Sir Rupert Netherton of what you were doing."

The earl grabbed her by the shoulders. "You did what? Good God! Do you know what you've done?"

"I think I do. You can never go back to England."

"It will be a damned sight more difficult for me now," said Traverhurst. "I must say, Miss Harwood, your talent for fiction has misled you and may have grave consequences."

"I don't understand," said Valeria.

"I am not nor have I ever been a Bonapartist spy."

"Then what are you doing here in disguise? And what about the gold?"

"I have delivered the gold to a certain gentleman who

has in return given me documents of military intelligence, which I shall endeavor to take back to London. I am hopeful that this information will hasten Bonaparte's defeat.''

Valeria regarded him skeptically. "You are telling me that you are a spy for England? That seems highly unlikely.''

Traverhurst looked insulted. "Oh, yes, you think it more likely that I am a villainous traitor.''

"I was not aware that the government engaged earls to be spies.''

"I admit it is not a common practice, but some years ago, the prime minister asked me to investigate a delicate matter because of my connnections in France. I have been a government agent since that time. I was asked to go on this mission because of my familiarity with the region. Do not forget that I spent much of my childhood here and have many relations nearby.''

Valeria began to feel confused. "But everything fit. I didn't want it to, but it did. Julian said there were rumors about a highly placed member of society being a spy. Although Sir Rupert Netherton could not say anything about it, I was sure he thought you were the spy.''

The earl directed a look of incredulity at Valeria and then he burst into laughter. "Netherton! Oh, this is famous! Good God, Valeria! Netherton is the spy!''

"What?''

"I suspected him first, knowing him to be an unprincipled scoundrel. Some years ago, I saw him cheating at cards. Oh, he denied it, of course, and I could not actually prove it. I think it is not at all surprising that a man who would cheat at cards would betray his country for blunt.''

"Oh, Traverhurst,'' cried Valeria. "I might have believed you had you not tried to implicate Sir Rupert! How could you expect me to give credence to such a preposterous story?''

"Damn it, Valeria,'' snapped the earl, now furious with her. "So you cannot believe Netherton a turncoat, but you can believe it of me! You think I am capable of deceit and dishonor!'' Valeria made no reply and seemed to be fighting back tears. Traverhurst frowned and continued, "I see it is useless to say anything further. You had best go back inside. I'll escort you back to Calais in the morning.''

"That won't be necessary, Lord Traverhurst.''

"I see. You would not want any further association with me. Very well, Miss Harwood. How will you get back? Do you have money?''

Valeria shook her head. "But I shall manage, my lord.''

The earl took some coins from his pocket and extended them to her. "Take this. It will be enough to get you home.''

"I do not want your money,'' she said.

The earl scowled. "Of course, ill-gotten gain.'' He grabbed her hand and forcibly put the coins into it. Then he turned and stalked off.

"Wait!'' cried Valeria.

He turned around. "What is it?''

"What are you going to do?''

"Can't you guess? At first light I'm off to take my place in Napoleon's army!'' With these sarcastic words, Traverhurst turned and was gone.

Valeria watched his retreating form and then she looked down at the coins in her hand. Clutching them tightly and trying to retain her composure, Valeria went back into the inn.

25

VALERIA was glad when the faint light of early morning appeared at the window of the rude room at the inn. She had hardly slept at all and was eager to leave her uncomfortable accommodations. Coming into the main room of the inn, she found it empty except for the innkeeper and a maid.

Thinking of Traverhurst, Valeria wondered if he was gone. She addressed the maid. "Would you know if the tall dark-haired man is still here?"

The maid smiled. "You mean the handsome one? Oh, I saw him but a few moments ago. He was going to the stables."

Valeria looked thoughtful and had the urge to go and see him before he left. But no, there was no purpose in that. He would only tell her more outrageous stories. She frowned, wondering if she would ever see him again. No, he would not dare show his face in England now.

"Would mademoiselle like something to eat?" inquired the maid.

Valeria sighed. "Perhaps some coffee."

"I shall fetch you some, mademoiselle."

After thanking the servant, Valeria sat down at a table in an obscure corner of the room.

Suddenly, two men burst into the inn. From their mud-splattered clothes, Valeria decided that they had been riding for a time. "Innkeeper," one of them demanded.

The proprietor hurried toward them. "How may I assist you, monsieur?"

"We are looking for a man, an English gentleman. Is he here?"

"An English gentleman here, monsieur? Indeed not."

The other man regarded the innkeeper impatiently. "He may not be dressed like an English gentleman. He is a tall, dark man."

"I have no Englishmen here of any sort," insisted the innkeeper. "I can always spot an Englishman the first time he opens his mouth. No, I fear you must seek him elsewhere, monsieur. Do excuse me, gentlemen." The proprietor bowed slightly and then hurried away, seemingly anxious to get away from the two strangers, who had the look of highwaymen.

"My God! He must have been through here," muttered one of the men after the innkeeper had gone. "We could not have missed him."

"Well," returned his companion, "perhaps he did not stop here. Do not fear, DuSable, we shall find him. But we must search here in case that oaf of an innkeeper is mistaken. Netherton's note said Traverhurst's French is very good. Perhaps he could be taken for a Frenchman."

The man named DuSable nodded. "If he did not go this way, I do not know where he could be. Maybe he is not even in France."

"Netherton said the girl told him Traverhurst was going to Dover, and Netherton has always been a most accurate informant. This is Traverhurst's most likely path."

DuSable shrugged. "I wonder why it is so important to kill this English lord?"

"He is an enemy of France and an enemy of the emperor. That is reason enough for me."

"And for me," said DuSable. "Come, let us go and search this place." The two men hastened out.

Valeria sat frozen with fear and astonishment. Netherton! So it was true! Sir Rupert was the traitor! And these dreadful men wanted to kill Traverhurst! Jumping to her feet, Valeria rushed out of the inn toward the stables. There she found the earl leading a horse from one of the stalls. "Traverhurst!" The earl turned to her in surprise and she continued. "You must hurry! There are two men here. They want to kill you!"

This information did not seem to startle Traverhurst as much as Valeria had expected. "Where are they?" he said evenly.

"In the inn. I think they are searching the rooms! Oh, Traverhurst, I have been such a great gudgeon not believing you! Netherton is the traitor! Oh, you must hurry! Do not waste a moment!"

The earl nodded and looked at the cart horse. "I fear this nag will not do." He eyed the other horses and quickly selected a big black gelding. "This is the only decent animal here," he said, taking up a bridle and expertly placing it on the horse's head. The earl then started to saddle the steed.

"You are not going to steal that horse?" exclaimed Valeria in surprise.

He looked over at her and smiled. "Indeed, I am, Madame Oracle." He tightened the cinch and turned back to her. "Come, you're going with me."

"I'd just slow you down."

"Don't argue, Valeria. I'm not leaving you here with those cutthroats."

She did not protest further, but allowed him to lift her up onto the big horse. Then swinging himself up behind her, the earl directed his mount out of the stable. Once on the road and some distance from the inn, Traverhurst tightened his arm about Valeria's waist. "Here we go," he said, kicking the horse sharply. The gelding raced down the road. Valeria, despite her fear, could not be unaware of the pleasant sensation of having the earl's arms around her. In addition to this, her relief at knowing he was no traitor was tremendous.

It was some time before the earl slowed the big animal. Valeria turned to look at him. "Do you think they are following us?"

"It is very likely."

"Can we get back to Calais?"

He shook his head. "I don't think it wise to attempt it.

It would be better to get help. My uncle's estate is not far from here. Going there would be the best plan. We'll get off this main road ahead."

Traverhurst urged the horse onward and they soon found themselves on a narrow country lane. Although it was hardly an occasion for sightseeing, Valeria noted the loveliness of the landscape with its tranquil farmland and gently rolling hills. They traveled for a time, neither of them speaking. Finally, the earl pulled up his horse and glanced back. "I think we're safe for a time. Why don't we rest the horse for a bit?" Traverhurst dismounted and lifted Valeria down. "Damn good animal," he said, giving the gelding a pat.

"Yes," she said. "He is a good horse." She paused awkwardly. "Oh, Traverhurst, how can you ever forgive me? Not only did I believe you a traitor, but I made Netherton aware of your plans."

He smiled slightly. "You are a meddlesome woman, Madame Oracle."

Heartened by his expression, Valeria regarded him hopefully. "Then you don't despise me?"

Traverhurst grinned and in response, pulled Valeria to him, enfolding her in his arms. He then kissed her long and passionately. When their lips finally parted, Valeria gazed into his gray eyes. "Oh, Traverhurst, I am so in love with you."

"And I adore you, my darling Valeria." He brought his mouth once again to hers and Valeria responded eagerly. Finally the earl pulled away. "I fear, my love, this is not the time. We'd best go. The estate is not far."

She nodded reluctantly. Valeria had been so lost in Traverhurst's embrace that she had momentarily forgotten the danger. She thought of the two men who were probably pursuing them. "Yes, we must hurry," she agreed. Soon the two of them were once again mounted and on their way.

As they rode along, Valeria poured out the tale of how she had come to the conclusion that the earl was a Bonapartist spy. Traverhurst grinned. "And that is why you came to Seahold? To get evidence against me?"

"I hoped I wouldn't find any. But what was I to think with that dreadful Dorsey? It seemed quite sinister. Do you know what agony it was to be in love with a man whom I thought to be an enemy agent?"

He smiled and tightened his arm around her waist. "And do you know what agony it was to think you cared nothing for me? That night at your stepmother's house I was so damned miserable."

"Poor Traverhurst," said Valeria, leaning back and kissing him gently. He grinned and returned the kiss with fervor.

They continued on in this matter for a time, but again the sober realization of their peril came to them. The earl increased the horse's speed, and soon they arrived at the estate of the Duc de Chevreuse. "This is my uncle's estate where I spent much of my early boyhood. We will be safe here."

Valeria stared at the splendid residence visible some distance away. She was struck by the beauty of the magnificent castle and its lovely pastoral setting. "Oh, Traverhurst, how grand it is. Your man told Sally it was like a fairy castle, and that it is."

The earl was regarding the castle fondly. "There is no place I love better, save for Seahold, of course. A pity we come here under such circumstances. I hope my uncle is at home."

They rode toward the house and were met by an elderly servant. The man eyed them warily and then there was a glint of recognition in his eyes. "Is it you, my lord?"

"It is indeed, Rambeau. Is my uncle here?"

The old man shook his head. "The duke and duchess are in Paris. Do you know what is happening there, my lord? We have heard nothing and are worried."

Traverhurst shook his head. "I fear I do not know, Rambeau. I am sure that there is no cause for worry. I doubt that my uncle is in any danger." He smiled. "However, I cannot say the same for myself."

Rambeau looked alarmed. "You are in danger, my lord?"

"It appears so. We may have been followed by cut-throats. They may be here shortly."

"Do not fear, my lord. I shall post guards."

"They had best be well armed, my friend," said Traverhurst.

The elderly servant nodded and hurried away. The earl dismounted and helped Valeria down from the horse. They then made their way inside. A stout woman appeared and, seeing Traverhurst, regarded him in astonishment. She then clutched her hands to her ample bosom. "My lord!"

"Madame Marquette!"

Valeria smiled as the woman rushed to Traverhurst and embraced him. "You are so cruel to stay so long in England."

"I promise I shall not do so in future," replied the earl. He glanced over at Valeria. "Miss Harwood, this is Madame Marquette. She was the housekeeper to my grand-father and now to the current duke, my uncle. This is Miss Harwood, madame."

Madame Marquette eyed Valeria with keen interest and then curtsied deeply. "But my lord," said Madame Marquette, "why are you dressed like that?"

"It is a very long story, one which I prefer not to tell at the moment. We have both had something of an ordeal. We would be grateful for some food and some different clothes."

"Of course, my lord," said the housekeeper eagerly. "Why, mademoiselle is very nearly the duchess's size. I shall see to you, mademoiselle, and I shall call Pierre to attend you, my lord."

Taking Valeria in hand, the housekeeper soon found a suitable dress. When she rejoined the earl a short time later, Valeria was attired in a stylish gown of pale green muslin that fitted her perfectly. It appeared that the earl was less fortunate. His lordship was considerably taller than his uncle and the sleeves of the coat Traverhurst was wearing were lamentably short. "I am glad that Bouchot can't see me," said the earl with a grin.

"But I daresay he would not have approved of your other attire either," said Valeria, smiling mischievously.

''Though I must say, I thought those clothes quite charming.''

''Then I shall endeavor to make them the fashion in town.''

Valeria laughed. ''I fear that that would be beyond even your abilities.''

''But you look lovely, Valeria.''

She blushed. ''The duchess has good taste.''

''I have good taste,'' he said with a smile.

Valeria blushed again and walked toward him. ''Do you think those men will come here?''

''I cannot deny it is a possibility, but some of the servants are standing guard. We will rest here a short while and then we will have an escort back to Calais.'' He smiled. ''And then back to England.''

''I daresay Maria and Julian are in high fidgets wondering what has happened to me.''

''Your brother will be even more in high fidgets when he finds out you have been with me. I fear you are hopelessly compromised, Madame Oracle.''

She smiled. ''Yes, I suppose I am.''

''So you have no recourse but to marry me.''

''I fear there is no alternative,'' she said with mock seriousness. She then smiled. ''But perhaps there are worse fates.''

He laughed. ''Come here, saucy wench,'' he said, grabbing her around the waist. Then, pulling her to him, he stopped her laughter with a kiss.

''What a pity to interrupt such a charming scene.''

A man's voice made them spring apart. Valeria gasped. There stood one of the men from the inn, the one called DuSable. In his hand was a pistol, wich he was directing at Traverhurst.

''I see I am unexpected.''

''God's death,'' said the earl. ''How did you get in here?''

DuSable regarded him contemptuously. ''Did you think a few stupid servants would stop me?''

''And where is your friend?'' asked Traverhurst, watching the intruder intently.

"Do not trouble yourself about that, Englishman," said DuSable. He turned to Valeria. "Get out of the way, woman."

Valeria drew closer to the earl. "I will not."

DuSable grinned. "As you wish, madame, but I assure you, I have no qualms about killing you both."

"For God's sake, Valeria," said Traverhurst, "do as he says." When she made no move to do so, the earl pushed her from him. "Now stay there!"

Valeria stood motionless, a horrified expression on her face. DuSable turned his attention to Traverhurst. "So, Englishman, perhaps it would be wise for you to say a prayer."

"The minute you fire that gun, the servants will be in here," said Traverhurst.

"Don't make me laugh. They are sheep. Indeed, you are the only wolf here. Perhaps it is a pity to kill you, but one follows orders."

"I am a wealthy man. I can pay you well for sparing me."

DuSable spat contemptuously. "Do you think I am like that dog Netherton, that I would do this for money? I am a patriot, monsieur. I work for my country and my emperor."

As DuSable spoke, Valeria glanced about the room. A short distance from her was a table on which was a heavy vase. Noting that the Frenchman seemed to forget her presence during his fervent reply, she took the opportunity to step toward the table.

"So you call yourself a patriot," said Traverhurst scornfully. "Assassin is a more accurate word."

DuSable grinned. "Perhaps you are right. Good-bye, Englishman." Just as the Frenchman was about to pull the trigger, Valeria snatched up the vase and hurled it toward him. The heavy object hit him squarely on the shoulder, causing his arm to fly up and the gun to go off wildly toward the ceiling. Traverhurst rushed DuSable and punched him hard in the midsection. The blow felled the Frenchman but he leaped up quickly and, glowering, charged for the earl.

Traverhurst stood waiting and suddenly DuSable lashed

out at him. Ducking the Frenchman's fist, the earl pulled his arm back and, with all the force he could muster, landed a crushing blow to his opponent's face. DuSable fell back, hitting the floor hard and then collapsing in a seemingly lifeless heap.

"Oh, Traverhurst!" Valeria ran to the earl and threw her arms around him.

"My lord, are you all right?" The servant Rambeau, followed by two others, hurried into the room.

"Yes, Rambeau, but there is another one."

"Oh, that blackguard. We have him, my lord."

"Was anyone injured?" asked Traverhurst.

Rambeau grinned. "Only the blackguard, my lord." He glanced over at the inert body of DuSable. "Two blackguards, it appears. I don't know how that one got past us. I am so sorry, my lord."

"No harm done, Rambeau, thanks to my lady here." He smiled down at Valeria. "Splendid work, Madame Oracle. However, I daresay, my uncle the duke will never forgive you."

"Never forgive me?" Valeria regarded him quizzically.

Traverhurst nodded with mock gravity. "It was his favorite Chinese vase, you know." Valeria laughed and joyously kissed his smiling face.

❧ 26 ❧

THE STYLISH carriage pulled up to the London residence of the Viscount Harwood. The door to the equipage was flung open and out jumped the Earl of Traverhurst, who then assisted Valeria down. They had just come from the Princess Lubetska's house where the butler had informed them that her highness was with the Harwoods, anxiously waiting for word of Valeria. Valeria and Traverhurst had, therefore, made haste to Julian's townhouse.

The earl offered Valeria his arm. "Courage, my darling. It can be no worse facing your brother than that DuSable fellow."

Valeria smiled. "Perhaps not. But I do hope no one will resort to fisticuffs."

Traverhurst grinned. "You have my word I shall not. But I do not know about you."

She laughed and they made their way to the door. They were met by Julian's butler, who did not disguise his joy at seeing Valeria. He hurriedly led them into the drawing room where they found Maria, Fanny, and Julian. The two ladies let out ecstatic cries and rushed to embrace Valeria. "My darling girl," exclaimed Maria, "we were so worried about you!"

"Indeed we were, miss," said Julian, his joy at seeing his sister soon replaced with disapproval at finding her returned with Traverhurst. He turned to the earl. "I expect you have an explanation, Traverhurst. Where has my sister been these past four days?''

"Alas, Harwood, I fear she has been with me.''

"What in thunder!'' shouted the viscount. "You must answer to me for this outrage, Traverhurst!''

"Do not be so tedious as to demand satisfaction, Harwood,'' said the earl. "After all, we are to be brothers-in-law.''

"By God, I won't hear of it!'' cried Julian. He looked at Valeria. "Are you mad, miss? You cannot want to be shackled to this fellow.''

"There is no one I would rather be shackled to, Julian,'' said Valeria, taking the earl's arm and smiling fondly up at him.

"This is outrageous!'' muttered Julian.

"But it is marvelous!'' cried Maria. "Oh, Valeria, I am so happy for you.'' The princess embraced Valeria again and then Traverhurst.

"Fanny, tell Valeria she should have nothing to do with this man,'' said Julian.

Fanny smiled. "Oh, Julian, do not be such a stick. It is clear she loves him.'' She looked at Traverhurst. "And I think her feelings are reciprocated.

"You are very right, Lady Harwood,'' said the earl. "We will be married as soon as possible.''

"Without even asking my permission?'' sputtered Julian.

"Quit speaking such fustian, Julian,'' said Valeria, smiling at her brother. "Don't be a pea-goose. Be sensible and give us your blessing. After all, no one else will marry me now.''

"Well, I want to know where you were,'' demanded Julian.

"In France, Harwood,'' said Traverhurst matter-of-factly. "Picardy is so pleasant this time of year.''

"What the devil?'' cried Julian.

Valeria laughed. "Calm yourself, Julian. We shall explain everything to you. But we had best all sit down first.''

They had scarcely been seated when the butler arrived to announce a visitor. "Sir Rupert Netherton, my lord.''

Valeria and Traverhurst exchanged a glance. "I am most anxious to see that gentleman," said the earl.

Julian looked over at the butler. "Very well, show him in, Eliot."

Sir Rupert Netherton entered the drawing room and stopped short at seeing Valeria and Traverhurst. "Miss Harwood, you are returned."

"And so am I," said Traverhurst, rising to his feet and approaching Netherton.

"Traverhurst," said Sir Rupert, looking rather uncomfortable.

"I daresay you did not expect to see Lord Traverhurst," said Valeria. "We were in France, both of us."

"Valeria!" said Julian, shocked that his sister would admit such a thing.

Valeria ignored her brother. "We met two associates of yours, Sir Rupert. One a Monsieur DuSable. A charming man."

"I fear I do not know the gentleman," replied Netherton uneasily.

"Indeed?" said Traverhurst. "He mentioned you particularly. What did he say Valeria? Oh yes, he said you were a dog."

"Traverhurst!" cried Julian. "What is the meaning of this?"

"How dare you?" said Netherton. "Really, I do not think I should have to endure such insults. I shall leave."

"That sounds quite prudent, Netherton," said Traverhurst. "But if I may be so bold, I suggest you leave the country. The king's justice goes hard on such as you. I have reported everything to the prime minister and I must say, he was not altogether pleased to hear about you."

Sir Rupert's face grew pale. He did not reply, but rushed out of the room.

"What is going on here?" said Julian.

"Yes, what is wrong with Sir Rupert?" said Fanny.

"What is wrong, Fanny," said Valeria, "is that Julian's dearest friend is the traitor he has talked of so often."

"What humbug!" cried Julian.

"It is true," said Valeria. "At this moment, soldiers

wait at his house to arrest him. I am sorry, Julian, but I swear to you it is the truth. In time you will believe it.''

"Oh, this is terrible," said Maria.

"It is utter nonsense," said Julian stubbornly.

"I shall not try to convince you, Harwood," said Traverhurst. "I think I had best take Valeria back to Princess Lubetska's home where she might rest."

"That is a splendid idea," said Maria. She kissed Valeria. "You go with Traverhurst."

"Aren't you going with them?" said Julian.

"Oh, dear, no," said Maria, smiling conspiratorally at Valeria. "I must stay and talk to Fanny."

"Then I shall see you later," said Valeria. She quickly kissed Fanny and a befuddled-looking Julian and then she and Traverhurst took their leave.

Once back inside the carriage, Valeria sighed. "Poor Julian, I fear he has had a dreadful shock."

"Yes," said the earl, "finding out that you are going to marry me is a dreadful shock."

Valeria laughed. "I meant about Rupert. He could not believe it."

"He is as hard to convince as you are," said Traverhurst, taking her hands and raising them to his lips. "We had quite an adventure, didn't we, my love? It was as if we were in one of your novels."

Valeria nodded. "Indeed, but then, my dearest Traverhurst, I always thought you were so much like one of my characters."

"Like your hero Captain Hannibal Wolfe?" said the earl. "I am very flattered."

Valeria smiled mischievously. "I meant like my villainous Morveau."

They both burst into laughter and the earl caught her up into his arms and kissed her soundly.